THE YUKON KID

Books by
JAMES B. HENDRYX

The Yukon Kid
Raw Gold
Corporal Downey Takes the Trail
Blood on the Yukon Trail
Man of the North
Gold—and the Mounted
Frozen Inlet Post
Downey of the Mounted
North
Oak and Iron
Prairie Flowers
Snowdrift
The Foot of the Rainbow
The Gold Girl
The Gun Brand
The Promise
The Texan
Without Gloves
Connie Morgan in Alaska
Connie Morgan in the Cattle Country
Connie Morgan in the Fur Country
Connie Morgan in the Lumber Camps
Connie Morgan with the Forest Rangers
Connie Morgan with the Mounted
Connie Morgan Hits the Trail

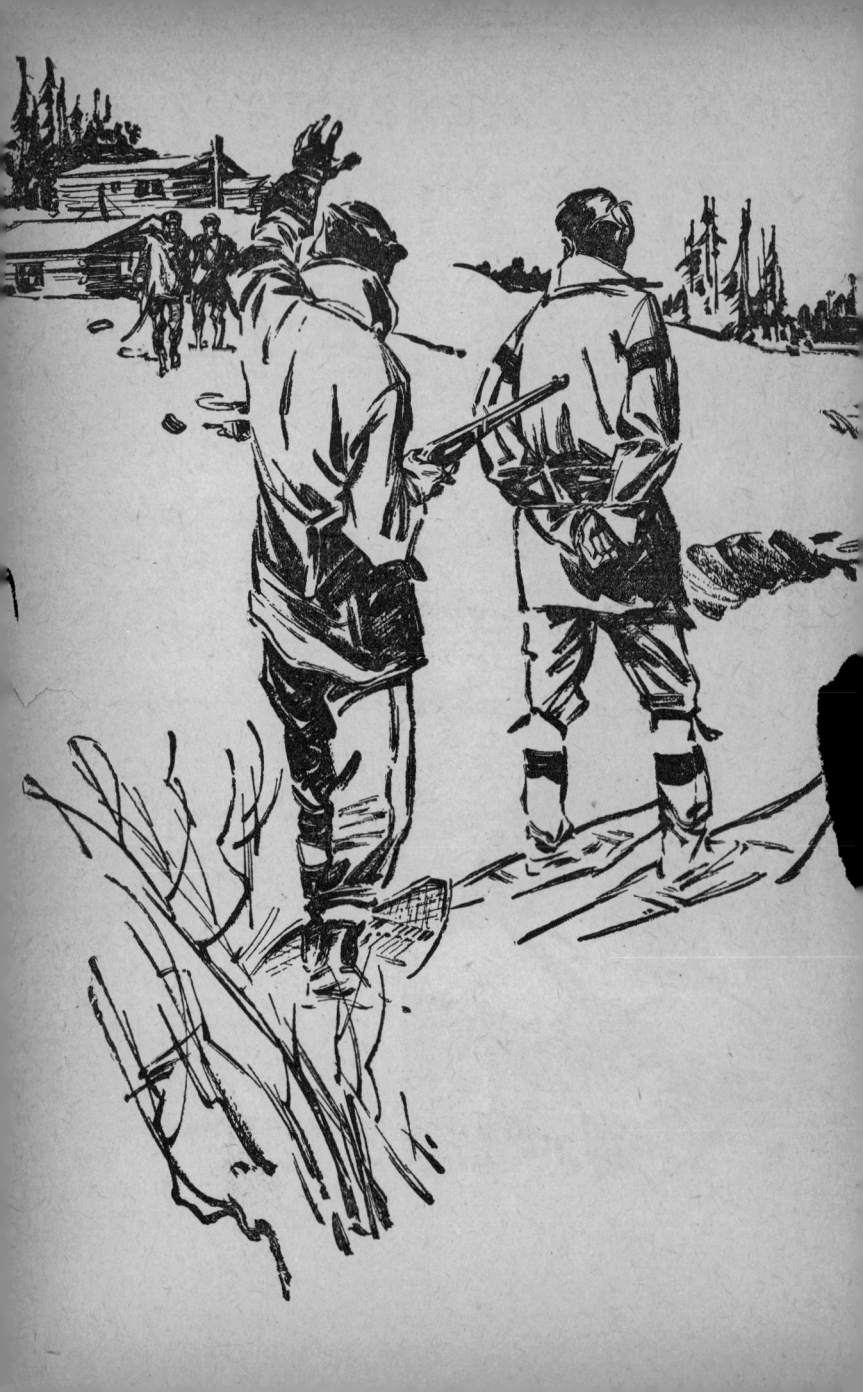

JAMES B. HENDRYX
THE YUKON KID

TRIANGLE BOOKS
NEW YORK

Triangle Books Edition Published November 1943
By arrangement with Doubleday, Doran & Company, Inc.

COPYRIGHT, 1933, 1934, BY JAMES B. HENDRYX

All rights reserved

TRIANGLE BOOKS, 14 West Forty-ninth Street,
New York, N. Y.

PRINTED AND BOUND IN THE UNITED STATES OF AMERICA
BY THE AMERICAN BOOK—STRATFORD PRESS, INC., N. Y. C.

CONTENTS

CHAPTER		PAGE
I	Gold	1
II	"I Hate You!"	10
III	Kitty Goes Outside	17
IV	The Passing of Big Tim	24
V	The Widow O'Brien	35
VI	Humdrum	46
VII	An Assault and Battery	54
VIII	The Yukon Kid	64
IX	A Barkeeper Gives Advice	76
X	Almost a Robbery	81

CONTENTS

CHAPTER		PAGE
XI	On the Trail	91
XII	In Seattle	96
XIII	Disappointment	105
XIV	Flight	118
XV	$1,000 Reward	129
XVI	Mr. Jones of Edmonton	138
XVII	The Building of a Crime	152
XVIII	Beyond the End of Steel	163
XIX	The Police Take the Trail	170
XX	Corporal Downey Plays a Lone Hand	180
XXI	An Attempt at Claim Jumping	191
XXII	Two Hundred Thousand for a Claim!	202
XXIII	The Yukon Kid Stakes a Claim	214
XXIV	The Giant Lets Go	222
XXV	In the Bottom of the Shaft	233
XXVI	The Yukon Kid Always Pays	244
XXVII	Homeward Bound	252
XXVIII	Dawson	267
XXIX	Corporal Downey Gives Advice	275
XXX	The Sourdoughs' Banquet	284

THE YUKON KID

CHAPTER I

Gold

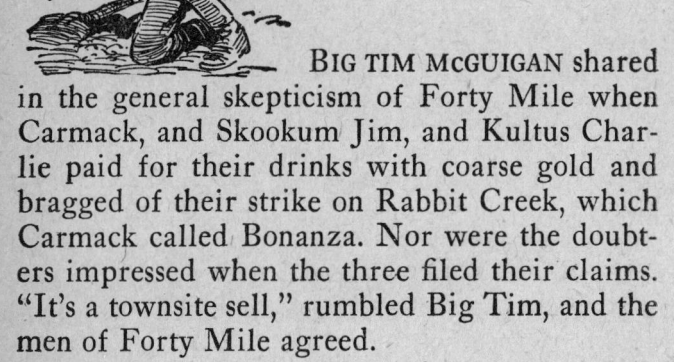

BIG TIM MCGUIGAN shared in the general skepticism of Forty Mile when Carmack, and Skookum Jim, and Kultus Charlie paid for their drinks with coarse gold and bragged of their strike on Rabbit Creek, which Carmack called Bonanza. Nor were the doubters impressed when the three filed their claims. "It's a townsite sell," rumbled Big Tim, and the men of Forty Mile agreed.

In vain Carmack reiterated his tale of how Skookum Jim, whiling away an idle hour, had panned more than a dollar from the dirt at the roots of a birch tree, and of how he himself had panned thirteen ounces before dark.

"Yuh never panned thirteen ounces in thirteen months, Carmack," grinned Old Bettles, returning his glass to the bar and wiping his lips on the back of his hand. "Not when a fish hook an' a rifle'll git you a livin', you didn't."

"Here's the gold," replied Carmack, thumping the bar with his sack.

"Yeh, Larue's gold," jeered Camillo Bill. "Larue's slick—but we wasn't made in a minute, neither. He figures on tolin' us up there to buy lots on his townsite."

"Larue don't even know about it," denied Carmack. "We didn't see him comin' down."

"It's Larue's gold, all right," opined Moosehide Charlie. "Who in hell ever heard of Carmack blowin' his own dust fer a drink?"

"I never had none before but what I needed," defended Carmack. "But now I got plenty! I'm buyin' another. Licker up, you frost hounds! I'll see you all on Bonanza by spring. Only there ain't room fer you all—an' them that's too late will be cussin' theirselves out fer fools."

"Frost houn's—hell!" cried Old Bettles with a drunken grin. "We're the wolves an' the foxes what can't be trapped. Come on, boys, we'll swaller Larue's bait while the swallerin's good—but we won't leave nary foot in his trap. Drink up! Here's to his goddam townsite!"

They drank, and drank again when Carmack bought another round, and as they drank they laughed in rough good nature and jibed and twitted the squaw man who, half drunk, now, held undeviatingly to his tale.

Only young Tommy Haldane did not laugh. He drank sparingly, and from his place at the end of the bar he watched Carmack's face. As the bartender weighed in the gold from the squaw man's sack, young Haldane spread his handkerchief on the bar beside the scales, at the same time tendering his own sack. "Give me that gold," he said, "and weigh in out of mine."

The bartender grinned: "What's the matter, kid? Want to change yer luck? Want to carry some stampede gold in yer poke? Don't let his talk fool you none. The boys has got him pegged right. Larue picked a hell of a man to start a stampede with—he ain't convincin'."

He obligingly dumped the gold from the scales into the outspread handkerchief and dribbled a like amount from Tommy's sack onto the scales. Nobody noticed the little byplay. Old Bettles was singing, and the others were joining in. Knotting the handkerchief about the gold, Tommy Haldane pocketed his sack, and presently he strolled out the door and made his way to his own little cabin near the bank of the mighty Yukon. For a long, long time he lay belly-wise on the floor, and stared intently at the play of the sunlight that streamed through his window upon two little piles of gold.

In the twilight that lingers long, even in the shortening days of late August, over Aurora land, he walked to the cabin of Big Tim McGuigan at the farther side of the camp. The door of the Antlers Saloon stood open, and from the interior sounded the tin-pan notes of the dance-hall piano, the raucous laughter of many men, and the voice of Old Bettles raised in drunken song:

> *"In the days of old,*
> *In the days of gold,*
> *In the days of 'forty-nine . . ."*

Kitty McGuigan looked up from her little plot of transplanted wildflowers as the voice of her father boomed hearty welcome from the doorway: "Hello, lad! Why ain't ye helpin' Carmack spend Larue's gold?"

Tommy Haldane's lips smiled as his eyes involuntarily sought the eyes of Irish blue that had lighted with quick gladness as the girl rose from her knees and tossed away a handful of weeds. "I'd rather be here, wouldn't I, mavourneen?" he answered as he reached for a hand, brown and hard like a boy's, with the earth of the flower bed still upon it.

White teeth showed as the girl smiled. "Well, if you hadn't rather be here you'd better travel long and travel far, Tommy Haldane! I didn't know you were in from the crick."

"Cleaned her up yesterday. Sixty-seven ounces. Hit camp this afternoon."

"Sixty-seven ounces!" cried the girl. "That's more than a thousand dollars."

"Yup. But I've be'n eighty days gettin' it. That's not so good—with everything high as it is. It's cost me better than four hundred."

"But even that's good, Tommy. Dad hasn't panned that much, sniping the bars, this summer. Have you, Daddy?"

"No. But another summer I'll be takin' to the cricks meself," said Big Tim. "You'd ought to be'n in the Antlers today an' heard Carmack braggin' about a strike he claimed he made up-river." The big Irishman scratched a match on the lintel log, and puffed blue clouds from his pipe. He grinned fondly as he pointed at the girl with his pipe stem: "I've helt to the bars this summer on account o' not leavin' her. Back in camp every night like a hen wid one chicken to look after. But the shoe'll be on the other fut next summer, ye spalpeen. It'll be ye herdin' the chicken, an' snipin' the bars, an' Big Tim McGuigan off to hell an' gone on the cricks. Ye're saddlin' a load onto ye'reself, lad. 'Tis what's brought the stoop av age to me own shoulders."

Hand in hand the two laughed as their eyes rested affectionately upon the huge upstanding figure that completely filled the doorway of the little cabin. At fifty Big Tim McGuigan was counted the strongest man on the river. Then the laugh faded from the lips of Tommy Haldane, and the eyes that met Big Tim's were grave.

"I was in the Antlers this afternoon an' I heard Carmack. I guess next summer there won't be any of us snipin' the bars."

Big Tim frowned. "What d'ye mean, lad? Sure, ye ain't givin' serious heed to the brag av the squaw man! Us old-timers—we know the game. It's a trick av Larue's to start a stampede to his townsite. Ask Old Bettles, or Moosehide Charlie, or Camillo Bill, or Swiftwater Bill, av ye won't take my word. Them's men that knows."

"I know what you all think. I heard Carmack, an' I heard you all. An' I suppose I'm the only man in Forty Mile right now that believes Carmack's right an' you're wrong. Call it foolishness, if you want to. Call it ignorance. Call it a hunch. Anyhow, it's what I believe, an' I can't help it."

Blue eyes glanced anxiously into the face of the speaker. "What are you going to do, Tommy?"

"I'm goin' to play my hunch. I'm goin' upriver."

Big Tim snorted his disgust. "An' when ye git there ye'll find Larue waitin' to sell ye a nice corner lot in his townsite!"

The younger man nodded: "An' if the townsite's located right, an' the price is right, maybe I'll buy it. A man might do worse than own lots in the right townsite."

"Ye talk like a fool, Tommy Haldane! An' how ye goin' upriver? Ye'll have to take yer outfit—even yer grub, fer Carmack says game's scarce. That'll mean a polin' boat an' anyways one pardner. Ye'll find no one in Forty Mile damn' fool enough to go wid ye."

"I figured maybe you'd go," answered the other.

"Me! Ye'll not ketch me kihootin' off upriver on the word av a drunken squaw man an' two lousy Siwashes! Be reasonable, lad. Peck away at the bars till the freeze-up. When the priest comes along ye two can git marrit, an' I'll move over into ye're cabin an' ye can have this—it's bigger. Then ye can settle down an' winter like a white man should."

Tommy Haldane felt the girl's fingers tighten about his own. He noted the sparkle in the blue eyes, and the slightly heightened color of the tanned cheeks. But there was a stubborn set to his lips as he shook his head slowly.

"There's plenty of men in Forty Mile right now that won't winter in cabins this winter," he said. "You don't know it—an' they don't—but *I* do. Better come along an' help me ride my hunch, Tim. She's big! The biggest thing this river ever saw."

The girl's fingers suddenly released his own and she took a swift step backward. "You don't love me, Tommy Haldane, or you'd stay!"

The cheeks were a deep red, and Tommy smiled into eyes that flashed dangerously. "Love you, Kitty! It's because I love you so much that I'm goin'. It's because I love you that I won't see you cooped up all your life in a ten-by-twelve log shack while I snipe bars an' hardly average wages. It ain't dollars I want—it's millions!"

The earnestness of the tone more than the words carried conviction. The angry flash died in the blue eyes, and Kitty stepped close and laid her hand on Haldane's arm.

"I know you love me, Tommy. I didn't mean it. But—upriver—and winter coming on—anything might happen. And I'd rather have you than the millions."

"It's the luck of the game, girl," laughed Tommy. "I want you to have both."

"Aye—the luck o' the game," echoed Big Tim. "A man must ride his hunch, lass." His face was grave, and his eyes were regarding Tommy Haldane searchingly. "Ever since——" He paused abruptly, cleared his throat noisily, and proceeded in a tone that sounded unwontedly gruff. "Fer a long time it's be'n my job to mother as well as to daddy Kitty. I've done the job as best I might. When I seen how things was shapin' between ye, I watched ye closer than ye know. Ye're a good lad—an' the makin's av a fine man, Tommy Haldane. Ye're good enough fer Kitty. I could not say more of any man. 'Tis not that I want to discourage ye, lad. If your hunch says upriver—upriver ye go. An' ye'll be right—whether there's gold there or none. A man must ride his hunch. But, knowin' ye as I do, 'tis hard fer me to fathom how ye gathered a pullin' hunch from the drunken mouthin's av Carmack."

"Light the lamp, Tim, an' I'll show you." The voice sounded tense with suppressed excitement. Only for an instant did Big Tim hesitate as his shrewd glance searched the face of the younger man. Was it possible that this mere boy had tumbled onto something that the sourdoughs in the Antlers had missed? Abruptly he turned and held the flame of a match to the wick of the tin bracket lamp.

CHAPTER II

"I Hate You!"

The three gathered close about the rude table as Tommy Haldane removed the lamp from its bracket and set it before them. From his pocket he produced a knotted handkerchief and his own sack of dust. "Get a couple of pieces of paper," he said. And when Kitty hastened to comply, he turned to Big Tim: "You know gold. You've panned it on Birch Creek, an' Beaver, an' a dozen others. An' you've sniped the bars on the rivers. You've handled gold from Circle, an' Mastodon, an' Forty Mile, an' you've seen it in the blowers. You've seen nuggets an' flour gold, too. But you never saw gold like this." Unknotting the handkerchief, he poured its contents onto one of the squares of writing paper which Kitty had placed on the table, while upon the other he shook a like amount from his own sack. Then he sat back and watched as Big Tim and Kitty bent their heads

"I HATE YOU!"

close over the two little piles of gold that glowed with a soft sheen in the dull yellow light of the tin lamp.

It seemed a long time before Big Tim raised his head. "Well, what about it?" he asked. "It's coarse gold. But I've seen coarse gold before."

"That color?"

"Color!" Big Tim's head once more bent over the two squares of paper, and for many minutes the only sound in the little room was the ticking of the clock on its shelf as the girl and her father studied the yellow grains, moving the lamp a bit to that side or this, prodding, separating the grains with their fingers. The girl was the first to look up. "This first pile is darker," she said. "But what difference does that make, Tommy?"

Big Tim was on his feet, his eyes shining with excitement, and suddenly Tommy Haldane felt his hand crushed in a mighty grip. "She's right, lad! 'Tis new gold! New to the river! Where'd ye git it? An' what's this got to do with Carmack?"

"That's the gold Carmack is shoving over the bar at the Antlers to pay for the drinks he's buyin'. The gold you fellows said was Larue's."

"But how come ye to have it?"

"I traded with the bartender as he was about to dump it off the scales. I stood where I could watch Carmack's face an', drunk or not—squaw man or not—I figured he was tellin' the truth. I stood at the end of the bar, right by the scales. It was late afternoon an' a streak of sunlight slanted in through the window. I was watchin' the blue smoke with the little dust particles floatin' around in it when the bartender shook the gold into the scales from Carmack's sack. In the sunlight the gold looked dark—almost red—different from any I'd seen. So when he had weighed in, I paid out of my own sack an' had him dump Carmack's gold into my handkerchief. He thought I wanted to carry around some stampede gold for luck. He still thinks so, an' he warned me not to count on what Carmack said—same as you did."

"I know'd ye was smart, lad!" The voice of Big Tim boomed proudly. "But I didn't know ye was that smart—the only man in a roomful av sourdoughs to notice the difference in the color av the gold! Come on—we'll go an' tell the boys!"

But young Haldane shook his head. "Not yet, Tim. We don't know for sure whether there's anything in this or not. They wouldn't listen to Carmack, but a lot of 'em'll listen to you. There's no use startin' a stampede till we're sure. Let's you an' me throw a light outfit into a canoe, an' hit upriver an' look around a little. We can stake an' be back in a month—twenty days, if we're lucky. Then we can get a polin' boat an' a winter's outfit an' hit back up again. An' believe me—we'll go back on the head of a stampede! Polin' boats are goin' to be worth what a man'll pay for 'em a month from now."

"Why don't you wait till spring?" asked Kitty. "If no one believes Carmack, the gold will be there in the spring."

"Spring—hell!—lass," cried Big Tim. "If there's a crick where gold lays so thick that a lazy loafer like Carmack can pan out thirteen ounces in half a day, it ain't goin' to stay hid long! Carmack's headin' down to Circle. There'll be someone there'll believe him. Even if they don't, what's to hinder someone else from happenin' along jest like Carmack done? There's good men upriver right now—Bob Henderson, an' plenty more, an' if one av them comes bustin' downriver wid word av a strike, there'll be a different story to tell. The lad's right. We'll go while the goin's good, an' stake in ahead av the rush. Then we'll drop down an' let 'em all in. I'm like Tommy—I got a hunch —an' my hunch says there'll be history made on the Yukon this winter—an' we'll be in on the makin'."

"Take me with you," urged the girl.

But Big Tim shook his head. For a long time he sat smoking, his eyes on the two yellow splotches. "Av this thing is as big as it well might be," he said, at length, "hell's goin' to pop on the Yukon. The stampede from Forty Mile an' from Circle won't be nothin'! When word av the strike reaches the outside they'll be the damn'dest stampede av chechakos the world ever seen. Good men will come—an' mixed in wid 'em'll be the scum an' the riffraff av the world. In such case a woman's goin' to be a care an' a hinderance to a man. He couldn't take her the places he might have to go—an' he wouldn't leave her behind. If the strike peters out, things will be about the same by spring as now. The two av ye are young—ye've plenty time ahead av ye. If the gold lays thick as Carmack says, the next two, three years are goin' to be hell on the rivers—an' no place fer a woman. An' if it lays thick, two, three years will make the everlastin' fortunes of them that get in on the head av it." Big Tim's eyes rested affectionately on the girl: "Ye'll not be the one, lass, to willy stand in the way av yer man. Ye've an aunt in Seattle—Kate O'Brien, a widdy woman, ye're mither's sister. She never thought much av me—never got over hatin' me fer takin' yer mother way off to the north country. She is a great hand to talk. But she won't turn down her own kin if ye ask her to keep ye a while, if I pay her good. She's a long eye fer a dollar, has Kate. They's a party goin' to start fer the outside a-Saturday, the government geologist an' his wife, an' I can arrange fer ye to go wid 'em. Give

Tommy an' me a year—two years, Kitty, widout hinderance, an' ye can live where ye like, an' as ye like, anywheres in the world, fer the rest av yer life."

"But I don't want to wait a year or two years!" cried the girl impetuously. "We're going to be married this fall, aren't we, Tommy? And I wouldn't hinder! I'd help! I've always lived on the Yukon! I'm no chechako!" The blue eyes that had flashed defiantly as her father talked, now sought Tommy's in swift appeal. Surely Tommy would side with her! They could be married and . . . Clammy fingers seemed clutching at her heart. Her cheeks paled, and the light of confidence faded from the appealing eyes. The red lips drooped wistfully, and the little room seemed suddenly shrouded in a misty film.

Tommy Haldane's lips were closed and there was a set she had come to know to the stubborn jaw. When finally he spoke his voice sounded far away and hard: "Tim's right, dear. We'll be most likely winterin' in a tent, an' if game's scarce it's goin' to be a hard winter—too hard for a man to expose the woman he loves to, if there's any other way. We can't leave you here because every sourdough in Forty Mile will be winterin' on Carmack's creek. An' I wouldn't winter a dog with the scum that'll be left behind. You go to your aunt, an' when I make my pile I'll come for you. If there was a priest here we could be married now—then I could pay for your keep——"

"Marry you!" The girl's eyes flashed black—thunderheads obscuring a blue sky. She had backed against the table, a hand on either side of her gripping its edge tensely, as the words fairly hurled themselves from her lips: "I won't marry you, Tommy Haldane! Now, or any other time! Not if you were the last man in the world, I wouldn't! I hate you! Who are you to think you could winter where I couldn't? I was born in the North! I've lived in the North for nineteen years. And you're a chechako. I'll go outside if dad sends me—and I'll stay outside! I hate the North, and the camps, and everything about them! I'll go where people *live!* And you never need to come for me, either! Go pan your red gold! And then come back to Forty Mile and spend it. There'll be girls here—girls that couldn't winter in tents—and wouldn't if they could! They'll help you spend your red gold, Tommy Haldane! To hell with you!"

arms closed convulsively about his mighty shoulders. And then he had turned away and was walking slowly up the bank, his blanket coat blending into the formless blur of faces....

In his little cabin Tommy Haldane was drinking grimly—savagely—drinking alone. He didn't like whisky, but one of the quart bottles on the table before him was nearly empty, and Tommy Haldane was very drunk. He had never been drunk before, and the room reeled dizzily. Shouts from the river bank reached his ears and their import percolated to his befuddled consciousness. Clumsily his fingers closed about the neck of the bottle, and he conveyed it uncertainly to his lips and swallowed two huge gulps, choking and gagging as the fiery liquor burned its way down. "Kittish goin' ou'shide," he mumbled thickly. "A'ri' Kitty—G'bye. Shaysh to hell wish me—goin' to hell fa'sh I can. Me'n Ol' Bettles goin' t'hell. She won' mar' me—don' blame 'er—wouldn' mar' no drunken bashtard neasher. G'bye...."

Big Tim McGuigan found him later in the evening asleep in his chair with an empty bottle in his lap. Removing his boots he carried him to his bunk and left the room, closing the door behind him. Until dark he worked at the stowing of a two-man outfit into a canoe. At daylight he was back in Tommy Haldane's cabin. Tommy lay as he had left him, breathing heavily. Big

Tim lighted the fire and put on the coffee pot. Then he roused the sleeper, a task that called for much shaking and the proper dashing of ice-cold water. Finally, after much half coherent mumbling, and demands to "le' me 'lone," Tommy swung his feet to the floor and sat upon the edge of the bed with his head in his hands, the picture of dejection and physical misery.

"Oh, God, Tim," he moaned, "I think I'm goin' to die."

"Don't ye wisht ye could?" grinned Big Tim. "But ye'd make a hell av a lookin' corpse wid ye're eyes like two coals in a gob av dough."

"Give me a drink, Tim—I could drink a gallon—I'm burnin' up."

Reaching for a glass, Big Tim splashed it half full of whisky from the bottle that remained on the table and held it close under the other's nose.

"O'Rourke!" exploded Tommy Haldane. And again: "O'Rourke! O'Rourke!"

"McGuigan's the name—not O'Rourke—though 'tis a good Irish name, at that——"

"Get that damn' stuff out of here! It's water I want—a whole bucketful!"

Big Tim's grin widened: "Sure, the hair av the dog is good fer the bite, they claim. Ye'll never make even a middlin' drunkard av ye can't swaller a pint or two before ye get up."

With a moan Tommy lurched across the floor, seized the water pail in his two hands, and raising it to his lips sucked in its cold contents in great gulps. When he had finished, Big Tim handed him a cup of black coffee: "Drink four, five av these, lad. 'Twill set ye up fine. I'll have breakfast ready in a minute."

"Breakfast!" cried Tommy, in disgust. "I couldn't eat any breakfast. I never want to see food again."

"It ain't sea food—it's pancakes," chuckled Big Tim, as he refilled the other's cup with coffee. "Come on—eat a bite, lad, an' wash it down wid the coffee. It'll settle ye're stummick. We'll want to be startin' pretty quick."

"Startin'? Startin' where?"

"Why, upriver, av course. Where d'ye think we'd be startin'?"

"Get some other pardner, Tim. I'm not goin'. I don't give a damn for the gold."

Big Tim answered nothing and the meal proceeded, Tommy managing to eat a sourdough pancake or two, and drink numerous cups of black coffee. When it was over and the dishes washed, Big Tim glanced about the cabin.

"Throw what clothes ye'll want in yer pack sack, an' we'll be goin'," he said.

"I tell you I'm not goin'."

"Ye may think ye ain't—but ye are. Av I have

to lick ye first it won't take long—but, ye're goin'. Ye're a welcher, an' a piker, an' a tin horn——"

"You lie!"

"That's better——"

"It's because I don't want the gold. I don't need it—now. What I've got'll last longer than *I* will, if this is how that damn' whisky makes a man feel."

"Don't fool ye'rself, lad. Ye'll be needin' all ye can git. The McGuigans can spend money. An' Kitty's a chip off the old block."

"Kitty! She'll never marry me!"

"No?"

"You heard her tell me to my face she wouldn't."

"Sure an' I did. An' I heard her mother tell me the same thing forty or fifty times. But she married me—an' neither ever regretted it. An' I heard Kitty tell ye 'to hell wid ye'—but ye don't have to go. Show 'em who wears the pants to start out wid. Do what they *ask* ye to, lad—but, never what they *tell* ye to. Ye've made a damn' fool av ye'rself once wid the whisky—let that do ye. Git ye're hands on all the gold ye can in the next year or so, and then go outside after Kitty McGuigan. An' ye'll bring her back av ye have to knock her down an' drag her back. Where's ye're guts, lad? D'ye want some damn' chechako to git her? I don't."

KITTY GOES OUTSIDE

"But she said——"

"Said—hell!" snorted Big Tim in disgust. "Av ye give heed to what they say, ye'll be at war all ye're life. Them tantrums is the pop valve women's got to keep 'em from bustin'."

A slow grin twisted the lips of Tommy Haldane. Without a word he collected a change of clothing and dumped it into his pack sack. Then his eye fell on the bottle of whisky from which Big Tim had poured the nauseating draught. With a shudder he seized the bottle by the neck and hurled it out through the door.

"Come on," he said, "I'm ready."

CHAPTER IV

The Passing of Big Tim

For eleven days Big Tim and Tommy Haldane prospected the Bonanza moose pasture. Then they staked adjoining claims that preëmpted a thousand feet on the creek and extended from rim to rim. On the evening before they were to start back for Forty Mile the two sat long over their pipes and their tea.

Big Tim's eyes regarded the little sacks of dust that lay on the blankets: "Two hundred ounces if there's a grain," he murmured, in an awed voice. "Two hundred ounces fer two men in eleven days—an' the prospectin' we done besides! An' it all come out av the grass roots! She's big, Tommy. She's so big they can't no one see the end of it. Carmack didn't know the half—not the hundredth part of it—nor the thousandth. Bed rock will tell the tale."

"We panned it from the creek, an' we panned it from the rims," said Tommy. "The whole valley's rotten with gold."

"Aye, lad—but she's spotted. Some will win, an' some will lose—'tis the luck av the game. Buy claims, Tommy. Buy claims, an' buy options. She's the biggest game ever played—an' the claims is the chips in the game. A man can't win every time he throws in a chip—but he don't have to. An' this ain't the only crick. A year from now, every crick, an' feeder an' gulch, an' pup, an' draw will be staked fer miles around. 'Twas a grand hunch ye had, lad. There'll be a stampede like no stampede ever was—an' we're on the head av it! From up the river, an' down the river, an' over the hills they'll come. An' fer one that wins, there'll be ten that loses. They'll drown, an' they'll freeze, an' they'll starve, an' thieve, an' murder. 'Tis every man fer himself, Tommy—an' the devil will git his share."

"There'll be a different story when we hit the Antlers," grinned Tommy. "They won't think we're toutin' Larue's townsite."

"They'll tear out the front gittin' to the river," laughed Big Tim.

"A man might do worse than get a corner on polin' boats."

"Never stop to shoot skunks on a moose hunt, lad. But we'd do well to buy us the pick av them before we spring the news. An', mind ye, not a word to anyone till we hit Forty Mile. We'll collect all the boys an' spring the word in the

Antlers. This first stampede will be a stampede av sourdoughs—an' they'll all start from scratch. An' the damn' chechakos can fight amongst themselves fer the tailin's."

That night it snowed, and it was snowing furiously next day when their canoe shot out onto the Yukon. Tommy, being the better canoeman, paddled the stern with the bulk of the outfit loaded abaft of midship to balance the weight of Big Tim in the bow. In so far as possible, they held close to the shore as an occasional rift in the wind-whipped snow gave them their bearings. Rains in the hills had swollen many of the feeders, and time and again in passing their mouths the two found themselves surrounded by a clutter of drift logs and the branches of uprooted trees.

Tommy felt a sudden jar as an uprooted tree rolled in the current beside the canoe. Placing his paddle on the trunk, Big Tim gave a mighty shove. There was a nasty scraping sound as the light craft shuddered throughout her length, and then the voice of Big Tim shouting through the storm: "Hell an' damnation! We've punched a hole in her!"

Tommy felt ice-cold water about his knees. "Plug her!" he yelled. "Plug her with your cap!" At the same moment he swung the canoe toward shore.

"There's a hell av a hole in the bow!" called

THE PASSING OF BIG TIM

Big Tim, and Tommy could see that he was pulling off his blanket coat. The water was inches deep about his knees, and a sudden rift in the storm showed the shore a full quarter of a mile away. Unknowingly, the current had swept them well out into the river, and Tommy saw at a glance they would never make it at the rate the water was pouring into the canoe. Dropping his paddle, he slashed the pack lashings with his knife and, grabbing up the coffeepot, ripped the lid off and began to bail furiously.

"I've got my cap an' my coat rammed in, but she's still leakin' like a sieve!" cried Big Tim.

With his free hand Tommy tossed him the frying-pan. "Bail! Bail like hell!" he cried. "If we can gain on her I can paddle in a few minutes an' we'll make shore."

But despite their best efforts the water slowly rose in the canoe. "Can ye swim?" yelled Big Tim.

"Not a lick," answered Tommy, throwing water as fast as his arm would move.

" 'Tis up to me, then!" called the big man. "She's gainin' on us—but, wid my weight out av here the bow'll rise so the hole will be clear av the water."

"Stay where you are!" Tommy screamed, as he saw the other shifting his weight. "By God, we'll both go down together!"

"Ye're a fool! 'Twill be child's play fer me!"

The man was on his feet, now—balancing precariously—the snow driving into his wind-tossed hair. "But—av anything should happen, an' I didn't make it—look after Kitty, lad! An' —in the Antlers—tell the boys that word av the strike is a present from Big Tim McGuigan!"

"Sit down!" yelled Tommy, and the next instant he was using everything he had in the balancing of the water-logged canoe. As Big Tim dived clear, the craft careened and rolled drunkenly. There was a rush of water toward the stern as the lightened bow rose clear of the water, and when the canoe steadied, Tommy bailed with redoubled fury.

In vain his eyes swept the surface of the rushing current for sight of Big Tim's head. Only a few yards of water were visible, the whole vast surface of the river being obscured by the long slanting lines of wind-driven snow. Once he called out loudly as an object bobbed up alongside. But it was only the end of a log spinning slowly in the current. He was gaining rapidly on the water, now. As Big Tim had figured, the hole in the bow was lifted above the surface of the river.

When the canoe attained some semblance of buoyancy Tommy tossed aside his coffee pot, and picking up his paddle, made all haste for shore. Pulling the canoe clear, he built a fire, and picking up his rifle, made his way upriver for a half mile or more. "He couldn't have landed above here," he reasoned after several minutes of shouting and shooting his rifle. "If he made shore, he's below."

Replenishing his fire as he passed, Tommy proceeded downriver, searching the shore, shooting, shouting. Nearly two miles, he walked, until a swollen confluent forced him to turn back.

Toward evening, when the storm ceased, he dropped down a short distance to a point that jutted out into the river. Here he collected wood, and built a fire whose light would be visible from several miles of shore. All night he tended his fire, sleeping fitfully—calling and shooting at intervals. At daylight, he again patrolled the shore upriver, searching the waterline, and alert for tracks in the snow. Breakfasting hurriedly, he plugged the hole in the canoe as best he could, and proceeded slowly downstream, close in—searching the shore.

Ten miles below, he gave it up. Surely Big Tim would have landed before this. No matter how strong a swimmer a man was, he couldn't have remained in that icy water long enough to have been carried so far down, and lived.

Hot tears filled the lad's eyes as realization of the fact of Big Tim's passing forced itself upon him. It was more than the loss of a partner —it was a personal loss—the loss of a loved one.

"It will kill Kitty," he croaked in a voice that was half a sob. "God!—how they loved each other."

Grimly, with tight-pressed lips, he drove his canoe toward Forty Mile. The vision of Big Tim rose before his eyes—Big Tim as he stood in the bow of the canoe, his hair flying in the wind, and the slanting lines of snow beating against him. His lips had smiled, and his kindly eyes had seemed to glow with a strange fire— and then he was gone. "They'll drown, an' they'll freeze, an' they'll starve, an' thieve, an' murder," he had said, back there on Bonanza. And now he was gone—the first fulfillment of his own prophecy.

Twilight was deepening, and the sourdoughs had forgathered in the Antlers saloon. Camillo Bill thumped the bar with the bottom of the leather box and with a twist of the wrist, spread the five dice on the board. "Four fours," he read. "I'll leave 'em."

Moosehide Charlie gathered the cubes and shook. "It's on me," he announced. "Three sixes is all I can find. What's become of Big Tim McGuigan?" he asked as Camillo poured his liquor. "I ain't seen him since Kitty left."

"Off on a prospectin' trip with young Haldane. I seen him that night, an' he said they was goin' up to look over this here Bonanza Crick."

"Hell! Big Tim wouldn't fall fer nothin'

Carmack said!" opined Moosehide. "Here's luck."

Camillo Bill grinned: "I guess 'twasn't so much what Carmack said, as gettin' the kid out of camp fer a while. Big Tim didn't let on much, but it seems Kitty turned young Haldane down. Leastwise, he wasn't there to say good-bye when she left, an' Curley said he sold the kid a couple of bottles of hooch that day—an' bein' as he ain't much of a hand fer licker, it ain't so hard to figure."

"Funny! I've seen 'em go plumb to hell, that way, on account of women. What did she turn him down fer? Haldane's a damn' good kid."

Camillo Bill shrugged: "Women's women, Moosehide," he answered, sagely. "They take notions. It don't have to be *fer* nothin'."

> *In the days of old,*
> *In the days of gold,*
> *In the days of 'forty-nine . . .*

Old Bettles got as far as he ever got with his song, forgot he was singing, and laid a hand upon a shoulder of each: "What you two short-horns prongin' about? Figurin' on beatin' Carmack out of his strike?"

"Talkin' about Big Tim—him an' young Haldane pulled out the day after Kitty left."

"Damn' fine gal, little Quitty McGigan. I c'n

remember when she wasn't no more'n so high." Bettles demonstrated vaguely, with a sweep of the arm that started as high as he could reach, and ended an inch from the floor.

"You saved her life once all right, old-timer," said Camillo Bill with approval.

"Betcher life I did. Do it again, too. Betcher that damn' doc'll come nex' time. Knocked him cold as a wedge. Knock half a dozen doctors cold as a dozen wedges any day fer Kitty. She's more sourdough'n we are. She was born here—an' we wasn't. Damn' fine gal. Goin' to bring me thousan' oranges. Goin' to have orange punch on my birthday."

"Birthday—hell!" grinned Moosehide. "You just had your hundredth birthday last week."

Bettles blinked owlishly: "Hun'reth birthday? How'n hell I had a hun'reth birthday when I wan't only sixty-two? Anyway, I never had no orange punch that birthday. Goin' to have 'nother birthday in the spring. Hell's fire! I'd shove *Chris'mas* six months ahead fer orange punch!"

All eyes turned toward a newcomer who had entered the door and moved swiftly across the room. It was young Tommy Haldane, and he halted directly before Camillo Bill, Moosehide Charlie, and Old Bettles. His face looked white and drawn and the words that fell from between stiff lips sounded, somehow, mechanical—wooden:

"Big Tim McGuigan's dead," he said.

"Dead!"

"Big Tim—gone!"

"God Almighty, kid—tell us about it." Camillo Bill shoved the whisky bottle toward the lad, but he shook his head. He leaned for a moment against the bar, while men crowded about as the word passed from lip to lip. The dance-hall piano was stilled, and the girls n_ ered curiously about the edges of the crowd and listened as Tommy Haldane recovered himself, and with every eye in the house on his face, told the story from beginning to er ' thudding the little sacks of gold onto the bar as he proclaimed the richness of the strike.

But not one eye glanced toward the gold as the sourdoughs followed his words to the moment of Big Tim McGuigan's plunge from the bow of the sinking canoe. They were living those moments themselves, those bearded men of the North—they saw Big Tim, hatless, coatless —the snow beating into his wind-tossed hair— they heard his words—saw the smile on his face —and they heard the splash with which the mighty Yukon swallowed this comrade of many a long snow trail. "An'," concluded Tommy, "he said, 'in the Antlers—tell the boys that word of the strike is a present from Big Tim McGuigan!' "

There was a silence, broken here and there by queer throat sounds. On the outer edge of the crowd a girl was sobbing aloud.

Camillo Bill was the first to find his voice: "Line up, boys," he said, in words that sounded husky and strange. The tension was broken, and men eagerly lined the bar. "All filled?" asked Camillo Bill. "Well—here's to Big Tim McGuigan—*He couldn't swim a damn' stroke! Me—I know!*"

CHAPTER V

The Widow O'Brien

IN SEATTLE, the purser of the boat exchanged Kitty McGuigan's gold for currency, and placed her in a cab with directions to the driver for delivery to her aunt. Thus it was that when the cab drew up before the door of a large house on a street of modest residences, Mrs. Kate O'Brien peered askance from behind the parlor curtains of her boarding house—for genteel folks only—salesladies, clerks, and the like—no lumberjacks, sailors, nor longshoresmen need apply.

Mrs. O'Brien had not always kept a boarding house for genteel folks only, on a modest residential street. Her first ventures had been on the waterfront. So, when from behind her curtains she saw that the cabby had swung to the sidewalk, not a conventional trunk, nor a genteel suitcase, not even a passé valise, but an ample duffel bag of heavy waterproofed canvas, her lips grimmed, and the light of battle kindled in her black eyes. For such dunnage was unpleasantly reminiscent of the ungenteel days on the waterfront.

Her lips were still grim, though the battle light somewhat mollified as her eyes took measure of the girl who was ascending the steps to the porch, followed by the cabby carrying the offending baggage. The girl wore a man's hat of soft felt, a man's shirt of blue flannel, and a skirt of heavy, dark material. Surprise, with more than a suggestion of grudging admiration, registered in the woman's eyes as she answered the jangling pull-bell, and stared into the face that showed beneath the brim of the felt hat—a beautiful face by any standard of measure, with its eyes of Irish blue—its naturally red lips, and its clear tanned skin that bespoke health and wholesomeness.

The girl was speaking in a tone rich and throaty that seemed somehow vaguely reminiscent of another voice: "Are you Mrs. Kate O'Brien?"

"That's me." The voice was neither hostile, nor cordial. The woman felt that the blue eyes were taking her measure. She waited, her ample frame blocking the doorway, while the girl drew an envelope from the pocket of her shirt.

"I have a letter for you," she said.

In silence the woman read the missive to the

last word. "So you're Maggie's girl? Maggie's, an' that Tim McGuigan's? Well, I guess you be, all right. You've got Maggie's eyes, an' her voice too. Come on in." She turned to the cabby: "Set that war bag in the hall."

"How much do I owe you?" asked Kitty, producing a roll of bills from her shirt pocket.

"Dollar an' a half, mum."

"No you don't! You thievin' land pirate! Give him a dollar an' let him take his rack of bones an' git back where he belongs."

"It's worth——"

But the door slammed on the protest, and Mrs. Kate O'Brien motioned the girl into a room separated from the hall by a portière of threaded beads and long polished sticks of bamboo that rattled softly into place behind them. "Go on in the parlor an' we can talk, though land knows I'm busy enough—what with the help like it is." The woman indicated a patent rocking chair of golden oak and polished nickel, and seated herself upon the edge of a haircloth sofa stuffed to uncomfortable roundness. "So yer ma's dead, huh? Tim McGuigan wrote me about 'leven, twelve years ago. Well, a body couldn't expect nothin' else—an' I told her so—goin' way off to the end of nowheres where there ain't nothin' but polar bears an' ice an' snow!"

The blue Irish eyes took on a slightly darker hue: "I've lived there all my life, and I never saw a polar bear," answered the girl quietly. "And I'd hate a country where there was no ice and snow. People die here, now and then, don't they?"

"Why, of course, folks dies. But we've got hospitals, an' doctors, an' drug stores, an' everything."

"But people die?"

"Some does; an' some don't. But——"

"Just the same up there, and we have no hospitals, nor drug stores—and only a few doctors. My mother loved the country. Will you have room for me, here?"

"Well—my rates is nine dollars a week, in advance—board an' lodgin', except the two front rooms which is twelve—but they're took—Mr. Snook, ladies underwear Harmon & Babbit's got the north one, an' Miss Gibbs, head operator Mildew exchange's got the south—the other boarders thinks they're engaged—an' if they ain't they'd ought to be—or married—or somethin'—the way they carry on there's goin' to be a vacant room front south pretty quick 'cause I can git fourteen a week fer it from Mr. Ginsberg, floorwalker gents furnishin's Harmon & Babbit—he's Jewish, but no one'd know it if they didn't look at him er hear him talk—an' that Miss Gibbs, she's personal non grattle around here—that's Latin when you don't like folks—Mr. Heidgerken, he use' to run a business college till he died of the heart disease a year back, learnt me that—he use' to talk so grand they couldn't hardly no one figger out what he was drivin' at—he cert'nly was educated swell. Anyway, I'd ruther fill up my house with men than women, they don't kick so much an' they're easier satisfied—except when they die, an' then it's a terrible mess—what with folks runnin' in, an' runnin' out, an' the undertakers an' all, an' the house smellin' of whatever they u.. ~ 'em—I had 'em take Mr. Heidgerken down to the public parlors fer the funeral, what with folks trackin' in an' all—it's bad enough to have the undertaker's wagon without a hearse an' maybe a string of cabs standin' around in front of the door—an' folks goin' by rubberin' at the house like it was my fault a man should die of the heart disease, which he'd prob'ly had it before he ever come here. I can let you have a back room, single bed, dresser, one window, an' 'lectric light, right next to the ladies' toilet, an' bath twict a week—an' bein' as you're anyways half my own kith an' kin, you might say, I'll let you have it fer seven a week if you'd like to kind of help around, or if you want to git you a job it'll be nine a week."

Kitty sat spellbound as her aunt, without apparent effort, unburdened herself. She heaved a deep sigh of relief, and the red lips curved into just the suggestion of a smile at the realization that she was experiencing the sensation of having shot a rapid.

"I'll take the room," she said, "and for the present, at least, I'll be glad to help all I can."

"That'll be all right. It'll be seven, in advance."

Kitty slipped the roll of bills from the pocket of her shirt. "I'll be here at least six months," she said, "so I'll pay you in advance for twenty-six weeks, that will be—let's see, a hundred and eighty-two dollars."

"Land's sakes! How do I know—without a pencil? They must have good schools where you come from, anyway."

"I've never been to a school. We don't have them."

"It can't be a body's born knowin' that six months is twenty-six weeks, an' seven dollars a week is a hundred an' eighty-two dollars, no matter how smart they be."

"After my mother died, Daddy and the other boys taught me all I know."

"Other boys? Funny Maggie never wrote me about havin' no boys! She wrote me after she'd had you—an' I thought that's all she had."

Kitty laughed: "Oh, I haven't any brothers or sisters. I meant the boys—the boys of Forty Mile. They're all grown men—some of them old enough to be my grandfather. And I just love them all!"

"Fer heaven's sakes! Ain't they no women to teach school?"

"N-o-o—not to teach school, even if there was a school. There's the dance-hall girls—and some others that have a cabin down by the flats."

"Humph," snorted Mrs. O'Brien, "you don't need to go into particulars! Fine country, I'd say, to fetch up a girl in! You bet I give Tim McGuigan a piece of my mind when him an' Maggie come an' told us—my Pat was livin' then, God rest his soul—he was a contractor an' made good money, an' he'd give Tim McGuigan as good a sewer job as a man'd want— three-sixty a day, an' eight-hour shifts Tim was gittin' when him an' Maggie was married—not that it wasn't partly Maggie's fault, she was always kind of uppity an' wasn't never satisfied with Tim in the sewers, so they saved up, an' when they had enough Tim boughten two tickets fer this here Alaska an' away they went, but me an' Pat stuck to the sewers an' when Pat got killed in a cave-in, which if the laggin' had be'n clear of knots an' shakes like the specifications, he'd be'n alive an' kickin' today, like my lawyer said when I sued the city an' got five thousan' dollars fer him, which the lawyer got half of an' I got two thousan' five hundred, an' a thousan' dollars from the life insurance company, an' the three thousan' one hundred an' fourteen-twenty-seven we had in the bank, an'

I sold Pat's outfit to Riley & Corrigan, the dirty bums—bran' new concrete mixer only be'n used fourteen months you might say, an' all the rest of the stuff, shovels an' picks an' wheelbarrows an' block-an'-tackles, an' the Lord knows what Pat didn't have, an' all they'd pay me was seven hundred an' sixty-eight-fifty fer it as good as new.

"An' now Corrigan's alderman an' Riley gits all the contracts, but Riley's drunk every night an' prob'ly he'll die of the snakes which would serve him right—robbin' a poor widdy woman! An' I bought a house that was fer sale down by the docks an' started a boardin' house, but it wasn't genteel what with the sailors an' stevedores an' whatnot, gittin' drunk, or drunk, or gittin' over bein' drunk—an' tryin' to run women in on me nights—so I sold out an' bought another place an' it wasn't no better what with the loggers an' lumberjacks worse'n the sailors. So I says to myself, 'to hell with the riffraff,' an' I sold out an' bought this place, an' if I do say it as maybe shouldn't, it's genteel—an' that reminds me, dearie, them clothes you got ain't fitten fer no lady to wear around a genteel boardin' house—they're half men's an' look a sight—'safternoon I'll set that good-fer-nothin' housemaid washin' winders, an' tell the cook what to git fer supper, an' I'll go with you an' do some shoppin'. Harmon & Babbit's got a sale on in ladies underwear. I heard Mr. Snook tellin' Miss Gibbs this mornin' an' he'll interdoose us to the clerk in the dresses an' maybe we'll git a price—yes, you was right, it's one hundred an' eighty-two fer twenty-six weeks, an' I can put it in the bank when we're down that way."

As she talked the woman had moved from the stuffed sofa to a desk and without a moment's hesitation in the stream of words, had performed the necessary mathematical calculation, and stood now before the girl who counted the bills into an eagerly outstretched hand.

"An' now, dearie," she continued as she folded the bills and, after a mighty exhalation, managed to stuff them between a tight-fitting corset and an ample bosom, "I'll show you your room an' call Ellie, an' she can help you upstairs with that outlandish contraption which you'll be throwin' away most of the stuff in it when you get you some decent clothes. It's half past eleven a'ready an' I don't want it settin' around the hall when the ladies an' gentlemen come to dinner, except maybe Mr. Snook which about half the time he eats his dinners at a restaurant somewheres, he wanted I should knock off fer it, but I says to him 'rates is rates, Mr. Snook. Dinner's here fer you an' if you don't choose to eat it it ain't my fault!' So he——"

In desperation Kitty interrupted the discourse that threatened to flow on and on indefinitely. "I don't need any help, thanks," she said, and to prove it swung the duffel bag to her shoulder while her aunt's eyes rounded in amazement. "Land's sakes, but you're strong! A body'd thought it was breakin' that cabby in two to set it in the hall!"

"I can travel all day with sixty pounds," she answered, as she followed the woman who panted and wheezed up the stairs with one hand on the banister.

As the girl swung the bag to the floor of her room, the woman lingered in the doorway. "I'll have Ellie fetch your dinner up so you won't have to come down the way you be. They'd talk, an' I don't want they should see kin of mine rigged out like a lumberjack. 'Course Mr. Snook, he'll have to, but I'll get him off to one side an' explain. We could do your shoppin' somewheres else, but Mr. Snook always gives me a price."

When the woman had gone, Kitty McGuigan closed the door and locked it, and seating herself on the edge of the bed she stared for a long time at the gaily lithographed reproduction of Rosa Bonheur's Horse Fair—but she saw no horses. In her mind's eye she was staring at high-flung, snow-burdened peaks rearing out of mighty distances, at dark, spruce-clad terraces with the Yukon rolling between—at Forty

Mile, with its rude log houses grouped in friendly proximity, its rabble of fighting, fly-tortured dogs, and the beach with its clutter of fish racks, and drying nets, overturned canoes, and poling boats, and amid the clutter a crowd of gaudy-shirted bearded men waving caps and handkerchiefs. . . . "Good-bye, Kitty!" . . . "Good-bye." . . . The boats and the men and the dogs and the nets blurred together, and with an aching throat, she buried her face in the pillow and sobbed and sobbed.

CHAPTER VI

Humdrum

The jaw of Mr. Oswald Snook, ladies' underwear—he called it "lingeree," and fondled it as though he loved it—dropped as he stared in undisguised admiration into the face of the girl who stood beside his landlady on the other side of his counter: "This is my niece, Kitty McGuigan, that I was tellin' you about this noon, Mr. Snook. She jest come from way up in Alaska——"

"Please' to meet you, Miss McGuigan," simpered Mr. Snook, and turned to shake a manicured finger at the older woman: "Now, Mis' O'Brien, I'd ought to known you was kidding me. You always would have your little joke. Why, Miss McGuigan's pos*tive*ly swell looking."

"I didn't say she wasn't—get her out of them clothes," defended the aunt. "In one of them print percales she'll knock their eye out. Her ma always run more to looks than what I did——"

"Size thirty-eight," appraised Mr. Snook, eyeing the girl professionally. "I'll give you a note to Miss Sippy, ready to wear, and she'll give you a price." He smiled ingratiatingly into the face of the girl: "But Miss McGuigan don't have to doll up to make a hit with me. I think the clothes she's got on become her fine. There's a sort of a sayvoor fare about 'em that's chick. Us artists in dress, we notice them things. But then there's something big and elemental in my nature, Miss McGuigan, that longs to get right out and conquer some of these here icebergs and wild places you read about. My grandfather, on my mother's side, lives twenty miles back from the railroad! What do you think of that?"

"My," said Kitty McGuigan. "And is he still alive?"

"Yes, indeed he is. Don't get to town sometimes for a week at a stretch. That's the life. I always say I envy him, though I don't know as I'd care to live quite so far away. One misses so much in the way of culture, don't you think, Miss McGuigan?"

"Sometimes I do," answered the girl, dryly.

"My grandfather's a great hunter. He shot a deer last fall, and there's wolves been heard within a few miles of his house. I suppose there's lots of wild animals up in Alaska, Miss McGuigan?"

"Oh, yes—lots of them."

"I suppose some of 'em are fierce, too, aren't they?"

"Yes. The ones we hate most are the chechakos. But, thank goodness they're scarce."

"Ah—yes," said Mr. Snook, a trifle vaguely, as he removed a carefully folded, lavender-bordered handkerchief from his pocket, flicked at his nose with it and, returning it still folded, patted it into place. "Yes, I remember, now— it was only a few days ago I was talking with our Mr. Bratty, furs third floor, and he was saying that it was hard to get any genuine chechako any more, but they make a very good imitation out of—of, I think he said skunk."

"That would be the nearest thing to it," answered Kitty, without so much as the quiver of an eyelash.

"But I suppose you can get the genuine article up there?"

"They're not very plentiful, but I wear a summer parka made entirely of matched chechako skins."

"I'll bet it's beautiful, all right. But what is a parka? You see, Miss McGuigan, to be perfectly frank with you, I'm one of these people who aren't ashamed to ask questions. If I don't know all about a thing I come right out and admit it. A parka, I suppose, is some kind of a coat?"

"Yes—with a hood to it."

"Oh, yes. I've seen pictures of 'em! So that's what they call a parka? Well, well! But is it so cold up there that you have to wear a chechako parka in summer?"

"Well, there are some hot days when even a chechako parka is uncomfortable—like the third of July this year when the thermometer got up to forty below. We nearly suffocated, but a cool breeze sprang up in the evening—that's one thing we can count on—our nights are generally cool."

"What do you mean?" gasped the astonished Mr. Snook. "Forty below zero in the summer?"

"Well, not exactly zero, as you understand it here. You see, the ordinary thermometer is no good on the Yukon because the mercury would be solid all winter. So we make our own thermometers by fixing the thigh bone of a chechako so it stands upright in a pan of gold dust, and it registers by the contraction and expansion of the dust which of course, can never become solid even in the coldest weather."

"Well, well, now isn't that clever? And simple, too, isn't it? Do you know, Miss McGuigan, I just love to hear how they do things in different parts of the world. I think it broadens a man, don't you?"

"Yes, indeed," answered Kitty, smothering an almost uncontrollable desire to shriek. If the boys were only here, she was thinking—they would talk of it for months on the Yukon. The voice of her aunt cut in on the thought: "Young folks is young folks, but you'll have plenty of time to talk some other time. I got to be gettin' along, an' we've got dresses an' shoes an' stockin's an' hats to get, yet. You can talk this evenin'. That is," she added with a knowing grin, "if Miss Gibbs'll give Mr. Snook the chance."

Mr. Snook simpered: "Now, now, Miss O'Brien. It ain't my fault if I'm pop'lar with the ladies. Miss Gibbs ain't got no strings on me, in spite of what they say. She ain't deuce high with Miss McGuigan. She lacks her charm, an' she ain't had the broadening influences of travel." He smiled benignly upon Kitty. "Just step to this end, Miss McGuigan, an' I'll show you something nifty in thirty-eights."

Kitty McGuigan smiled to herself all the way home as she listened to her aunt's untiring patter. Even Seattle had its compensations, and she would be back on the Yukon in the spring. She had no faith in Carmack's strike even if her father and Tommy Haldane had. Dear old daddy—he did what he thought was best for me. And Tommy is a dear, too—but, I'll never forgive him for not coming to say good-bye."

At supper that evening—for at Mrs.

O'Brien's genteel boarding house the evening meal was supper—Kitty was properly introduced as "my niece from Alaska," her repeated explanation to her aunt that the upper Yukon country was not in Alaska, carrying no weight whatever.

Mr. Snook smiled and smirked with the familiarity of old acquaintance, and a look that brought a blush to Kitty's cheeks at the realization that he knew exactly what she was wearing beneath the printed percale—a look that caused the nose of the lynx-eyed Miss Gibbs to elevate perceptibly, and put a sneer into the words with which she acknowledged the introduction: "Ah, Alaska. How interesting," she drawled. "I suppose you eat nothing but bears, up there?"

"Two, each morning for breakfast," answered Kitty, sweetly. "One fried on one side, and the other on the other. For lunch I generally take a boiled seal, or half a dozen raw fish, and in the evening I like half a cold moose and some Eskimo ice cream."

Miss Gibbs flushed scarlet at the laugh that went up from the other boarders. But she came back for more: "What is Eskimo ice cream?" she asked with a disdainful wrinkling of the nose. "It sounds almost as appetizing as the rest of the food."

"Oh, it is," answered Kitty innocently. "You

milk a reindeer on a snowball, and then eat it—the reindeer, of course. The snowball freezes so fast it explodes and kills the reindeer."

The other lady boarders and Mr. Snook went off into further gales of laughter, and even the elderly Mr. Latham, the undertaker's assistant, broke all precedent by emitting an audible cackle. While Miss Gibbs, with an acrimonious remark anent fresh country girls, relapsed into seething silence.

Later, in the parlor, Miss Daffy, notions, Harmon & Babbit, confided to Kitty with a friendly little squeeze of the hand: "It tickled us most to death the way you got Gibbs's goat, dearie. She sure got a grouch when she seen how you was cuttin' her out with Snookie. He's an awful nice man, Snookie is, and so intellectual. But Gibbs has hogged him ever since she come. She thinks she's awful swell because she's head operator at the Mildew exchange, but us girls call her the 'Wrong Number.'"

Somehow the winter passed with Kitty earning her two dollars allowance on board and room by doing more work about the house than the paid servant—a fact that she realized, but did not resent, as it gave her something to do until such time as her father should send for her to come back to her beloved Yukon. She discovered the public library and spent hours in poring over volumes whose range included Voltaire and Laura Jean Libbey. She went to dances with Mr. Snook or Mr. Ginsberg, and soon became known as the best dancer on the floor. About Christmas-time the twelve-dollar Miss Gibbs relinquished her room which was immediately engaged by the fourteen-dollar Mr. Ginsberg. The Bonheur lithograph was replaced on the wall by the black-and-white drawings of a young artist named Gibson whose men somehow always reminded her of Tommy Haldane—not that they were dressed like Tommy, but, somehow just to look at them you knew instinctively that they were clean and wholesome, and eminently fit to be tacked upon the wall of her room.

During the winter, also, she refused four offers of marriage from Mr. Snook, who was always so nice about it, but never seemed to take the refusals as final; and one from Mr. Ginsberg—who was not nice about it at all.

CHAPTER VII

An Assault and Battery

ONE day, in April, Kitty saw a man enter a store. A gun store it was, and he was a bearded man dressed in a blanket coat and mukluks. A great wave of homesickness swept over her. Visions of the ice-locked Yukon, lying grim and silent between its snow-clad hills—spruce spires—wind-swept headlands—smoke rising lazily from cabins half buried in snow—dog teams, and the shouting of men. . . . "Good-bye, Kitty." . . . "Good-bye." . . .

She walked past the store into which the man had disappeared. Turned, and walked past it again. She had seen blanket coats in Seattle—but mukluks! Only a man from the North—her North—would have mukluks. The third time she hesitated, and then entered the store. The man was looking at rifles. Several lay on the counter before him, and he would pick one up, work the action, throw it to his shoulder, lower

AN ASSAULT AND BATTERY 55

it again and meticulously examine the sights—discard it—pick up another. Gradually Kitty edged nearer, fascinated—unnoticed by either the man, or the clerk behind the counter. His choice seemed to have narrowed to one of two weapons. He would pick one up, sight it, lay it down, and pick up the other. Finally, he seemed to have settled on one of the two guns. It was then that, to her utmost confusion, Kitty heard her own voice speaking. "It'll jam in the cold," she said. "The oil gums it."

Both the clerk and the man stared, and Kitty felt the blood flood her cheeks in a fiery wave. "Camillo Bill had one," she said in desperation. "But——"

"Camillo Bill!" cried the man, his scrutinizing eyes lighting. "What do you know about Camillo Bill?"

"Oh, I know him well, and Moosehide Charlie, and Swiftwater Bill, and Old Bettles——"

A huge hand thrust out impulsively: "Put 'er there, Miss! You sure talk my language. I hail from Circle."

"I live in Forty Mile."

"Sure, I know'd that when you started reelin' off them sourdoughs. Yer a long ways from home, Miss, ain't you? An' of course you know there ain't no Forty Mile, no more—no Circle, neither, you might say——"

"No Forty Mile! No Circle! What do you mean?"

"Why—the big strike upriver jest about emptied them camps."

"You don't mean Carmack's strike!"

"I sure do. That damn' squaw man jest nach'elly raised hell with them camps when he begun pryin' gold out of the grass roots up on Bonanza."

"We can't permit that kind of language in the presence of a lady," protested the clerk.

The big man favored him with a single pitying glance: "Yer bib's wet, sonny," he said. "Man's talk might be too strong fer you—but not fer her. She's a human bein'."

"You mean they've all gone up to the new diggings?" There was a note of disappointment in the tone. Kitty had been so sure that Carmack's strike would not amount to anything. Who ever heard of a squaw man doing anything worth while? Her father had said that if the strike did pan out big it would be a year—maybe two years.

"All of 'em that's worth a damn has," answered the man. "You know the kind that wouldn't—an' even they'll move up this spring. She's big! An' there's goin' to be a Godamighty stampede when the news hits the outside. Me—I'm takin' in two ton of flour an' pork. Grub's worth what a man'll pay fer it a'ready. Wisht I

AN ASSAULT AND BATTERY 57

could buy forty ton, an' I wouldn't never have to do another tap all my life."

"Do you know Big Tim McGuigan?"

"Big Tim! I can't claim I know'd him, personal. I wisht I had. By God, Miss—there was a man! Big Tim is history on the Yukon by now. All up an' down the river you can hear it—wherever moose meat's chewed an' round oaths is swore—how Big Tim McGuigan couldn't swim a lick, an' how in the thick of a whirlin' snowstorm he dove out of a canoe plumb into the middle of the big river so his pardner could make shore. He wasn't never seen again, Miss—but, up in the Big Country the sourdoughs will be tellin' about Big Tim till the Yukon runs uphill!"

Kitty McGuigan never knew how she got out of the gun store, nor did she know that more than one pedestrian turned for a second look at the beautiful girl who, with tight pressed lips and white tense face, passed them on the streets, her blue eyes staring straight before her. She realized nothing until she found herself seated in a little park, staring dry-eyed out over the waters of Lake Washington.

Her world had suddenly crashed about her ears. The big lovable man, who had been both a father and a mother to her almost ever since she could remember, was dead. Never again would she see the laughter light his blue eyes, nor hear his big booming voice expound the tenets of his homely philosophy. All that was gone—and she was down here—and up there on the Yukon the bearded men who had loved him were telling the story of his passing. Then came the tears—hot, scalding tears and sobs that shook the very bench on which she sat.

"What's the matter, miss?" A stick of polished wood rested upon the back of the bench beside her, and through a blur of tears, she looked up into the kindly eyes of the blue-coated figure who was regarding her with genuine concern.

"My—my father is—dead," she said, striving mightily to control the sobs.

"Aw, that's too bad, miss—too bad. I'm—I'm sorry." The tears flowed afresh at the note of honest sympathy in the voice. "We must all die, miss. One day, an' one tomorrow. 'Tis a thing we all must face. I'll bet he was a fine man."

"The finest man in all the word," she answered, pressing her tear-drenched handkerchief to her eyes.

The helmeted head nodded slowly: "'Tis worth all he's lived through—no matter what it was, to have a daughter sayin' that about um. I've a gurl av my own—an' if she'll be sayin' that when I'm gone, 'twill be all I'll ask. Was—was he sick long?" the sympathetic voice asked, awkwardly.

"He was drowned—in the Yukon," faltered the girl. "I—— A man just told me."

"Did he go up on the gold rush?"

"No—we lived there—always. I was born there. My name is Kitty McGuigan—Big Tim, the sourdoughs called my father. They loved him."

"I'll bet they did. Well, miss—jest sit here as long as ye like. 'Tis better than bein' cooped between the walls av a room. I'll jest keep an eye out, an' if any folks come this path I'll turn 'em aside—one way an' another." Slow footsteps sounded on the gravel, and when Kitty looked up, the policeman had gone and in her lap lay a clean white handkerchief of ample proportion. Gratefully she pressed the handkerchief to her face. It smelled strongly of cigars.

In groping, disjointed spasms Kitty tried vainly to frame her future. She would return to the Yukon—she would remain in Seattle and get a job, and be known as Miss McGuigan, laces and ribbons, Harmon & Babbit, and stay on at her aunt's boarding house and maybe marry Mr. Snook, after all, and keep house in a tiny flat with people living above and below you. Even that would be better than having to listen to the everlasting torrent of words that poured from the lips of her aunt. Why hadn't Tommy Haldane written of her father's death? How long ago was it he had died? It must have been before the freeze-up, because the man had said he dived from a canoe—and the break-up had not yet come to the Yukon.

Her money was pitifully low, and she was already two weeks in arrears at her aunt's—a fact that had by no means passed without comment. Her explanation that it would only be a short time till she heard from her father had been met with whining explanations of how hard the times were, and that the Widow O'Brien always got her rent in advance. Only that morning Kitty had fled the house with the determination to get a job of some kind, if only to escape the necessity of listening to her aunt bemoaning the fact that the fourteen-dollar Mr. Ginsberg had "given notice," and she would probably have to rent the room out for twelve.

And then she had foll—— the man in the mukluks into the gun store. There would be no more money from her father. And Tommy Haldane would never come—she remembered the look on Tommy Haldane's face when she told him, back there in the little cabin, that she would never marry him. No, Tommy Haldane would never come. In the excitement of the big strike he had probably forgotten her very existence.

Wearily, the girl rose and walked back along the pathway. Where it merged into a driveway she paused and glanced about for sight of the

AN ASSAULT AND BATTERY 61

policeman. She wanted to thank him for the handkerchief. But he was nowhere in sight. She considered retracing her steps and leaving it on the bench where he could find it. Instead, she thrust it into the bosom of her blouse. She would keep it always. Tears were very near the surface again as she remembered the kindly, awkward sympathy of his words. He was not like the others—Mr. Snook, and Mr. Ginsberg. He understood. He was more like the men she had known back there on the Yukon. Vaguely she wondered whether he would join the stampede that her father and the stranger in the gun store had predicted would come. She hoped he would. He wouldn't be like the other chechakos. He would fit. She hoped that he would find lots and lots of gold.

It was mid-afternoon when she finally reached the boarding house. She had eaten nothing since breakfast, and she suddenly realized she was hungry. As she was about to ascend the stairs her aunt beckoned her into the parlor. "The mail's here," she said, meaningly, "an' there ain't no word from yer pa. I don't like to be hard on no one, 'specially my own kin. But business is business, an' it's goin' on three weeks now that you're behind. Last time I let anyone get behind it was Miss Lambert, which she was copy clerk down to the railroad. She always paid up all right till they switched over to men an' she got fired. She hunted another job, but she couldn't seem to find none, an' when it had run along two weeks I jest told her out an' out, she'd have to go, what with me turnin' down folks most every day that could afford to pay fer the room. Few days later they found her floatin' in the bay, an' when the time come to bust into her trunk that I'd held fer her board, I could only git 'leven dollars fer the stuff, trunk an' all—an' she owed me eighteen! They'll git you, one way an' another if you ain't watchin'. So, you see, you couldn't hardly expect me to keep you much longer without I see the color of your money. But you've helped around quite a bit, an' I don't want to be hard on you, so I'll keep you till the end of the week, an' in the meantime you better git out an' rustle you a job. You can't depend nothin' on Tim McGuigan——"

Kitty felt herself growing strangely cold, and when she spoke her voice sounded unfamiliar and hard: "My father," she said, "is dead."

"Dead!" cried the woman, as though striving to grasp the import of the word. Her voice rose in a tone of outraged bitterness: "Dead! An' him owin' me fer two weeks' board! Ain't that like the dirty loafer! Good riddance, I'd say, what with——"

Kitty McGuigan's right arm shot out with incredible swiftness and her doubled fist landed squarely upon the Widow O'Brien's mouth with

AN ASSAULT AND BATTERY 63

a force that sent her reeling backward and mixed her false teeth with her tonsils. "That," the girl found herself saying in a voice of deadly calm, "is for the girl they found in the bay. And these are for Big Tim." The blows landed in staccato succession, each clean from the shoulder in the approved manner of Forty Mile— one eye, the other, the nose, and the point of the flabby chin. And the Widow O'Brien crashed backward onto the stuffed haircloth sofa, and slid peacefully onto the floor.

Kitty whirled at the sound of a shriek to see the face of Ellie, the housemaid, staring wide-eyed through the parted portières. She took a step forward and the face disappeared as she heard Ellie run shrieking up the stairs.

Sudden panic seized Kitty. Seattle was not Forty Mile. She could doubtless be arrested for what she had done—much as her aunt deserved it. And it seemed to the excited girl that every policeman from the hilltops to the bay must hear Ellie's terrified shrieks. Swiftly she crossed the hall and let herself out the door. And the next moment, she was hurrying down the street.

CHAPTER VIII

The Yukon Kid

IN THE Antlers saloon not an eye had shifted from Tommy Haldane's face for so much as a glance at the little sacks that he had tossed onto the bar in confirmation of his story of the strike, until the last word that told of the passing of Big Tim McGuigan had been spoken. They were taking his measure—these men—and not a word, not the flicker of an eyelash, nor the movement of a muscle escaped them.

During the long tense moments of his recital, Tommy Haldane had stood on trial for his life. The lad was no chechako. His two years on the river had been in the nature of a novitiate. But, Big Tim was of the cult. And when Tommy finished speaking not a sourdough in the room but knew he had spoken the truth. From that moment Tommy Haldane, too, would be reckoned a sourdough—a man to rub shoulders with such men as Camillo Bill, and Moosehide Charlie, and Old Bettles.

THE YUKON KID

Camillo Bill had voiced the sentiment of the whole when he had ordered the round of drinks. Reverently, and in silence, they had drunk to Big Tim. As he returned his glass to the bar Old Bettles, himself dean of the sourdoughs, thrust out his hand—a hand that would have been the first to grasp a rope if the story had not rung true: "It was hell, kid—we know. But it's the luck of the game. Big Tim McGuigan was a man!"

Then others were crowding close, all talking at once—and the talk was of gold. Forty Mile did not go to bed that night. Huge fires lit the beach where men swore and jostled each other and threw heavy packs into poling boats and canoes, and others built rafts and rigged them with tracklines.

Tommy Haldane sought out the gold commissioner and recorded a claim in his own name, and one in Kitty McGuigan's. He bought a poling boat, hired a breed to help him, and with the gold he had shaken from the grass roots of Bonanza, he bought supplies at the Alaska Commercial Company's store and helped his breed pack them to the boat. By morning the A. C. company's shelves held little except squaw cloth, and silk dresses for the dance-hall girls.

In the gray light of early morning a group of sourdoughs foregathered at the front end of the bar. Tommy Haldane was among them. Old Bettles bought a round of drinks.

"How about lettin' Kitty know?" asked Swiftwater Bill, his eyes traveling the circle of the faces. "It's sure goin' to be hell on her."

"I can't write," said Moosehide Charlie.

"I don't know where she's at," admitted Camillo Bill.

"It's up to you, kid," opined Old Bettles, as the eyes of all focused on Tommy Haldane's face. "You must know where she's at—an'—then —besides——"

"She'll come bustin' back, hell-bent, when she hears," predicted Camillo Bill. "She never had no other home. She's a sourdough clean down to her mukluks."

Moosehide Charlie nodded affirmation: "We're her folks. She'll come back to us when she hears."

Old Bettles drained his glass and motioned to Curley behind the bar: "Fetch a pencil an' paper," he ordered, and turned to Tommy. "It's hell, kid—but it's up to you. Not only you was the last to see Big Tim—but—seems like she'd ruther hear it from you. She'll come back quicker fer you than——"

Tommy Haldane shook his head gravely: "No. Kitty hates me, now. The last thing she told me was that she'd never marry me——"

Swiftwater Bill laughed: "Where's yer guts, Kid? I'll bet two to one, she———"

Tommy interrupted him: "You could bet ten to one—or a hundred to one, Swiftwater—an' win. She's goin' to marry me—but not now. She'd come back, all right—as soon as she heard. But, she'd come back to you boys—not to me. She loves the last man of you. But—do we want her back? Big Tim an' I foresaw this stampede. That's why he sent her outside. She appealed to me—but, I thought like Big Tim. That's why she hates me. What'll Forty Mile be like in a week? You wouldn't winter a dog here—neither would I. It's goin' to be tough up on Bonanza—livin' in tents. An' grub's goin' to be short before the break-up. Next summer the whole damn' country's goin' to fill up with chechakos. As Moosehide says, you boys are her folks. You want to do the best by her—same as Big Tim an' I did. She's winterin' with her aunt in Seattle. In the spring I'm goin' down there an' tell her. An' I aim to bring her back. She'll be Mrs. Tommy Haldane, then—an' we'll come back to our folks on the river. That's how it looks to me. But—I won't set up my judgment against yours. We'll take a vote on it. Seems like I just couldn't write about it, boys—but, if you all say so, I will."

"The Kid's right," said Camillo Bill, and the others nodded.

"But that ain't no sign we shouldn't have another little drink," opined Bettles. "Fill 'em up, Curley—an' git that pencil an' paper off'n the bar—it's in the road.

> *"In the days of old,*
> *In the days of gold,*
> *In the days of 'forty-nine. . . .*

Here's gold in yer poke, you frost hounds!"

As they filled the glasses the bartender eyed them sadly: "It's goin' to be mighty lonesome 'round here when you boys is gone," he said. "The boss is goin' on up an' stake fer me an' him, an' then he's goin' to try to git some kind of a shack together up on Larue's townsite so we can move up."

"We'll all pitch in an' roll his shack up fer him," said Moosehide Charlie. "It's goin' to be gosh-awful lonesome fer us, too—what with the long nights, an' livin' in tents most likely—jest a-waitin' fer the break-up."

Tommy Haldane spoke up: "I'm goin' to try my hand at winter minin'," he said.

The others stared in astonishment. Swiftwater Bill laughed: "You'd ought to do good at it, kid. I rec'lect one time me an' Bettles, here, we winter-mined up on the Koyukok. It was the year of the two winters—the time spring come in hind end first an' April backed clean up into

February. So me an' Bettles, we figures that if we're goin' to do any minin' at all it'll have to be winter minin', so we goes at it. An' we done fairly good too—panned out sometimes as high as eleven ounces of snow to the pan—not to say nothin' of a lot of ice nuggets in the way of coarse stuff. It was eleven ounces, wasn't it, Bettles?"

"W-e-e-l," said Old Bettles, doubtfully, "the way I rec'lect it, you're a little bit high, Swiftwater. Seems to me that the pure snow we panned never run higher'n around seven ounces to the pan. It was ice nuggets an' all run her up to eleven."

Tommy Haldane grinned into the serious faces of the two sourdoughs: "Have all the fun you want. But, if my scheme works, I'll bet you'll all be winter minin'—and pannin' out gold—not snow."

"What is this here scheme you got, son, fer beatin' the devil at his own game?" queried Camillo Bill. "Tell us about it—an' we'll tell you why it won't work."

"Why, it isn't much of a scheme—just common sense. Suppose you scraped away the snow an' built a cordwood fire on the ground. It would thaw the gravel a few inches deep under the fire, wouldn't it? Then suppose you got busy an' shoveled out that thawed gravel an' built another fire when you got down to the frost again —you could keep that up all winter couldn't you

—an' go down as deep as you wanted? Take it where the dirt is as rich as I know that dirt on Bonanza to be, a man could make damn' good money at it."

Moosehide Charlie looked at Swiftwater Bill, and Camillo Bill looked at Old Bettles. The latter was the first to speak: "Sounds reasonable, kid," he said, with a perfectly straight face. "Yes, sir—reasonable an' easy. 'Course, they was one little item that bothered me, first off—but I see, now, how you could fix that. Havin' shoveled this here dirt out, they wouldn't be no water to sluice it with. But all you'd have to do would be to go up onto the headwaters an' build a big fire an' thaw out the crick. That could be a kind of a community fire—a big 'un—everyone havin' claims on that crick, bein' assessed a certain amount of cordwood to keep it goin'. 'Course them that had claims quite a piece down from headwaters—they'd be kind of out of luck, on account, the water'd be half froze—kind of thick an' gummy like. But they could sort of mix their dirt into it, an' then sort of work the gold out by pullin'—like these here taffy pulls the girls has around Chris'mas. Er, another way would be to have a string of booster fires all along the crick to keep it thawed the hull len'th."

Tommy Haldane joined in the roar of laughter that greeted Old Bettles' suggestions. "Drink up, boys, it's on me," he said. "Then I'll tell you another one. I don't figure to sluice out till spring. Just throw it onto a dump an' in the spring sluice her out when you've got the water. You could pan out enough in a pan or an old piece of canvas inside a tent if you wanted to, to keep an' eye on how she was runnin'—an' plenty for expenses, too. That way you'll be workin' in a dry hole. An' in the spring instead of sloshin' around in ice water, you'll be sluicin' a dump that's high an' dry."

Once again the sourdoughs looked into each other's faces. But this time there was no latent laughter in the shrewd eyes. After a silence, Camillo Bill's lips twisted into a slow grin: "That sort of a squeaky, gratin' sound we hear is caused by four set of brains bein' called upon sudden to do the onexpected phenomenon of thinkin'. Fer my part I admit I ain't got no comeback to the kid's proposition. The only thing I can think of to say is: if winter minin's as simple as all that, why in hell ain't it be'n done before?"

"Which ain't so much of an argument, when you come to think about it," said Swiftwater Bill, thoughtfully. "A wheel looks simple as hell to us, now. But I'll bet folks drug their stuff over the ground fer a long while before some son-of-a-gun figured out it would be easier to roll it. Boys, maybe winter minin's come. It was the kid, here, that first noticed the difference in the color of Carmack's gold. Looks like our heads runs more to whiskers than brains. Me—I'm a-goin' to try it jest like he says."

"I'm feelin' in need of another jolt of brain oil," said Bettles. "Boys it sure looks from here like our winter vacation is all shot to hell."

"It's plumb daylight," announced Moosehide Charlie, glancing toward the windows. "Come on—let's go!"

As the sourdoughs turned from the bar after a last drink "on the house," the bartender proffered Old Bettles a quart bottle: "Better stick that in yer pack," he said.

"What fer?" asked Bettles, in surprise.

"Well, you be'n hittin' her up pretty strong since you hit camp, an' you ain't so young as you was onct. I thought maybe a little hooker in the mornin' an' evenin' would kind of let you down easy."

"Look-a-here son," said the old man. "I'm obliged to you. But don't never ask no one to take no likker on the trail. It's all right in a camp. A camp would be a damn' poor place without it. But it ain't no good on the trail. When I git to where I need any lettin' down that I can't git out of b'iled tea an' moose meat, I'll quit the trail, an' git me a job curryin' the pyanner in some dance hall."

That winter the snow clouds that hung low over Bonanza reflected back the red glow of a hundred fires. Winter mining had come to the Yukon. Men working in pairs, and in threes and fours, chopped cordwood by day and tended their fires by night, and shoveled the dirt into dumps to await the coming of spring. The sound of axes and the creak of rude windlasses carried far on the keen air to mingle with the shouts of bearded men.

As Big Tim McGuigan had said, the valley was spotted. Not every claim showed pay. Test panning showed some fabulously rich claims, and there were many that showed richer than anything heretofore uncovered in the North. Those whose claims showed lean, prospected other valleys and feeders and draws, or worked for wages on the better claims. Fifteen dollars a day was going wages, and young Tommy Haldane worked five men besides himself on his claims which were among the richest in the whole valley.

On the first run of water he sluiced his dump and the clean-up netted him four thousand, two hundred and forty ounces—nearly sixty-eight thousand dollars—and, owing to the crude construction of his sluice, most of the flour gold had got away. His deepest shaft was less than twelve feet below the surface, and bed rock—no one knew where. It was then he realized that he and Kitty McGuigan were rich beyond their wildest dreams. Kitty McGuigan . . . fondly he recalled each little mannerism and trick of expression—each glint of the eyes of Irish blue. He would go to her, now—would tell her of the death of Big Tim—would assure her of his own great love, steadfast and undying—and then—of the gold that lay in their gravel.

It was the fourteenth of May that year when the ice went out of the Yukon. That evening Tommy sought out Camillo Bill and Old Bettles, whose claims adjoined his above Discovery. "I'm goin' outside," he announced. "Goin' out to fetch Kitty."

"That's the stuff, kid. Good luck!" said Camillo Bill.

"Tell her not to fergit my oranges," reminded Bettles. "We'll have a proper saloon, here, I hope, agin you git back, an' then I'll pull a birthday party."

"I wish you boys would kind of keep an eye on the claims till we get back," said Tommy. "I'd hate to see 'em get jumped or anything."

Old Bettles chuckled: "If you have as good luck fetchin' back Kitty as we'll have keepin' jumpers off them claims, kid, you'll be married an' have a large family agin Michaelmas Day—an' I don't know what time of year that comes, neither."

Early next morning Tommy pulled out amid the yells and farewells of the assembled miners. "Hooray fer the Yukon Kid!" cried someone.

The new name struck the fancy of the bearded men of the high North. Others took up the cry—and, as the Yukon Kid he was destined to be known ever after. A sourdough among the sourdoughs. For not a man among them but knew of his part in the validation of Carmack's strike, and also that this beardless youngster was the father of winter mining—and for many a year to come the word of the Yukon Kid was to be eagerly awaited upon matters of importance.

CHAPTER IX

A Barkeeper Gives Advice

In dawson, Tommy and the two men he had brought with him to help transport the gold from Bonanza, piled many little mooseskin sacks on the bar of the New Antlers saloon, which shared the patronage of the sourdoughs with the Tivoli, a few doors down the street.

"Weigh 'em in, Frank, an' give me a receipt," he said to the proprietor, who had been the saloon keeper at Forty Mile, in the days of that camp's glory.

As the man weighed-in the dust and made the necessary notation, he shook his head, regretfully: "Too bad Old Tim couldn't of lived to see it," he said. "By God, there was a man!"

Tommy nodded: "I guess no one knows that as well as I do. I'd give every damn ounce of it —an' the claims to boot, to have Old Tim back."

"There ain't no one doubts that, son. But that's the way she goes. It's the luck of the game. Some loses; an' some wins. This'll come in mighty fine fer Kitty. The boys tells me you've cut her in—full pardners on everything."

"Sure I have! Old Tim an' I were pardners —an' she's his only heir."

Frank Weed's eyes twinkled knowingly, and a smile curved the lips that gripped the butt of his cigar: "An' I s'pose that's as fer as it goes, eh? Jest her bein' Old Tim's heir?"

Tommy Haldane's lips answered the grin; "Well—I'm goin' to marry her—if she'll have me. I'm headin' down to Seattle after her, right now. An' by the way—I'd better stow a few of them sacks in my pocket for expenses. There'll be a diamond ring, an' whatnot."

"She'll have you, all right enough," grinned Weed. "Hell! after winterin' in a city like she done, she'd marry Old Bettles to git back here on the Yukon! This is her country, Tommy—an' we're her folks. She'll be homesick fer the sight of us."

"She said she hated the North, an' everything about it—me most of all," said Tommy, glumly. "She said she'd never marry me."

Weed's grin widened: "There's a hell of a lot of women you never fought with," he observed. "Let me give you a tip, Kid. Never believe a damn' word they say when they're mad. An', only about half what they say, when they ain't," he added, cynically.

"Wonder how much of this dust I'll need?" speculated Tommy. "I don't want to pack no more'n I have to. It's heavy."

"If it was me I'd take it all," advised the proprietor.

"All of it! Cripes—it's a thousan' miles to Skagway! An' it weighs better'n two hundred an' fifty pounds!"

"Two sixty-five, to be exact," corrected Weed. "But you got a couple of men here to help you. If you pay them two, three thousan' dollars in wages, you've still made a good profit."

"Profit? What do you mean?"

"Figure it out fer yerself—here, on the river, gold goes fer sixteen dollars an ounce—don't it? Well, in the States, it fetches a few cents better'n twenty dollars. That's a little better'n four dollars an ounce profit—right around seventeen thousan' dollars on what you've got here. That'll pay fer yer men's wages, an' a damn' good weddin' throw'd in, without makin' a dent in yer pile."

Tommy nodded: "That's right," he said. "An' I can stick the money in the bank, down there for an ace in the hole, in case anything happened up here."

"That's business, Tommy," agreed the proprietor. "You'll get along."

"They ain't callin' him Tommy Haldane no

more, up on Bonanza," informed one of his hirelings, proudly. "He's the Yukon Kid."

"The Yukon Kid is right!" agreed Weed, heartily. "Him, bein', what you might say, the daddy of this camp—the name fits him like a new glove."

Tommy grinned, and with a motion of the hand, indicated the little knot of men about the roulette wheel, and those in the chairs along the wall. "Give 'em what they want," he said. "I'm buyin' a drink before I start. When I get back with Kitty, I'll set 'em up to a real blow-out."

"Step up an' name yer licker, boys," called Weed. "The Yukon Kid is buyin' a drink. He's goin' outside."

The men, chechakos for the most part, who had come in on the van of the big stampede, surged to the bar and filled their glasses.

"Drink up—an' good luck to you," said Tommy, lighting a cigar.

"Wher's yourn?" asked one of two stubble-jowled chechakos who had crowded in beside him.

"I don't drink. Tried it once, an' damn' near died."

"Huh," grunted the man. "Well, I s'pose whisky's fer men—not kids. You got to be hard-boiled, here—er you don't last. This ain't no country fer Sunday School boys. So yer quittin', eh?"

"No—not quittin'. I'll be back."

"Huh," grunted the chechako, incredulously, his eyes on the sacks ranged on the bar in front of Tommy. "What's in them bags?"

"Dust."

"Dust! You mean gold?" exclaimed the other stubble-jowled man, his eyes widening.

On the other side of the bar Frank Weed, who had overheard the conversation, answered the man with a grin: "No, no! Not gold! H-e-l-l—no!" His words carried to the farthest reaches of the room. "Up on the Bonanza, where the Kid come from, they're so damn' tidy an' neat that when they sweep out their tent of a-mornin', they sack up the dust out of the dustpan an' fetch it fifty miles down to the big river to dump it, so it won't litter up Bonanza."

And amid guffaws of loud laughter, the two stubble-faced ones slunk scowling from the room.

CHAPTER X

Almost a Robbery

ON THE river bank the little sacks of gold were made up into three equal packs and placed amidships in the canoe. The Yukon Kid was traveling light. Grub was cut to a minimum, and the men took only one blanket apiece. There would be no long portages until the head of Lake Lindeman was reached, and then the canoe would be left behind.

Paddling steadily, the three forced the light craft upriver, holding well inshore to take advantage of backwaters and eddies. They met boats during the day—singly, and in little flotillas. There were a few canoes among them, but for the most part, they were rudely constructed of green, whipsawed lumber.

"The chechakos is sure pilin' in on us," observed the man in the bow. "The half of 'em won't make no strike."

"Half of 'em!" grinned the Kid, from the

stern. "They'll do damn well if one in a hundred makes a strike! What do they know about minin'? There won't half of 'em make even wages. An', if you think this is a stampede wait till this fall—an' next spring. Word of the big strike ain't had time to get spread good, yet. When it does, there'll be a real stampede. I want to get back an' do some more prospectin' before these damn chechakos get spread all over the country. Prospectin', an' buyin' claims—that's my job from now on! I'll hire the men to work 'em."

"That's all right—if a man's got the dust to buy 'em with, an' the brains to pick 'em," agreed the man in the middle. "But, take me, now, it seems like I allus had better luck with my hands."

"You two boys are all right," said the Yukon Kid. "If you stick by me, you won't be sorry. I've got a hunch I'll be buildin' up quite a big outfit—an' I'll need good men. You savvy minin', an' you savvy the country. I can use you. From now on your wages will be an ounce a day, an' grub. Whenever you think you can better it, you're welcome to quit."

"Guess we won't be quittin' on you," said the man in the bow. "If the chechakos is goin' to come bilin' in like you say, they're goin' to have to eat one another—there sure ain't goin' to be grub enough in the Yukon fer 'em."

ALMOST A ROBBERY

"That's right," snickered the man in the middle: "An ounce a day, an' grub, looks a damn' sight better than nothin' a day, an' git et."

The sun sank lower, throwing the shadow of the mountains over the surface of the great river, the Kid glanced more and more frequently over his shoulder to scrutinize the canoe that had been following at a distance all day. It was a two-man canoe, evidently lightly loaded, and it hugged the bank, hanging back out of sight in rounding points and headlands. He had not mentioned this canoe to his men. The gathering gloom was rendering it almost invisible, when, far in the forefront, the Kid saw another canoe, headed downriver, swing into a little cove at the mouth of a creek.

Twenty minutes later, when they reached the cove, the three chechakos had pulled their canoe from the water, and were already building their supper fire.

The Kid headed the canoe for the mouth of the creek. "We'll shove up around a bend," he said, "an' camp."

"Hey there!" called one of the chechakos, as they passed close beside the little fire on the beach. "How far is it to Dawson?"

"About thirty miles—maybe thirty-five," answered the Kid. "Make it in half a day. You've got good water all the way."

When the first bend of the small creek cut

them off from sight of the river, the three beached the canoe, threw the packs out of it, and drew it from the water.

"You boys get busy with supper, while I cache this dust," said the Kid. "An' make it snappy. Fry up some sow belly, an' douse yer fire as soon as the tea boils. We'll have light enough to eat by. The moon'll break over the hills directly."

"Figger, mebbe, them three chechakos might give us a call?" asked one of the men.

"No. They prob'ly think we're a prospectin' outfit headin' on up the crick. Our smoke's driftin' away from 'em, an' anyway, they won't wander far from their fire. Prob'ly plenty tired after a day at the paddles. I kind of figger they're goin' to have callers, after a while—an' we want to be in on the meetin'."

The two men glanced at each other in perplexity, but obeyed without question. The moon rose, and shortly the fire was doused, and squatting there in the half-light, the three munched bannocks and salt pork, and drank scalding tea.

"It's like this," explained the Kid, when supper was over. "There's be'n a canoe followin' us all day. It's a two-man outfit, an' they've hung back so's to just keep us in sight. I shouldn't be surprised if it was them two chechakos that was interested in what was in our little sacks—the ones that Frank Weed made a fool of in the Antlers. Their canoe was floatin' high, so they're travelin' light. My guess is that they're figurin' on jumpin' us tonight an' grabbin' off that dust. Dim as the light was, they couldn't have seen this other outfit head into the cove—but, they saw us head in—you bet! They'll think the other outfit is us. When they slip up to stage their hold-up, we're goin' to be sittin' right in the edge of the brush with guns on 'em."

"Like in a duck blind over a settin' of decoys," grinned one of the men.

"Exactly," laughed the Kid. "It's goin' to be comical as hell to see 'em when they find out those three ain't us."

"Yeah," snickered the other man, "but, that ain't goin' to be half as comical as them decoys'll be when they wake up to look into the muzzles of a couple of guns. Chechakos ain't got none too much guts, nohow. I'm glad I ain't their washwoman."

"We'll be slippin' over there, now," said the Kid. "Easy's the word. We'll slip in as close as we can. There'll be light enough out there on the river bank to see our sights. I don't expect we'll have to do no shootin', anyhow."

Making their way noiselessly through the bush, the three sourdoughs paused in the shelter of the spruce scrub to survey the scene. Twenty yards away, on a narrow strip of shingle at the water's edge, three blanketed forms sprawled beside the glowing embers of a little fire. The three were apparently asleep, and pointing to a clump of low willows within six or eight yards of the sleepers, the Kid led the way, wriggling across the dozen yards of rocky exposed ground on his belly. The two followed, and cocking their rifles, squatted beside their leader in the shadow of the low willow clump.

The red glow of the embers waned and blackened. The moon rose higher, blazoning the broad surface of the Yukon with a rippling path of silver. From some high ridge to the eastward, a wolf howled. An hour passed. And, a half. Then, noiseless as a shadow, a dark shape rounded the point and crept close along the shore. Nearer it came—and nearer, forging slowly against the current. Nosing into the moon's path, it loomed sharp and distinct against the silvery background—two men in a canoe. In the shadow of the willows, the three shifted their rifles and held their breath. The canoe beached without a sound. And, without a sound, its two occupants exchanged paddles for rifles and stepped ashore. Dark masks covered their faces to the eyes. Silently they advanced, and three paces from the sleepers they paused.

"Set up!" commanded the larger of the two, roughly. "We come fer them tent sweepin's!"

The blanketed forms stirred—sat up, to gaze in wide-eyed bewilderment into the muzzles of two rifles.

"What—what the hell?"

"What d'you mean—tent sweepin's?"

The third merely elevated his hands, his mouth working wordlessly.

"You know what we mean—them bags of dust you had in the saloon! Come on—dig 'em up, er, by God! we'll blow you to hell!"

"We ain't—we ain't got no dust! We ain't got started, yet!"

"We ain't be'n in no saloon! We come downriver!"

The shorter of the two robbers leaned forward, staring into the three faces that showed pasty-white in the moonlight. "Good God!" he cried, suddenly. "It ain't them!"

"Wher' be they, then?" demanded the larger one, savagely. "Them three that come upriver? We seen 'em head in here! Wher's the Yukon Kid?"

"Right here," answered a smooth voice from the willow clump. "There's three rifles on you. Drop those guns, or we'll cut you in two!"

Two rifles clattered onto the sand, and two pairs of hands reached high above two masked faces. The three blanketed ones scrambled to their feet in complete bewilderment as the Kid and his two men stepped from the willows.

"What the hell?" asked one, his eyes sweeping the circle of faces.

"Only that these two damn' chechakos tried

to rob us," explained the Kid. "They followed us up from Dawson. I've be'n watching 'em all day. They thought you was us."

"What you goin' to do with 'em?" asked one, eyeing the two masked figures with disfavor.

"Tie 'em up till mornin', an' then hang 'em," answered the Kid. "Robbers ain't wanted on the Yukon." He turned to his men. "Jerk them masks off, an' tie up their hands an' feet. I'll slip over an' get the blankets. We'll take turns—one of us'll watch 'em, while two sleep." The Kid tossed one of the men a babiche line he had brought from the canoe. "Tie their hands an' feet separate, an' then tie 'em back to back. That way they can't squirm around an' fool with the knots."

"My God!—don't hang us," begged the larger of the two—the one who had taunted the Kid in the Antlers. "It was only a joke. We thought you was only a kid, an' we'd scare you!"

"You paddled a hell of a ways to pull off a damn' poor joke," answered the Kid, dryly. "We'll just call the hangin' a joke, too. But, the joke'll be on you."

"But—we didn't rob no one!" protested the smaller of the two, as the thongs drew tightly about his wrists. "We only done it to scare you!"

"You didn't scare no one, either—you damn' liars!"

"The hell an' they didn't!" cried one of the

three chechakos. "I was so damn scairt I couldn't talk—an' I had a hell of a lot to say, too!"

The Kid grinned: "You've got to be hard-boiled, here, or you don't last. Ask that big guy. He knows. He told me that this mornin'. He's hard-boiled as hell, standin' in front of a bar drinkin' free whisky. But, he ain't so hard, now. Listen to him beg!"

Trussed like roast turkeys, lying back to back on the ground, the two were whining and begging for their lives.

"Shut up!" ordered the Kid, contemptuously kicking a spurt of sand into the larger one's mouth. "If you keep that up we'll hang you tonight instead of waitin' till mornin'. We aim to catch us some sleep."

As he went to fetch the blankets, one of the three chechakos followed him to the edge of the scrub. He was a kindly-faced man, and the Kid saw that he was disturbed.

"Ain't there somethin' else you can do besides hang them fellas?" he asked.

"They held guns on you an' threatened to blow you to hell," reminded the Kid.

"I know. But even so—I'd hate to see 'em hung. I—I wouldn't sleep all night fer thinkin' about it. I—I guess I ain't hard-boiled."

A slow grin twisted the Kid's lips. "Go get yer sleep," he advised. "We ain't goin' to hang 'em. But it'll do 'em good to put in a night thinkin' we are. In the mornin' we'll give 'em breakfast, an' throw 'em in their canoe with their hands tied an' no paddles an' shove 'em out on the river with a sign tied on 'em that they're thieves. The boys'll feed 'em from time to time, an' keep passin' 'em on."

"On? On—to where?"

"Why—clean on down into Alaska. On to the ocean, I guess. We don't want men like them in the Yukon. They'll be murderin' some poor devil for his dust."

"I guess that's right," admitted the other. "Anyhow—it's givin' 'em a break."

CHAPTER XI

On the Trail

AT LAKE LINDEMAN, head of the water trail, the three carefully cached the canoe, well away from the straggling camp of chechakos who were busily engaged in whipsawing lumber and building boats. Pack-laden, they paused for a few moments to look down upon the muddy camp, swarming like an anthill with activity.

The Kid shook his head, half contemptuously: "They're gold crazy," he said. "They can't see nothin' but gold. An' there won't one in a hundred of 'em get enough gold to worry about. Look at 'em—all buildin' boats to float down to the gold country in. They don't know how to build boats—an' when they get to where they're goin', they won't know how to dig gold! Seems like, when there's a gold stampede, men lose their heads. Take that bunch down there—there's several hundred of 'em, and out of that number there must be at least a dozen good carpenters—men who could build boats, and good ones. An', there must be anyway a few others that know how to saw lumber. If those skilled men looked around 'em they'd see the chance of a lifetime—a little portable sawmill to make the lumber—an' carpenters to build the boats. The others would fall all over themselves to buy those boats—at any price they're mind to ask for 'em. They could get rich, right here. But do you see 'em doin' it? Not by a damn' sight, you don't. The lumber makers an' the carpenters are passin' up a sure thing, doin' what they know how to do, to tackle the rankest kind of a gamble, doin' what they don't know how to do! An' that's the way it is all along the line. They can't see that every dollar's worth of gold that will be taken out of the Yukon is goin' to cost ten dollars in outfits, an' boats, an' grub, an' whisky, an' wages. It ain't the ones that uses their hands that's goin' to win out in this stampede—it's the ones that uses their heads. Believe me—I'm goin' to get mine! An' I'll never turn over another shovelful of gravel, neither!"

On the Chilkoot Summit, where the Mounted Police had established a customs station, the Kid paused to chat with Corporal White, who was off duty.

"Look at 'em," said the corporal, with a wave of his hand toward the long line of chechakos who were waiting to pass customs. "You'd think they was goin' to a picnic."

The Kid grinned; "What's your bet? How many of 'em'll get gold?"

"It ain't how many of 'em'll get gold, that's worryin' us," replied the corporal. "It's what they're goin' to eat! Look at that one that just come through! Look at the pack he's got! A night shirt, an' a tooth brush, an' enough flour, maybe, for another batch of pancakes! They won't be comin' in that way very long. The order's goin' out that no one will be admitted without he's got a year's provisions with him. It's goin' into effect pretty quick, now. It'll save a hell of a lot of starvin'."

"It sure will," agreed the Kid, and indicated the two men who accompanied him. "These two boys are workin' for me," he said. "They'll be comin' back through as soon as we get to Dyea. I'm goin' outside for a while—be back in a month. So long."

At Dyea the Kid sent his men back, and took passage for Seattle on a steamer that had just dumped a new load of chechakos on the beach. Leaning over the rail, he idly watched the last of the lightering to the beach, a grin of amusement on his lips. Meager outfits, inadequate for a week's camping on a farm wood lot, were sandwiched between cumbersome bales of goods and material that, by no stretch of the imagination, could be made to serve any useful purpose on the trail. "They'll abandon most of it at Sheep Camp," he mused aloud, as he remembered the straggling camp that sprawled on the American side, at the foot of the steep slope to the Chilcoot.

Suddenly he straightened, his eyes on the hodge-podge of milling humanity upon the beach. "By cripes!" he muttered. "What are they all goin' to do when that police order about a year's supply of grub goes through? They'll have to go back—back to Skagway—to Vancouver, or Seattle, maybe, to get it! Someone's overlookin' a bet! A store at Sheep Camp! Bacon an' tea, an' flour are goin' to be worth what a man'll pay for 'em, when that order goes through! An' four thousan' two hundred an' forty ounces of dust will buy a hell of a lot of tea, an' bacon, an' flour!"

As the ship steamed southward, the Kid's mind turned again and again to the possibilities for vast profit in a store at Sheep Camp. But—there were the two claims on Bonanza to be looked after—and there were other claims to be bought. He remembered Old Tim's advice—"buy claims"—"they're the chips in the game." He would buy claims—buy 'em, and sell 'em—and buy more—not only on Bonanza, but on a hundred other creeks! He must go back to the Yukon—but—this Sheep Camp store was too good a thing to pass up. He realized that his advance information had put him in a position to make a vast amount of money. Someone was going to make that money—someone with the brains to grasp the opportunity, and the capital to put it through. He had both. This was a sure thing. The buying and selling of claims was a gamble. Yet, one lucky claim might well be worth a dozen stores at Sheep Camp.

"By cripes, I'll hire someone to run the store!" he exclaimed, one day, as he stood alone in the shelter of the wheel house and watched the high wooded shores slip silently northward. But, who? He knew no one in Seattle. "Kitty might know," he muttered. "She's be'n there all winter. If she don't, her aunt will. It's a cinch her aunt'll know someone that's honest, an' has got sense enough to sell tea, an' bacon, an' flour."

Visionary plans for buying a portable sawmill to set up on Lake Lindeman, and engaging a crew of boat builders, flashed into his brain. But these he discarded. "A man," he observed, sagely, "might get into too *damn' many* things."

CHAPTER XII

In Seattle

IN SEATTLE the Kid exchanged his gold for bills of large denomination, which he rolled up and distributed among his pockets. He registered at a hotel, left his duffel bag in his room, and proceeded at once to the Widow O'Brien's boarding house at 2202 Blankenship Road.

Inquiring his way of a policeman, he struck out at a brisk walk, which slowed to a more leisurely pace as his brain struggled with the problem of what he would say to Kitty at the moment of their meeting. I'll say—"Well, Kitty, I've come for you, like I said I would. . . ." No, that would remind her right away that she told me she'd never marry me—that she hated me. . . . I'll say "Hello, Kitty. . . ." But, Gosh! I've got to say somethin' besides hello. . . . I—I've got to tell her about Big Tim. . . . That's goin' to be tough—an' maybe, she'll somehow blame me. . . . She might think there was

somethin' I could have done that I didn't do.
. . . But, no—Kitty's a sourdough. She'd know.
. . . She'll be glad to see anyone from up in the
Yukon. . . . But maybe she's learnt to like the
city. . . . Maybe she won't go back. . . . She
said she hated the North, an' hated me. . . .
Maybe Big Tim an' me was wrong, after all.
. . . Maybe we had ought to have let her stayed.
. . . We done what we thought was best. . . .
But take a woman, now, they might think they
know as much about things as a man—an' maybe
they do. . . . Big Tim seemed to know a lot
about women, to hear him talk. . . . I sure
wish he was here. . . . Take a man now, an' if
he don't do like you tell him, you can knock hell
out of him, or fire him, or somethin'. . . . But,
a woman—that's different. As he walked slowly
along the street, the Kid's eyes shifted occasion-
ally to the house numbers. "Twenty-one ninety-
six, twenty-one ninety-eight—twenty-two ought-
two," he muttered. "That's the house. Maybe
she ain't home." His lagging steps had carried
him past, and he proceeded on to the next corner. "Fella's got to kind of get his bearin's," he
explained. At the corner he paused and, though
it was not a hot day, he removed his hat, ran his
handkerchief around the leather band, and
mopped his forehead. "Maybe it would be better to wait till supper-time," he argued, as he
slowly retraced his steps, his eyes on the house.

"Cripes!" he muttered, angrily, as he turned abruptly from the sidewalk, mounted the steps, and pulled the bell. "Anyone would think I was afraid!"

A jangling sound from deep in the interior of the house was followed by a moment of silence. Then the door opened abruptly, and a figure of ample proportions blocked the entrance.

"Is this Mrs. Kate O'Brien?" asked the Kid.

"Yes, it is," snapped the woman, eyeing the high-laced pacs and flannel shirt with disapproval. "An' I don't take no loggers, nor neither sailors, nor mill hands, an' such-like. I run a genteel house for ladies an' gents an' don't want no riffraff, like when I run boardin' houses down on the waterfront. But a body had to do somethin', bein' left a widdy, an' all, an' I didn't know no better then, but I've learnt since. There's plenty of places down——"

"I ain't a logger, nor a sailor, nor a mill hand," interrupted the Kid. "I come from the Yukon, an'——"

"The Yukon!" Color mounted to the high-boned cheeks, and the porcine eyes took on a glitter. "You mean up there in Alasky?"

"Well, it ain't in Alaska, it's——"

"That's what that good fer nothin' hussy was always tellin' folks—'sif it made any difference, bein' all ice an' snow, anyway, but to hear her tell it you'd think it was the Garden of Eden, itself!"

"Is Miss Kitty McGuigan in?"

"In! In!" The woman's throat seemed to swell, rendering articulation momentarily difficult. "No, she ain't in! An' she better never show her face around here! What with runnin' out on me owin' two weeks' board an' lodgin' an' me lettin' her have a nine-dollar room fer seven, an' all she had to do was help a little around the house, an' on top of that, lightin' in on me an' knockin' me down in my own parlor—a blackjack she must of had hid in her clothes, an' then give me the boots to break my nose an' my lower plate an' knock my uppers half ways down my throat, an' give me a couple of shiners which it was two weeks before I was fit to be seen, an' as soon as I come to, I sent Ellie to fetch the police an' that lazy loafer of a Stromberg come, but the dumb Swede couldn't find her, an' all the rest of the police ain't no better from the chief down, which I went right down to headquarters myself an' made the complaint when I seen Stromberg wasn't doin' no good, an' me fit to be in bed with the beatin' she give me, but I wanted the chief should see them shiners fer himself, an' my busted plate, an' my nose way over to one side, an' I had to go in a cab, not bein' fit to be seen on the street, an' the dirty loafer charged me a dollar when I could go on the street car fer ten cents—er walk fer that matter, an' it cost me eight dollars fer a new plate, an' the doctor charged me five dollars more fer fixin' up my nose, an' he didn't get it none too straight, at that, as you kin see fer yerself—an' her my own kith an' kin which I'd took in, you might say, out of pity. It's like I says to Mr. Snook. 'Things is comin' to a pretty pass, Mr. Snook,' I says, 'when a body's own flesh an' blood, as you might say, hauls off an' pretty near kills 'em in their own parlor!' An' all because I asked her fer the fourteen dollars that was two weeks overdue, an' she says her father was dead, an' I know'd right away he wouldn't be sendin' her no more money—the dirty loafer to up an' die owin' a poor widdy woman fourteen dollars an' no way to pay it—an' that's just what I told her, even if he did marry my own sister, an' she hauled off an' pasted me one an' then kep' right on a hammerin' me, an' the next thing I know'd there was Ellie tryin' to lift me up off'n the floor, an' yellin' her fool head off instead of goin' fer the police which if they ketch her she'll find out she can't go around blackin' folks eyes an' bustin' their nose an' their plate in their own parlor— but, they won't ketch her—they've had two months an' ain't done nothin' yet, the lazy loafers, all they're good for is jumpin' on poor widdy women about exits an' fire escapes, which anyone kin see if this house got afire an' the roomers didn't have sense enough to run downstairs or jump out the windows they'd ort to git burnt. Who're you, an' what do you want with Kitty McGuigan, the ungrateful hussy, if I ever lay hands on her——"

"You won't," interrupted the Kid, dryly, "if you ever reached out to try it, she'd take up the job where she left off, an' knock them teeth clean on through you."

"Is that so!" shouted the woman, angrily, as the Kid descended the steps. Thrusting her head from the doorway, she glanced up and down the street. "If that lazy good fer nothin' Stromberg was ever where he'd ort to be when folks want him I'd have you pinched an' learnt that you can't go around insultin' respectable widdy women on their own stoop!"

As the Kid passed down the street he heard the door slam noisily. "Big Tim said she was a great hand to talk," he muttered. "But—God!"

Two blocks down, a big policeman was helping an aged woman to cross the street. When he had left her safely on the sidewalk, the Kid accosted him. "Are you Stromberg?" he asked.

"Yes, that's me. Somethin' I can do for you?"

"Do you know a Mrs. Kate O'Brien that runs a boardin' house up the street a-ways?"

"Who don't?" countered the officer, a grin widening the lips beneath the blond mustache.

The Kid returned the grin: "I've jest be'n talkin' to her——"

"I'll bet you mean she's been talkin' to you."

"You win," laughed the Kid. Then, his face became suddenly serious. "I went there," he said, "to find Kitty McGuigan. She's a niece of this Mrs. O'Brien, an' was boardin' with her. She's from the Yukon country, an' her dad was drowned last fall. I'm from there, too. I—we were goin' to be married an' go back. But it seems that, somehow, Kitty heard about her father's death, an' her aunt called him a dirty loafer, an' Kitty beat her up an' pulled her freight. I want to find her. Do you know anything about it?"

"She done a good job," answered the policeman. "The hired girl called me in an' Mrs. O'Brien sat on the sofy an' told me what come off. What with her bein' so damn' mad, an' her lips kind of mashed an' swole up an' her false teeth broke, I couldn't hardly understand her, but she wanted this Kitty McGuigan pinched fer everything short of murder. I seen it was jest a fambly row, an' went on about my business, figurin' that the woman had got about what was comin' to her, anyhow."

"But—where is Kitty McGuigan?"

"The big policeman shook his head. "I couldn't say. She's prob'ly found her another boardin' house, somewheres."

"But," persisted the Kid, "Mrs. O'Brien told me she went to headquarters an' complained directly to the chief, an' that all the police in Seattle had be'n huntin' her for two months. Surely they'd have located her, if she'd only changed boardin' houses."

Stromberg chuckled. "Hell, lad—there ain't no one huntin' her—an' never has be'n. She did go down an' raised hell with the chief, an' showed him her black eyes an' her busted teeth, an' he asked me about it, an' when I told him what I thought, he laughed an' tossed the notes he'd made in the waste basket. You see, I know'd this Miss McGuigan, in a way—used to pass her walkin' back an' forth along the street. I'd think how pretty she was, an' how there was a look in her eyes—like she was thinkin' about somethin' far away. An' it was always 'Good-mornin', or 'Good-evenin', officer,' an' a cheerful smile along with the words. When a girl like that beats anyone up, they've got it comin'. A policeman's got to use his head."

"How will I go about findin' her?"

"Well, you might try an ad in the papers, an' if that don't work, go down an' have a talk with the chief. It's part of our business to find missin' persons, an' I'll speak a word in his ear, in the meantime."

Thanking the officer, the Kid visited the office of Seattle's most important daily where an enterprising reporter, scenting a first-hand story of the Bonanza stampede, collared him for an interview that cracked the front page. The story carefully avoided mention of Kitty McGuigan, but it told of the death of Big Tim, of the fabulous wealth that lay buried in the gravel of Bonanza, of the new camp of Dawson, of the practical abandonment of Circle and Forty Mile, and wound up with the statement that Tom Haldane, recently of Forty Mile, was temporarily sojourning at a certain local hostelry.

At the close of the interview the reporter laid his hand on the Kid's shoulder. "Everyone in Seattle will read that story. You'll be hearing from your girl tomorrow. And, remember—I get the story of the wedding—and a release on that Kate O'Brien angle. Jeez—that's a pip! I'll take a camera man along and run a picture of the old gal with her war paint on. And, you better not talk to any other newspaper men—you couldn't trust the damn' crooks to lay off on the girl angle—and, if she's afraid of arrest for that knockout she handed the old lady, she might lay low and not get in touch with you."

The Yukon Kid returned to his hotel in high spirits. Kitty would read the story in the morning paper, and tomorrow he would hear from her!

CHAPTER XIII

Disappointment

AT BREAKFAST the following morning he read the story, and before the meal was finished he realized that, if Kitty McGuigan had not read the paper, everyone else in the city evidently had. A dozen reporters had broken in on the meal—and the lobby swarmed with people seeking first-hand information about the great gold strike.

Escaping from irate reporters and the clamoring populace, he sought refuge behind the locked door of his room, leaving word at the desk that he would see no one except Miss Kitty McGuigan, of Forty Mile, Y. T. He sent out for magazines, and spent the day in seclusion, having his meals served in his room to keep from being mobbed by the horde that demanded personal interviews.

During all that interminable day he read magazines, dozed, or paced up and down the floor waiting for word from Kitty. But, no word came. Nor did any word come on the next day, nor the next. The populace—even the reporters, sensing the futility of an interview, turned their thoughts elsewhere, and on the fourth day, the Kid visited the chief of police.

The kindly officer heard him through and nodded, thoughtfully. "I remember the O'Brien complaint," he said. "We disregarded it on Stromberg's say-so. Those family assault and battery cases are a nuisance. You better talk to Officer Kelly. After reading the story in the paper the other day, he said he had talked to Miss McGuigan along about the time of the O'Brien complaint. I'll call him in."

In answer to the chief's summons, a ruddy-faced patrolman entered and stood at attention.

"This is the young man that that piece in the paper was about the other day. He's trying to locate this McGuigan girl—the one that polished off her aunt, that time. You better sit down and tell him what you know about her. Take him into my private office—and you'll find cigars on the desk."

Seating himself in the chief's chair, Officer Kelly tendered a box of the chief's cigars, lighted one without removing the band, and settled back in comfort, motioning the Kid into a chair drawn close beside the desk.

"An' what was you wantin' of the gurl?" he

asked, in rich brogue, his eyes taking shrewd measure of the man before him.

The Kid told the story, and at its conclusion, the policeman blew a cloud of blue smoke at the ceiling, and cleared his throat.

"An' so this Big Tim—her father, jumped out av the canoe so you could git to shore—an' him not bein' able to swim a lick?"

The Kid nodded: "Yes. I tried to stop him, but it was no use."

"By God—there was a man! She said up there in the gold country they loved um."

"They did. Big Tim didn't have an enemy in the world. But—how did she know he was dead? An', when was it she talked to you?"

"Ut's like this—a couple months ago, ut was— I was walkin' me beat through the park an' I seen the gurl sittin' on a bench alone on wan of them walks clost beside the lake. When I got closter I seen she was cryin' fit to shake the bench, an' moppin' at her eyes with a handkerchief the size av a postage stamp. I stops an' asks her what's the matter, an' she looks up at me with her blue eyes swimmin' in tears. 'Me father's dead,' she says, an' off she goes in another fit av weepin'. I speaks a word or two av sympathy, an' she tells me he was drowned up in the Yukon. She said a man just told her— but, who he was, or where he told her, or how he know'd it, she didn't say. She said he belonged up North—that they loved him up there. I ain't much good in times like that—ut's a woman they want. A woman knows what to say. So I says a few words to comfort her as best I could, an' tells her to set there as long as she liked, an' I'd kind of keep an eye out an' turn folks along some other path, an' I seen how the damn' little handkerchief she had was all wadded an' wet, an' havin' a clean wan av me own, that the old woman had slipped into me pocket, I drops it on her lap, an' went on, knowin' she'd best be let alone."

"I want to thank you for that," said the Kid, his lips tight.

"Hell—'twas what any man would do. Well —I thinks no more about ut till, ut's mebbe, three or four days, an' I was in here at headquarters, when in barges a big two-hundred-pound woman with her nose all taped up, an' two as pretty a black eyes as you ever seen, an' a set av broken false teeth in her fist, an' she won't stop short av the chief, hisself. Well, be the lovin' God! I thought I'd heard wimmin talk! But, two minutes after she got started, I know'd different. The chief, an' the desk sergeant, which he'd follered her in when she brushed past um, they both tried to git in a word —but there wasn't no stoppin' her, short av murder. So they let her go till at last she run down. We heard how this McGuigan had married her sister an' drug her off up North to die, an' all about the sewer contractin' business a few years back, an' about this Kitty McGuigan comin' down an' boardin' with her, an' her payin' six months' board in advance, an' how, when she got two weeks in arrears waitin' for her father to send some more money, she kep' after her until three, four days ago the gurl comes in an' tells her her father is dead, an' when she tells the gurl her father's a good fer nothin' loafer fer dyin' on her that way, owin' two weeks board, the gurl up an' knocks her fer a row av apple trees. An' she done a good job, too. She messed up her mug in grand style! We sure was tickled with the results av the assault. Well, she claimed she'd complained to Stomberg, which he's the cop on the beat, an' he hadn't caught her yet. She demanded the gurl's arrest fer most everything that's in the books, short av actual murder.

"They got rid av her at last, an' when Stomberg come in the chief asked him about it, an' Stomberg told um 'twas his belief that the old slut got jist what was comin' to her. 'Twas only last year she throw'd a gurl out av her house with only the clothes on her back because she'd got a couple av weeks behind with her board. She was a gurl that had lost her job through no fault av her own an' was huntin' another. But, with no money, an' no place to sleep, an' nothin' to eat, the poor kid give ut up. They found her body floatin' in the bay a few days later."

The Kid drew in his breath sharply. "God! If——"

Officer Kelly laid a kindly hand on the younger man's shoulder: "There's be'n no floaters found in the last couple av months that could av be'n her."

"But, she had only the clothes on her back, an' no place to sleep, an' nothin' to eat, an' no money—just like that other girl!"

"Listen, son," said the policeman. "You jist got through tellin' me about Big Tim McGuigan jumpin' out av the canoe to sure death that you could git to shore. Would the daughter av a man like that quit? Not be a damn' sight, she wouldn't! She'd be game."

"You're right," replied the Kid. "She's alive, somewhere. An' I'm goin' to find her!"

"That's the talk! We'll go back now an' speak to the chief."

"We'll locate her within a few days if she's in Seattle," assured the chief. "I'll make it a general order for all ranks—and put some special men on the case, besides."

"It's funny she didn't read that piece in the paper an' come to the hotel."

"Not necessarily. She may not read the papers closely. Or, she may read another paper. That story was only in one issue."

"Would it do any good to post a reward for information about her?" asked the Kid, eagerly. "Run an ad in all the papers—an' keep it there for a month, if necessary?"

"It wouldn't do any harm," said the chief, "and it might help a lot."

The next moment his eyes widened as the Kid pulled a roll from a bulging pocket and stripped off ten one thousand dollar bills. "Good Lord!" he exclaimed. "You're not carrying that much cash around with you!"

"Sure. Why not? I figure I'll be needin' it one of these days to buy some bacon, an' flour, an' tea."

"To buy what!"

"Supplies—to ship up to Sheep Camp, at the foot of the Chilcoot. I got the tip that the Mounted Police are going to stop everyone going into the Yukon at the pass unless they've got a year's supplies along. An' the fellow that can sell 'em those supplies right there on the spot is goin' to be lucky. I've got to go back inside, but if I could find the right man to handle 'em, we'd both clean up big."

The chief turned to the uniformed officer with a smile: "There's your chance, Kelly. You've been wishing you had enough of a stake to get in on this gold rush. Don't like to lose a good man—but I don't want to stand in your way if you can clean up some real money."

"D'you mean," asked the officer, turning to the Kid, "that you're huntin' a man to handle them supplies?"

"Sure I mean it! Here's the cash to pay for 'em. Better than sixty thousan' dollars."

"Would I do?"

"You bet you would! It would kind of give me a chance to pay you back for that handkerchief. But first we've got to find Kitty."

The chief picked one of the big bills from the desk top, and handed back the other nine. "This ill be plenty for a reward," he said. "I'll attend to the ads." He turned to Kelly: "You better get into plain clothes," he said. "I'll detail you on this case and relieve you of all further duty. I'll put Stomberg on it, too—you're the only two that know the girl by sight. And, when you get ready to hit North I'll accept your resignation."

"Thanks, chief," said the officer. "I'll go home an' git out av me uniform. But furst we'll be stoppin' at the bank an' gittin' rid av that cash. There's plenty av rats in Seattle that would crack a man over the head for a tenth part av what Haldane's got on um. Sixty thousan' dollars—an' he carries it around in his pants! Sixty thousan' dollars will buy a hell av a lot av bacon, an' flour, an' tea."

For thirty days the Yukon Kid stayed around Seattle while the police combed the city for

Kitty McGuigan. Kelly and Stomberg worked night and day, and all regular patrolmen checked every girl on their beats. Continued disappointment was stamping its mark on the features of the Yukon Kid. A somber look crept into his eyes, and his lips rarely smiled. Kelly noted that he looked ten years older on the day the chief summoned him to the office and told him definitely that the girl was not in Seattle.

"What'll I do, now," asked the Kid. "What is there left to do?"

"The only thing I see is the private agencies. It's evident that, if she's still alive, she's gone some place else. There are representatives of two detective agencies here that have country-wide connections. You might take the case to them. It'll cost you plenty—but, they may be able to locate her."

"I don't give a damn what it costs," replied the Kid. "I'm takin' out a lot of dust—an' I'm goin' back an' take out a lot more. I'll pay 'em whatever they want. By God—they've got to find her!"

Accompanied by Kelly, the Kid visited the two agencies and made arrangements for their handling of the case. Each accepted the commission, though each admitted that without a photograph and with only such description as the Kid could furnish, the chance for success was small. Each arranged to send in a report, and a bill for expenses every thirty days until notified to quit.

As he was about to leave the last of the two offices, the manager cleared his throat: "Of course," he said, "the girl may be dead. But, if we found that she had taken the other way out, would you—er—be interested, then?"

"What do you mean—'the other way out'?" asked the Kid.

"Well—some girls, when they figure they've got plumb to the end of their rope take acid, or jump in the bay. Others—er—go down the line——"

Kelly grabbed the Kid's arm just in time to prevent the local manager of a nationally known detective agency from taking it on the chin. "Hold on, Haldane," soothed the big Irishman. "He's right. A lot of 'em go that road, lad—a hell av a lot av 'em. I've often thought the wans that jumps in the bay was the smartest—it's quicker. Me an' Stomberg checked up that angle unbeknownst to you. 'Twould av be'n bad policin' not to. It ain't always from choice they go. There's a traffic. We run acrost her trail, too——"

The color suddenly left the Yukon Kid's face, and he wrenched violently to free the arm that ex-Officer Kelly still held in a vise-like grip.

"Hold on, now, till you hear me out. 'Twas the only breath av a trail that anyone picked up

DISAPPOINTMENT

to pay—or go clear back to Skagway or Seattle, an' waste the rest of the summer doin' it."

"An' when I'm sold out, shall I go back an' git more?"

"Hell—no! Never kill good dogs by ridin' your sled. It won't be long before word goes back to the startin' points that there's teeth in the police order—then they'll all bring their year's supplies with 'em. No—when you sell out, stick the money in your pocket an' come on down to Dawson, an' we'll split it. You'll have a stake then, an' I'll let you in on somethin' else. I'm never goin' to dig any more gold. I'll hire men to dig it for me. An' buy more claims. An' hire more men. A man can make more with his head than he can with his hands. What we clean up on this deal is just a shoestring. You play along with me, Kelly. That handkerchief has got to be paid for."

CHAPTER XIV

Flight

WHEN Kitty McGuigan had turned several corners after abruptly quitting her aunt's boarding house, she slowed her pace and breathed easier. Her heart quickened as a policeman strolled toward her, but evidently he had not heard Ellie's screams, for he accorded her scarce a glance as he passed idly swinging his club on its tasselled cord.

She hailed a passing cable car and rode downtown with no object in view other than placing distance between herself and Ellie, whose terrified shrieks must certainly have roused the neighborhood.

A tempting display of food in the window of a short-order restaurant caught her eye, and she got off at the next corner and walked back. When she paid her check she counted her remaining change and found that it amounted to exactly four dollars and ninety-six cents.

Almost without volition she turned toward the waterfront. She wondered if any of the ships were northward bound, and suddenly realized that her four dollars and ninety-six cents would not finance any sort of a journey. Tears filled her eyes as she gazed longingly at the ships lying in their slips. . . . "Good-bye, Kitty." . . . "Good-bye." . . .

If she could only see one of the boys—any one of them would gladly toss her his whole sack of dust. Then she could go back—back to Forty Mile—back home—back to—no, not back to Tommy Haldane! Tommy didn't care—he hadn't even come down to the beach the day she went out of the North—out of his life forever.

She felt no slightest sense of compunction for the attack upon her aunt—rather a warm glow of satisfaction as of a deed well done. She shuddered as she thought of the girl they had found floating in the bay. The water looked greasy, and gray, and cold. And the water of the Yukon —ice-cold it must have been the day it closed forever over the body of Big Tim McGuigan as he dived from the canoe in the whirling blizzard.

She realized that her eyes were eagerly scanning the docks for sight of a blanket-coated figure in mukluks who would be loading two tons of flour and pork onto one of the ships. He was a sourdough, the man from Circle—he was home folks—he would see that she got back—but—back where? He had said there was no more Forty Mile—no more Circle. Anywhere on the Yukon would do—up on Bonanza where Carmack had made his strike. Old Bettles would be there, and Camillo Bill and Moosehide Charlie, and Swiftwater Bill, and Tommy—yes, and Tommy Haldane, too. She'd show Tommy Haldane that she could live in a tent and chew moose meat with any of them! Only it would never be in *his* tent! She hated Tommy Haldane!

"Looking for something, dearie?" asked a voice in her ear, and Kitty turned to meet the gaze of a pair of eyes that were regarding her with friendly concern. The eyes looked out from a face of ivory whiteness with cheeks the color of roses—a wonderful complexion, thought Kitty, for a woman of forty, or more. Her glance lowered from the face to the skirt of taffeta that shimmered and seemed to change color in the rays of the setting sun. Vaguely Kitty was aware that the woman had been walking behind her for a long time. She continued without giving the girl a chance to speak: "Excuse me if I'm wrong, but you looked like you was a stranger—like you was looking for somewheres you couldn't find. I thought maybe I could help. You see, I'm acquainted here."

As the woman smiled, Kitty noted the white,

even teeth that showed between lips that seemed startlingly red above the ivory chin.

"No, I'm not looking for anything—in particular," answered the girl. "I am just—just taking a walk."

The smile widened: "Well, now—so am I. Some folks likes to walk out in the parks—and that's nice, too, sometimes. But take me, now—I like it along the docks better—I like the smell of the water, an' the ships and things—don't you?"

"I think I like the wild country best," said Kitty, noticing for the first time that the breeze carried the odor of fish, and of tar.

"You from the country?" the woman asked with evident interest.

"From Forty Mile—on the Yukon."

"Yukon! Why, that's the place where they've just struck gold. They say it's richer than the California strike, 'way back. And the word is passing that there's going to be a big rush."

Kitty nodded: "Yes, if it's as rich as they think, there's bound to be a big stampede."

"Are you acquainted up there?"

Kitty smiled: "I know pretty near everyone, I guess."

"Do you want to go back?"

"Yes, indeed I do!" The desperate eagerness of the reply was not lost on the woman who laughed throatily.

"Well, now isn't that lucky—I've been thinking maybe I might go up there myself. But let's go some place where we can talk. There's a Chink in the next block where we can get a cup of tea." She paused, and added: "Unless you'd like something a little stronger—you look kind of fagged out. I know a quiet little place——"

Kitty shook her head. "No, thank you. I've had my supper—but, I wouldn't mind a cup of tea."

Seated at a teakwood table, fantastically inlaid with bits of nacre, the two talked and sipped their tea. At the end of an hour the woman had succeeded in learning pretty much all of Kitty's past history, and had adroitly disclosed nothing of her own. Finally she summed up: "It's lucky for both of us we ran onto each other. We ought to clean up big up there, what with you knowing the ropes, and all. And you can come home with me, dearie, and stay until everything's set to go. What with being pretty near broke, and no place to go, and the cops probably looking for you already, if your aunt's come to. I'll find out about the boats—if there's going to be a big rush, and we can get in on the first boat, we'd have the edge on them that waits till later. There'll be some of my girls want to go, too."

"Oh, have you got some girls of your own?" asked Kitty.

"Sure, I have," answered the woman with a bland smile. "Six of 'em. They're all good girls. You'll get along with 'em fine, when you get acquainted. We'll be going, now. It's too far to walk. I'll have the Chink call a cab."

Ten minutes later, the cab drew up to the curb and Kitty followed the woman across the sidewalk and up a flight of half a dozen steps where they paused before the door which the woman opened with a latchkey.

Kitty found herself in a small hallway from which heavily carpeted stairs led to the floor above. "Wait here, and I'll be right down," said the woman, and disappeared up the stairs.

Voices sounded from a room which opened off to the right—voices and the tinkle of glasses jostling against each other on a tray. Through the open door Kitty caught a glimpse of a waxed floor. An indescribable uneasiness assailed the girl. She sniffed the air, heavy with the fumes of beer and stale tobacco. A man's voice ceased, and there was a sudden burst of feminine laughter, and an oath in a girl's voice. A piano, loud and brassy, struck into a lively waltz. One swift step and Kitty stood in the doorway. At a glance her eyes swept the room. On an upholstered lounge a girl sat on a man's lap holding a beer glass to his lips. Other girls, in scantily cut gowns of flimsy brilliant material lounged in deep chairs, smoking. A man balanced on the floor, his arm about the waist of a girl in gold silk stockings, while a negro woman in snowy white apron was gathering empty glasses onto a tray. Leaning against the piano another man grinned drunkenly as his eyes swept Kitty from head to foot. He lurched toward her across the floor: "Look who's here!" he cried, thickly. "C'mon, kid—le's dance."

Sudden terror gripped the girl's heart. Like a blow the realization struck her. She knew, in a vague sort of way, of the women who lived in the cabin down by the flats in Forty Mile. Hot blood flooded her cheeks. The man was before her, now—his muddy eyes leering into her own, as he rolled the wet stub of a dead cigar between his thick lips. As his fingers touched her arm, something in Kitty's brain seemed to snap. Every muscle in her body tense, she jerked the arm free, and reaching low, with doubled fist, as Moosehide Charlie had taught her to do, she drove that fist squarely against the side of the man's jaw with every ounce of her hundred and fifty pounds behind it. In a frenzy of panic she whirled to the street door. Her fingers found the night latch, and amid a confusion of sounds, she slammed the door behind her and fled blindly down the street.

Darkness had fallen, and as she had done once before that day, she turned a corner, and another, and another. She was in a darker street now, but she had no slightest idea in what part of town. Certainly it was an unfamiliar part. She hurried on.

Two blocks ahead a street car shot across the street, and she hastened her steps. It seemed to the girl that hours passed as she waited for another car, her eyes shooting quick frightened glances down the street over which she had just come. Sounds of footsteps startled her, and her overwrought nerves peopled the shadows with lurking forms. With a shriek of wheels, a street car rounded a corner, and as it rumbled toward her she could scarce restrain herself from running to meet it.

She fairly leaped onto the platform, and as the car lurched along she kept her face turned from the window for fear a passing policeman might recognize her. Her brain worked rapidly. She must leave Seattle—now—tonight. It made no difference where she went—but, with two charges of assault against her, no doubt every policeman in the whole city was on the lookout for her. Recollection of the nice policeman in the park struck her with the force of a blow. Oh, why had she told him her name? The police would have a good description of her, now. She wondered what he would think when he found out she was a common criminal? She hoped he wouldn't be the one to arrest her. She couldn't look him in the face—after the kind words—

and the handkerchief. When the conductor collected her fare she asked him where the depot was.

"Where do you want to go to?" he asked.

"Tacoma," she said. She had often heard Tacoma discussed at her aunt's table. She had heard San Francisco and Portland favorably mentioned—but rightly guessed that with a total capital of four dollars and ninety-six cents these cities were unattainable. Tacoma, she knew, was much nearer.

The conductor glanced at his watch, and peered out the window. "We pass right clost," he said. "When we're on time you've got eight minutes to catch the train. You'll make it, all right—we're only about two minutes behind."

In the station Kitty bought a ticket and nervously watched the clock. A policeman passed through the waiting room, and the girl stooped low over the tying of her shoe. She breathed easier as he disappeared without recognizing her. But not until the train was actually under way did she feel entirely at ease. Even then she wondered whether the Tacoma police would have been notified.

In her relief at leaving Seattle behind she had given no thought to the future. She would find work of some kind, and maybe before the freeze-up she could save the money to go back to the Yukon. Once on the big river she would be all right. She would borrow enough for an outfit, and then she would hit out into the hills on her own. She'd make a strike, too! She'd show Tommy Haldane—she'd show him she was no chechako! He hadn't even come down to the beach to see her off. . . . "Good-bye, Kitty." . . . "Good-bye." . . .

In Tacoma she found a cheap hotel and engaged a room for the night, paying a dollar in advance, as she carried no baggage. She thought that the night clerk eyed her peculiarly as he handed her the key. She locked her door, and further barricaded herself with a chair back wedged beneath the knob.

It was late when she awoke the following morning. Dressing carefully, she left the hotel, bought a newspaper, and entered a restaurant. As she dallied over her breakfast she eagerly scanned each bit of news, and was relieved to find no mention of any assaults in Seattle, nor any broadcasting of her own name and description. The want ads met her eye and she considered numerous positions, finally deciding on one as waitress at the Grand Pacific Hotel.

The hostelry was an imposing structure, and Kitty walked past its entrance several times before she finally summoned the courage to enter. She met a kindly assistant manager to whom, when he asked for references, she explained that she had never worked any place before, that she was from the Yukon country, and that she had no baggage because she found that the things she had brought with her were of no use in a city. He smiled, and gave her the job. When he asked her name she answered without a moment's hesitation: "Kitty Flannigan." She was not sure that the Seattle newspapers had not carried the story of her doings, even if the Tacoma papers had ignored it—and her observing glance had taken in a familiar Seattle paper on the manager's desk. Anyway, Flannigan had been her mother's name and she reasoned she had a right to it.

CHAPTER XV

$1,000 Reward

WHEN Kitty had been a month at the hotel she was made cashier of the newly opened grill room, and her salary raised in accordance with her new position. She was happier now than she had been since that day in the gun store when the man from Circle told her of the death of Big Tim McGuigan. For, at her present salary it would not be long before she could save enough to go back to her beloved Yukon.

Then one day Miss Burns, the head waitress, stepped smilingly to her desk, a folded Seattle newspaper in her hand. "Ain't you glad your name ain't Kitty McGuigan instead of Kitty Flannigan?" she asked, indicating the advertisement that headed the personal want column of the paper. Kitty read

$1000 REWARD

One thousand dollars in gold will be paid for information as to the whereabouts of Miss Kitty McGuigan, formerly of Forty Mile, Yukon Ty., Canada, who disappeared from her boarding house at 2202 Blankenship Road, this city, on April 9.

Followed then a description that would have applied to one out of every four young ladies on the West Coast, and the request that any information be immediately communicated to the Chief of Police of the city of Seattle.

Kitty knew that her heart was racing wildly. She wanted to scream. She locked her ankles together beneath the desk for fear Miss Burns would see that her knees were trembling. But she managed to register little interest in the notice, and even laid down the paper with a smile.

"I wonder what she done?" speculated the interested Miss Burns. "Must of been something important, or the police wouldn't be offering no thousand-dollar reward. Gee, I wish I could lay my eyes on her. Think of having a thousand dollars all to once—and gold, too. I'll bet it would be heavy. Tell you what we'll do, Kitty—we'll go halves on it. You keep an' eye out for every dame that comes in here, and so will I. If you see her, you tip me off and I'll slip out and get Sweeny, the house dick, and he'll make the pinch, and we'll divide the reward. That would be five hundred apiece—but we'd prob'ly have to slip Sweeny a hundred. Even if the lazy bum made us split three ways with him it would be more than three hundred apiece. I could use three hundred, and I bet you could, too."

$1,000 REWARD 131

"Yes," answered Kitty. "I could use three hundred. We'll keep our eyes open."

It was the noon hour and the room was filling rapidly. Most of the patrons were business men, but Kitty noticed that from her position near the door, Miss Burns was according each woman who entered an appraising scrutiny. Her eyes dropped to the paper on her desk, and she turned it over to hide the headline that seemed to shriek its offer of one thousand dollars reward. Her brain raced madly. What had happened? Why should the police be offering a thousand dollars reward for her? Had her aunt died? And were the police seeking her to hang her? Her lips pressed tight in horror as she remembered the man she had seen hanged in Forty Mile when a miner's meeting found him guilty of robbing a cache. Maybe Miss Burns had recognized her from the description, and was only waiting the chance to slip Sweeny the word. She roused with a start. A man was waiting to pay his check. As she handed him his change she thought that he looked at her curiously.

The room had emptied when Kitty left her desk at three o'clock. She would be off until five, a girl from the office taking her place during the slack hours. Miss Burns was nowhere to be seen when Kitty hurried to her room. She counted the cash in her pocketbook and found that it amounted to sixty-two dollars and some loose change. She had been paid the day before. Hastily she dressed for the street, and threw her few belongings into a suitcase. She knew that leaving the hotel with the suitcase would arouse no suspicion, even if she were noticed, as it was her habit to carry her laundry back and forth in it. Hastening to the station she bought a ticket to San Francisco, and spent the hour before the departure of her train in the waiting room, her face screened by the newspaper in which she appeared deeply absorbed.

She bought all the Seattle, Tacoma, and Portland papers, and as the train rushed southward, she scanned them eagerly. Each carried the notice of the reward. She wondered whether the San Francisco papers would carry it, but consoled herself with the thought that San Francisco was a much larger city, and it would be easier to escape notice, especially as she realized that the description which she had reread many times was in no wise accurate.

Vaguely she wondered what they would be saying at the hotel when she failed to report for duty. She wondered if Miss Burns would suspect, and would telegraph the police to be on the lookout for her.

It was a chance she must take. She would be safer in San Francisco than in Tacoma, at any rate.

She found a cheap lodging house, and answered a garment manufacturer's ad under the "Help wanted—Female" classifieds. She breathed easier when she found that neither her landlady nor the manager of the shirt factory recognized her as the thousand-dollar Kitty McGuigan. After a short term of instruction she was given a machine, and assiduously devoted her time to the stitching of shirts at a wage that made Forty Mile seem a dream of a far-off and indefinite future.

The San Francisco newspapers carried the reward notice, as had the papers of the more northern coast cities, but Kitty felt a comparative sense of security in the fact that she came into daily contact with but few people. It was not like being the cashier of a well patronized grill room.

Within the month the reward notice was dropped from all papers simultaneously, and shortly thereafter Kitty quit the shirt factory to accept a more congenial and lucrative position in a candy store and ice cream parlor. Here she soon became known as a young lady eminently capable of taking care of herself, keeping the cheap mashers in their place, but readily accepting the invitations of the better element of the store's patrons—clear-eyed young mechanics and salesmen, for the most part—to dances at the various "athletic" and "social" clubs of which they were members. It was at one of these periodical balls that Kitty's dancing came into the notice of Morris Hertzbaum, a small-time theatrical producer and backer of road shows.

Mr. Hertzbaum, a connoisseur of dancing ability—talent, and a gift, he called it—lost no time in seeking an introduction, which was immediately followed by an interview in which he convincingly pointed out the folly—the crime, even—of hiding such talent between the four walls of a candy store. From the viewpoint of Mr. Hertzbaum, such a gift belonged to the public, and could not with a clear conscience, be withheld from the public. The fact that the public was willing to pay, every night and two afternoons a week to witness this gift, made it doubly advisable that it be not hidden between the four walls of a candy store. Of course, this talent was as yet only a talent in the rough—uncut, and unpolished, as it were. But, he, Morris Hertzbaum, in the fulfillment of his duty as public benefactor, would gladly finance the cutting and polishing providing Miss Flannigan would contract to appear under his management only, for a specified length of time, and at a salary to be determined—such salary, even at the outset, and dating from the evening of her first public appearance, to be at least double her present salary as a purveyor of ice cream and candy.

Kitty accepted. Her one recreation with the exception of books, was dancing. She loved it. And, if she could turn this congenial avocation into a profitable vocation, she would be foolish not to do it.

So she resigned her position in the candy store and devoted herself to her dancing under the more or less able tutelage of several masters of specialty, and the critical eye of Mr. Hertzbaum himself. Her undivided interest, her robust health, and the perfect coördination of mind and superbly muscled body enabled her to attack the work with a dash and a verve that forced words of praise and appreciation from the lips of hard-boiled trainers, and tears of joy from the watery eyes of Morris Hertzbaum. The obese and optimistic producer unblushingly predicted Broadway, for sure, and smacked his thick lips in anticipation of the golden harvest to come.

But, it's a long way to dance to Broadway.

A number dropped out of a vaudeville road company, and Hertzbaum replaced the act with

NADU THE SUBLIME

Genuine Nautch Girl from India.
Favorite of the late Rajah of Rammikan.
Who has appeared before all the Crowned Heads
OF EUROPE!

So Kitty McGuigan, alias, Kitty Flannigan, became Nadu, the Nautch Girl, with a darkly hinted Rammikan past—and as Nadu, the Nautch Girl, she danced from the mining towns of the Far West, through the tanks of Kansas and Nebraska and Iowa, and the sticks of Michigan, Wisconsin, and Minnesota, at a salary of forty dollars per week—if and when. But, there were many ifs, and many whens—and with the passing of the months Forty Mile seemed to sink farther and farther into the past. Yet, somehow, it always remained a goal. . . . "Good-bye, Kitty." . . . "Good-bye." . . .

Yes, sometime she was going back. The boys would be glad to see her. She'd show Tommy Haldane!

In far-off San Francisco, Mr. Morris Hertzbaum dined overheartily one evening and died of acute indigestion, and was gathered unto his fathers. The road show disbanded at Hallock, Minnesota, and Kitty, a seasoned trouper, now, found that her funds were just sufficient to take her to Winnipeg where she was fortunate in securing a minor rôle in a stock company.

A year had passed since she had fled in terror from her aunt's boarding house in Seattle. The newspapers were beginning to print more and more of news of the Yukon gold strike, and the names "Klondike," and "Alaska" were on everyone's lips. Kitty eagerly devoured every scrap of news that came her way, winnowing the true from the false with the discriminating understanding of a sourdough. Many a laugh she had over the feature stories of the Sunday newspapers—preposterous, distorted tales of snow and ice and famine—and of beasts that never were. She had long since become disillusioned. It was a long, long way to Broadway. It was a long, long way to Forty Mile. She despaired of ever seeing Broadway.

Jealously she guarded her small savings—begrudging each necessary expenditure—hoarding her pennies and her dimes against the day when her little bank book would show enough to her credit to pay her passage to Forty Mile—or to Dawson, rather, as the new camp was called that the papers said had sprung up in the shadow of Moosehide Mountain.

Then it was that one evening at an after-theater supper in the grill room of a hotel, she was introduced by the leading lady to Mr. Jones, of Edmonton.

CHAPTER XVI

Mr. Jones of Edmonton

MR. JONES of Edmonton was an old acquaintance of Mrs. Palm, leading lady of the Olympic All Star Stock Company—that is, he had met her upon the occasion of a previous visit to Winnipeg, some six months before. And it was upon the invitation of Mr. Jones that a half dozen of the Olympic thespians had foregathered after the theater to partake in what the hotel had to offer in the way of food and drink.

And, in the matter of food and drink, Mr. Jones did himself proud. But it became pointedly apparent to the little assembly that, after his introduction to Nadu, the Sublime, there were exactly five too many stars twinkling in the immediate firmament to suit the fancy of Mr. Jones of Edmonton—a realization that came as something of a relief to the leading lady, who was also the wife of the manager of the Olympic, for in eighteen hundred and ninety-seven, wives were wives in Winnipeg, and the Olympic, being a stock company, it wouldn't do to have folks talk *too* much.

Nevertheless, the company dined heartily and well, and drank heartily and not too well. A successful party, and a gay one, thought Mr. Jones of Edmonton as he chatted entertainingly with Nadu, the dancing girl, whom he had contrived to have seated on his right.

Mr. Jones drank sparingly, as was his habit, and when he noted that beyond a sip or two of her cocktail, Nadu drank nothing at all, he managed to convey his hearty approval in an intimate aside that passed unheard—but not unobserved by exactly five pairs of eyes. With many a nasty little dig Kitty would pay for her conquest, and knowing this, she took unaltruistic delight in smiling sweetly into the points of the green daggers that flashed in the eyes of the skinny ingénue and the leading lady's buxom understudy, as she pushed her conquest to the limit.

The next evening after the theater, Mr. Jones of Edmonton dined again with Nadu, the Nautch girl with the eyes of Irish blue—just they two alone at a little table in a far corner of the grill room. And the next night. And, yet, the night thereafter. The intervening afternoons, not being matinée days, had been spent, one in bicycling about the city and through the parks, and the other in taking a ride in the horseless carriage then on exhibition, that carried two passengers besides the driver over a fixed course for a certain sum. "They're trying to sell stock in a company to build the things," explained Mr. Jones, above the noise of the motor as they shot along at a speed of seven or eight miles an hour, gripping the seat arms with one hand and their hats with the other. "But they'll never amount to anything, except as a curiosity. Who'd buy them, anyway? Look at that team! Takes three men to hold 'em. The farmers would mob anyone that was fool enough to try to run one. I tell you, for getting over the roads, they'll never get anything that'll beat Old Dobbin. They'll never get me to sink a dollar into their confounded contraption. We bankers have to watch our step."

That night, after their late supper, Mr. Jones had boarded his train for home, promising to return in a month as his business would surely require a visit at that time—only he told it with smiling eyes, and a tone that conveyed to the girl that it was she, and not the business that would be responsible for the promised visit.

After Mr. Jones had gone, Kitty realized that his sojourn had been the one bright spot in her life since that day so long, long ago when she had stood facing Big Tim McGuigan and

Tommy Haldane in the little cabin on the Yukon.

She recalled the clear eyes and wholesome look of this young banker who had paid her such ardent court. She admired the smooth, suave manner of his speech, and the fact that, if not actually handsome, he was distinguished-looking with his gold pince-nez, and his carefully trimmed imperial. He had been generous to a fault, and thoughtful beyond any man she had known. A flush of pleasure heightened the color of her cheeks as she reached out and touched the petals of the two huge bouquets of flowers that all but hid the mirror behind her tiny dressing table. Never before had she been the recipient of flowers on the stage. And, he loved the things she loved. She remembered how his eyes had lighted when he found she could discuss with authority such matters as tump straps, and canoes, and rifles, and the hunting of big game. He, too, had spoken of these things as a sourdough, and not as a chechako. He had explained that each year he was wont to spend a month or six weeks far north of the railways. And she had told him, on their last evening together, something of her life before she became a trouper. She remembered how pleased he had seemed when she had told him that the Nautch girl stuff, and the Rajah of Rammikan, and her appearance before the crowned heads of Europe had been creations of the fertile brain of Mr. Morris Hertzbaum, late of San Francisco.

Long and earnestly Kitty stared at the face that stared back at her from among the petals of the drooping flowers. All her life she had lived among men. She knew men—their faults, and their virtues. Women she distrusted. But men she liked, or hated, or simply despised because unworthy to be either liked or hated. And men liked her. She possessed that indescribable something that has been succinctly termed "it," to a degree that would have surrounded her with men even had her physical charms been far less alluring. She did not fear men, but instinctively divining their motives, handled them with an ease and skill that baffled, but left no scars.

It was thus she had handled Mr. Jones of Edmonton who had wooed her with a finesse and an ardor that had led him to propose everything except marriage. She did not love Mr. Jones. The question she was trying to decide was: could she ever love him? And what of Tommy Haldane? Tommy Haldane was the only man she had ever loved, and he was the only man she had ever hurt. She had hurt him brutally—viciously, as the wolf hurts. She had been young, then—only two short years younger, in the cold reckoning of time—but, oh so much younger in the wisdom of the world. But—she *hated* Tommy Haldane! And, Tommy Haldane had not made good. He had turned out a weakling among those big men of the high North. Of this she was sure, for never in the Sunday feature stories from the Klondike, syndicated all over the United States and Canada, had she ever seen mention of his name. Swiftwater Bill, and Moosehide Charlie, and Camillo Bill, and Old Bettles, and a new name she had never heard, The Yukon Kid—these names had been blazoned from coast to coast as the elder heroes of the land of ice and snow.

But the name of Tommy Haldane had never even been mentioned. Even though she had convinced herself a thousand times that she hated him, she knew that his failure to make good had been a disappointment so bitter as to amount to poignant pain. If he had risen to the heights— and crashed in some mighty battle of gold, even though he came out penniless, she knew that her heart would have swelled with pride. If he had, even as Swiftwater Bill had done, scattered a fortune to the four winds in epic, hell-roaring debauch, she could have loved him for it, and have cheered him on as he plunged back into the wilderness to rip new fortunes from the guts of new creeks. But—to fail—when he had gone in among the first—that, she could not forgive.

Look at this Yukon Kid—the youngest of them all—and the most talked of! Scarcely a newspaper that did not spread his doings and his sayings before an admiring world. He had amassed millions. Had waged and won titanic battles. Held the North at heel! And Kitty had never even heard of him—some chechako, probably. The one chechako in thousands, who, by the indomitable force of him had made good.

There was a wistful droop to the lips in the mirror. She drew a long breath that seemed, somehow, to catch in her throat. Ah, well. . . .

Once more she was dining alone in the grill room of the hotel with Mr. Jones, of Edmonton. He seemed more ardent than ever, and some way, more serious. They talked long of the Yukon, and of the great stampede to the Klondike. Every day, now the newspapers were full of the news of the new North—of the jamming throngs that fought for place on the Seattle docks—of overcrowded steamers—of the vast army of pack-laden men that crawled like neverending snakes over the passes. And, under the spell of the talk of the land she loved, she found herself telling him more and more of the intimate little details of her life. She told him of Tommy Haldane—but, she spoke of her father as Flannigan. For, she never had learned the reason for the police reward, and she was far too wise to allow any man to get anything on her. As far as Mr. Jones of Edmonton knew, she was Kitty Flannigan—and her Seattle days were, to him, an uncut page.

Suddenly, he leaned toward her, and his hand closed firmly over her own as it idly toyed with a spoon. She noticed that his hand looked strong and capable and brown against the snowy whiteness of the linen. "Kitty," he said, "do you want to go back?"

"Back?" she repeated, dully, raising her eyes to his, which burned with an eager, devouring fire. "Back—where?"

"Back to the Yukon. To the Klondike. To Forty Mile—anywhere you want to go."

"What do you mean?"

"I mean, do you want to go North—with me?"

"But—I thought you were a banker," she said, the little puzzled wrinkles gathering between her eyes.

"I am a banker. But, I've got red blood in me, too. I want to get in on this thing. It's big! It's a man's job—a he-man's! I've read about it, and thought about it, and talked about it, until I'll be damned if I can keep out of it! It's your country, girl—and it can be my country. Let's go!"

For a long time Kitty sat staring straight before her. Forty Mile—home! What did the future hold for her here? What did it hold for her anywhere, outside? Swiftly and in sequence the events of the past two years swept before her—Seattle—Tacoma—San Francisco—the mining towns, and the one-night stands among the tanks and the sticks—Winnipeg, and the dreary round of stock—the vile insinuations of the understudy, and the barbed jibes of the nasty little ingénue. Forty Mile—home—the boys welcoming her back as they had tried to cheer her departure. . . . "Good-bye, Kitty." . . . "Good-bye." . . .

"Let's see," she said, unconsciously speaking in an audible whisper. "It was Old Bettles that wanted the oranges, and Moosehide Charlie the yellow shoes, size nine—and the red necktie for Swiftwater Bill——"

"What?" exclaimed the puzzled Mr. Jones.

The eyes of Irish blue were wet with tears. "Yes," answered Kitty McGuigan. "I'll go." Slowly she disengaged her hand from his and held it toward him, indicating the third finger of her left hand with the forefinger of her right. "But not," she added, "until there is a bona fide ring on there."

With a laugh he recaptured the hand. "I—I hoped you would add that, Kitty," he said.

"You knew I would," she corrected, simply.

"Do you love me?" he asked, bending low to press a burning kiss upon her hand.

A slow flush heightened the color of her

cheeks, but her eyes were not raised to his: "Would I marry a man I could not love?" she countered.

The words seemed to satisfy him. He leaned back in his chair, selecting a cigar from a pocket case, and removed the red-and-gold band with the air of one who would speak, but was at a loss to begin. He lighted the cigar and cleared his throat a bit nervously. "There's something I want to tell you, Kitty," he began. "I believe a man ought to come clean with the woman he loves—no dark secrets, or anything, you know," he added with a smile.

Kitty was instantly on her guard. So there was a secret—a dark secret in the life of Mr. Jones, of Edmonton? She felt a strange sinking of the heart, and Forty Mile, which had suddenly loomed so close, seemed to be receding far, far into the distance. She braced herself to hear the worst—better to know it now than—too late.

Mr. Jones noticed the almost imperceptible stiffening of the muscles of the hand that lay on the table, and smiled: "Don't get scared, dearest. It's nothing so terrible. Nothing that involves any moral turpitude, even though it might not stand the searchlight of cold ethics. Wait till you've heard, and I think you'll agree that in what I propose there is the element, at least, of grim justice.

"It goes back quite a while—to the time when

I was a boy, and my father owned the bank of which I am now the nominal president. As a matter of fact, I am merely an employee of a gang of unscrupulous scoundrels, who, through fraudulent representations, obtained a controlling interest in the stock of the bank which my father had spent the best years of his life in building up—and then kicked him out! They not only kicked him out, but they managed to depreciate the stock until the holdings my father had managed to retain were worthless. Then they reorganized, and my father died in poverty —a broken-hearted old man. My mother did not long survive him.

"As a gesture to public sentiment these men sent for me the day after I finished high school, and offered me a position in the bank—a miserable sop, tossed from the hands that had robbed my father, and murdered him as surely as though they had plunged a knife into his heart. I accepted—and for years I have been biding my time—have been awaiting the chance to strike in vengeance, if not, of the murder, at least of the robbery of my father. The time has come. At this very moment I am in position to wrest from these wolves of finance almost the exact amount of which they robbed my poor father.

"The plan is simple—and the stampede into the Klondike makes it safe. There is a development project on foot in Alberta that calls for the expenditure, thirty days from tomorrow, of two hundred and fifty thousand dollars in cash. I have been sent here with securities, and the authority to arrange for the shipment of the currency of that date. Instead of arranging for the shipment, I shall walk out of the bank here with the currency in my grip—and that is the last the world will ever know of John W. Jones.

"I have planned it all out—for years and years I have waited for this day. There is no chance to fail. The money will not be missed for thirty days—neither will I, for I stopped off here to arrange the details of the loan while on my annual vacation of six weeks in the wild country to the northward. When the loss is discovered, the police will spend months combing the Ontario wilderness—for I will leave a plain trail to the end of steel. Then—smooth shaven, and in the garb of a gold-rush stampeder, I will lose myself among the thousands of unidentifiable men who are pouring into the North.

"And, dearest, I have planned it so there is no chance in the world for you to become involved. Tonight I hand you the money for your journey to Dawson. Tomorrow, you leave—alone. You wait for me in Dawson, and when the coast is clear I will join you, and we will be married. You run no risk whatever, for if anything should happen before I can join you, no one can connect you with the matter in any way. To marry here would be a mistake—marriages are matters of record. What do you say?"

The man, who had been leaning forward speaking in a rapid, tense undertone, straightened in his chair, and nervously relighted his dead cigar, as he waited for the girl to speak.

For a long time Kitty remained silent. What this man proposed was robbery—pure and simple. It took no "searchlight of cold ethics" to determine that. Why beat about the bush? But —was there not a sort of grim justice in it? Kitty thought there was. But her early training—her innate honesty would not allow her to condone a robbery as a means of working justice. Old Bettles, or Camillo Bill, or Swiftwater Bill—any one of them might *kill* the men who had mortally wronged his father—but never rob them. Still—down here in the provinces, such vengeance would be called a murder, a more serious offence than robbery. They would hang a man for murder, yet the law had allowed the men who had as good as murdered the elder Jones to go scot free. There was no justice in that. At the thought of murder, a slow flush crept into the girl's face, and her lips pressed tight, as the headline of a certain newspaper advertisement seemed to leap at her out of the past: $1,000 REWARD! Who was she to sit in judgment upon the ethics of a man who struck for vengeance? When she, herself, because of an act of vengeance, was probably wanted for murder in Seattle at this very moment. The future lay before her, dull, drab, hopeless. Kitty suddenly realized that she was unutterably sick and weary of the whole horrid grind. Forty Mile—home—lay within her grasp. She had only to say the word. The North—her North was calling. One little word, and she could slip quietly out of this hateful life forever. It seemed to her that after this night when Forty Mile—the North—had seemed so near—she would shriek if she ever had to face another audience. Two hundred and fifty thousand dollars—a quarter of a million. . . . You're not as young as you once were, Kitty McGuigan. And, you'll be a long time dead. "Good-bye, Kitty." . . ."Good-bye." . . .

Her lips moved, and Mr. Jones of Edmonton leaned forward—tense, to catch the words:

"That's a lot of money," she said. "I'll go."

CHAPTER XVII

The Building of a Crime

MR. JOHN W. PORTER, president of the private bank of Cranch, Alberta, was one of those rare crooks who deliberately, and with the utmost sagacity and patience, spend years in building up to one big crime.

As clerk and general factotum to old Theodoric Rice, who owned the general store in the little Canadian prairie town, he daily drove his one-horse delivery wagon past the little wooden bank. And, daily he delivered groceries to the back door of Banker Edwards's home, which was the most pretentious home in the little town, having a porch along two sides and a cupola on one corner. And daily, in the store, he waited with deference on the fat Mrs. Edwards who wheezed, or the washed-out anemic Edwards daughter. Noons he clung idly to the rope that worked the canvas awning which protected the sidewalk display of foodstuffs from the sun—

THE BUILDING OF A CRIME 153

but not from the street dust, nor the flies—and watched the spare, and sharp-nosed, and side-whiskered Banker Edwards leave the bank and walk home to his dinner.

He noted that the people on the street always addressed Banker Edwards with deference and respect. The farmers when they sold their crops called first at the bank, and later, paid their store bills—or pleaded for further credit. Banker Edwards, it was said, owned many farms that had once been the property of others. He knew that poor old Theodoric Rice was hard put to meet the interest on the mortgage that Banker Edwards held on the store and its stock of goods.

He saw that the Edwards family pew in the little wooden church was the only cushioned pew. And he watched with interest on Sundays while Banker Edwards with thin-lipped piety took up the collection, for being a warden of the church as well as the treasurer of the parish, it was right and proper that he should attend to the gathering, as well as to the dispensation of the funds of the Lord.

And he noticed that frequently upon a Sunday, after the service, the futile little preacher and his futile little wife would turn in at the cupolaed mansion to dine upon the Banker Edwards' bounty.

All these things young John W. Porter saw and pondered.

But the true power and greatness of Banker Edwards was awesomely impressed upon the plastic mind of the grocer's clerk, when, in his function of Justice of the Peace, the banker had one day followed a thundering harangue on rectitude with a stiff jail sentence upon the person of a terrified and ragged youth who had been detected in filching a few dollars from the till of his employer, a dealer in lumber and lime. The sentence, Banker Edwards had made plain, was administered not only as a just punishment for a criminal act, but as a solemn lesson to other youths. And in the heart of at least one youth the lesson bore results. Then and there John W. Porter resolved never to filch a few dollars from the till of an employer. A farm, here and there. A grocery store, maybe. Why not even a bank?

From that day on, young John W. Porter became a closer student than ever of Banker Edwards. With a share of his slender wage he opened an account in the bank, being careful to add each week to the deposit and to make that deposit at the time of day that Banker Edwards himself was on duty.

He noticed that old Luke Digby, the only employee of Banker Edwards was beginning to drag his heels as he walked to and from his little house on the outskirts of the village. Whereupon he sought ways and means for insinuating himself further into the notice of Banker Edwards. Old Luke was wearing out. Sometime—a year, two years—five—and Banker Edwards would discard him and hire another. And young Porter reasoned that a bank could be looted easier from inside than out.

Just at this time fortune took a hand in bringing young Porter more forcibly to the attention of Banker Edwards than even the methodical regularity of his weekly deposits in the bank. A hold-back strap broke in the descent of a slight declivity, and the Edwards family horse went careening down the main street dragging the family phaëton upon the seat of which the fat Mrs. Edwards bounced alarmingly as she held the reins in a frozen grip, and shrieked her wild-eyed terror.

Out over the wheel of the Theodoric Rice delivery wagon vaulted young Porter. With a short dash, and a well-timed leap his fingers closed in a death grip on a cheek strap of the plunging Edwards horse. A buckle tongue ripped his bare arm from elbow to wrist. But he held on, and thereafter for the half of a muddy block he was dragged with his weight on the bit until the frantic horse fought to a stand almost directly in front of the bank where Banker Edwards, in shirt sleeves and skull cap, had rushed out onto the sidewalk attracted by the yells of the townsfolk. And there the banker stood, suggesting, directing in a high-pitched voice, stabbing the air with his pen: while the butcher, the blacksmith, and the Hebrew proprietor of the Eureka Clothing Store heaved, and pried, and pulled, and pushed in the extraction of the hysterically sobbing Mrs. Edwards from the bespattered phaëton.

Deposited safely on the sidewalk, she sniffled, and snuffled, and sobbed, and babbled, and declared to all and sundry in a voice that broke back and forth between a bellow and a squeal, that Rice's grocery boy was a *hee*-ro!

Meanwhile the hee-ro stood patiently holding the now docile horse, as he listened with a shamefaced grin to the panegyric, and to the laudatory accounts of eyewitnesses who, each trying to be heard above his neighbor, recounted the accident as he saw it. Albeit, he listened with a slant-eyed glance upon Banker Edwards, and carelessly shifted his position to bring his bloody arm and his mud-smeared garments into full view of the excited financier.

When the fat Mrs. Edwards had waddled into the bank, and the horse had been tied to the hitch rail, Banker Edwards patted the boy on the shoulder.

"You're a good young man," he admitted. "You think quick, and act quick, and you save your money. I've had my eye on you. Have Dr. Smith fix your arm up and then go to Levi's and pick out any suit in the store, and a shirt, and a pair of shoes. Tell him I sent you, and to charge the goods to me. I know merit when I see it, and I'm going to speak to Rice about raising your wages."

The following week young Porter got a raise, though he well knew that old Theodoric could ill afford it. He noted that Banker Edwards spoke to him, now, as he passed the store on his daily trips to dinner.

Sunday he donned his new fourteen-dollar suit of clothes, and his new yellow shoes, and went to church, where he devoutly bet with himself on the relative numbers of A's and E's in the verses of the hymnal, and tiring of that, speculated on the amount of money Banker Edwards would collect when he passed the plate. This, to young Porter, had always been the most interesting part of the service—he could tell by the tunk of the coins as they dropped onto the brass plate whether they were five- or ten-cent pieces, but the quarters and the big copper pennies sounded the same, and it was only by watching the boldness or the furtiveness of the contributor that he could arrive at anything like a fair estimate. Then, there was the weekly contribution of old Mrs. Plank which didn't tunk because it was in an envelope—but the thrill for which he always waited breathlessly was the grand tunk of the Edwards half-dollar that always went in last, and with a gesture, while the banker waited at the head of the aisle for the organ to stop playing. It was a noble sound—that last resounding tunk that fairly splattered the lesser coins aside—an opulent sound—the sound that differentiated Banker Edwards from the common herd.

When old Luke Digby keeled over on the sidewalk one hot day and was carried into the drug store, dead, John W. Porter relinquished his hold on Theodoric Rice's awning rope, walked across the street, quietly informed Banker Edwards of the fact, and applied for Luke's job. He got it.

He was twenty-one years old, then, and for the next five years he devoted himself so assiduously to banking in all its details that the directors came to realize that he knew more about the business than Banker Edwards, himself. He was an "up and coming" young man, and Banker Edwards was an old man.

Oftener and oftener they listened to his advice and acted upon it.

Business expanded, a bookkeeper and a teller were added to the staff, and Porter was made cashier. But Banker Edwards was still president.

Then young Porter further identified himself

THE BUILDING OF A CRIME 159

with the institution by marrying the washed-out and anemic Edwards daughter, a young woman as colorless of soul as she was of complexion.

The wooden bank building was torn down, and a brick one was erected on its site.

Shortly thereafter Banker Edwards died under circumstances that aroused suspicion only in the mind of the young physician whose silence was assured by virtue of the bank's holding his paper in a ruinous amount.

At the next directors' meeting young Porter was unanimously elected to fill the vacancy left by the demise of Edwards. He noted with a cynical grin that the passing of Banker Edwards had created no more than a ripple in the daily life of the village. It was Banker Porter, now—that was all. It was he, instead of Edwards, that haggled over loans with the farmers, and pried into the business affairs of the small merchants, and thundered disapproval of the small sins of the small town's evildoers—though he never sent a ragged urchin to jail for filching a few dollars from the till of an employer. It was he, now, who passed the plate in church. And he took a pious and wholly unaccountable delight in the mighty tunk of his own silver dollar—where Edwards had tunked but a half.

He owned no stock in the bank beyond that required by law of its officers. Why, he reasoned, should one rob himself?

Thus he settled into a state of rectitude and connubial boredom, relieved by frequent trips to the wilderness for hunting and fishing of which he had become passionately fond, and to the larger cities of the dominion where he became well and favorably known in a business way, as Mr. John W. Porter, president of the Farmers' and Drovers' Bank of Cranch, Alberta—and in a social way by whatever name and registry the spur of the moment suggested.

He became a connoisseur of dress, and of women. And, always he waited his chance. Several times he had been tempted, when, in anticipation of the bountiful harvest the vault would be stuffed with currency—small bills for the most part, ones and fives and tens and twenties—bulky stuff in any large amount. But always he had resisted the temptation. He had learned one lesson well—never filch a few dollars from the till of an employer.

Then, the St. Agnes Reclamation Project loomed on the horizon, and he knew that his chance had come. Heart and soul he worked for the project—arguing, pleading, browbeating, and cajoling stockholders and directors. Finally he carried his point—the Farmers' and Drovers' Bank would finance the St. Agnes project.

It was just at this point that, under the name of John W. Jones of Edmonton he met Kitty McGuigan, who came with Mrs. Palm and the others to the party in the grillroom of the Winnipeg Hotel. And under the name of Mr. Jones, a single man, he wooed her. When he returned to Winnipeg a month later he was all set to go. If Kitty would go with him, so much the better. Her beauty and the young verve and force of her ravished him and set him afire. And the ease and finesse with which she turned aside his proposals and played him along, intrigued his imagination. He wanted her as he had wanted no other woman in his life. He would have her. If he had to marry her to possess her—he would marry her. When you are wanted for the embezzlement of a quarter of a million dollars, a wife or two, more or less can add but little to your worries.

During that intervening month he had laid his plans. He concocted the story he told Kitty, arranged to take his regular trip into the wilderness, and agreed with the directors to arrange with the Winnipeg bank for the certain delivery of the necessary cash upon the proper date. He checked over his securities, packed his suitcase, kissed his wife a perfunctory good-bye, and stepped onto the train that was to whisk him forever from the little town of Cranch, Alberta.

Standing on the back platform of the rear car, a cynical smile on his lips, he watched the twinkling lights dim, and finally merge into the blackness of the prairie. It was for this moment he had lived. Go he must, now—whether Kitty accompanied him or not. He was not afraid to tell her of his contemplated crime. When she had heard the story that went with it, she might not approve, she might refuse to have anything further to do with him—but she would respect what he told her in confidence—she was no snitcher. If she turned his proposition down he would go alone—this Klondike stampede assured his getaway. It would be more futile than hunting for the proverbial needle in the haystack, for the police to single out one particular man among those toiling thousands on the passes—especially when the police of all Canada would be looking for the wrong man. Again he smiled cynically at the thought that soon after the discovery of the embezzlement, the body of John W. Porter would be buried— in dishonor, it is true. The farmers and the merchants would wag their heads and talk. And the stockholders and directors would whine and snivel.

Idly he wondered whether his wife would wear mourning.

CHAPTER XVIII

Beyond the End of Steel

When Kitty agreed to go North, Porter, alias Jones, handed her a liberal amount in crisp new bills for her passage. He advised that she go at once, and alone, as it would be just as well if they were not seen on the street or at the station together. When the girl protested that she ought to give notice, he countered with the question of whether Hertzbaum had given her notice when the road show disbanded and left her all but stranded among the sticks of northern Minnesota? And also whether she thought that if the Olympic All Star Stock Company should meet with reverses, Palm would give her notice?

"He would not," said Porter. "He would say: 'The show's busted. You'll have to hunt another job.'" And Kitty knew that he spoke the truth.

The following day at ten o'clock in the morning John W. Porter walked out of a certain bank in Winnipeg with two hundred and fifty thousand dollars in big bills in his grip. At eleven o'clock he boarded a train for the end of steel on a northward creeping branch line, and the following morning stepped off the train to grasp the hand of the smiling Pierre Gatineau, a guide who had often accompanied him into the wilds. From among several guides whom Porter was wont to employ he had selected Gatineau for this particular trip. And as he watched the guide stow his duffel into the waiting canoe, he nodded with approval as his eye checked the fact that the guide was, in height, and weight, and muscular development almost exactly his own double. It was for that he had been chosen.

At the Hudson's Bay Post at the far end of the lake Porter bought the supplies and laughed and joked with McGregor, the factor, as had been his wont. The factor later told the police that there had been nothing remarkable in the deportment of either Porter, who had traded with him for years, nor of Pierre Gatineau whom he had known always. They had come and had gone on as usual.

While the guide prepared supper that evening, miles from the post, Porter leaned back against his bed roll and smoked: "Well, Pierre, you and I have traveled a good many miles together, eh?"

"*Oui*," smiled the man, proudly, "An', ba' gos'

we git de feesh, we git de moose, we see de co'ntry, too, eh?"

"You bet we do! I'd rather have you than any guide I ever went in with. That's why I hired you for this trip. We're going a long way this time, Pierre. A hell of a long way. We'll be gone a long time!"

The guide looked up in surprise: "W'at yo' mean—hell of a long ways? Hell of a long t'am? W'ere yo' wan' to go?"

"Oh, no place in particular. We'll just keep on going and see where we come out. I'm tired. I'm going to take a long rest."

Pierre pondered, shoving his cap forward over one eye to scratch his head. "Mebbe-so, I ain' kin go so long," he hazarded.

"Why not? Don't I always pay you well? Don't you like to guide me—or what?"

"Oui, oui, yo' pay me better as mos' man. Me, I'm lak I guide yo'. Yo' paddle de canoe, an' yo' pack on de portage. Yo' ain' set back an' let Pierre do all de work. *Non.* But, me—I'm got de 'oman an' de leetle kids. I'm say to de 'oman, I'm be gon' seex week wit' M's'u Portaire. I'm feex it wit' de store to let de 'oman hav' de grub, de clo's—de t'ings she need an' I pay in seex week w'en I'm com' back. I'm ain' com' back in seex week—*voilà!* Dat store mans she say Pierre she no good—she no com' back an' pay. Yo' ain' kin git no mor' grub—no mor' clo's—eh?"

Porter laughed: "So that's it, is it? Well, Pierre, you know I'm rich—got lots of money. And you know I've often told you I like you."

"*Oui.*"

"If you thought your family would be taken care of, would you go on with me—stay in as long as I wanted to?"

The guide nodded: "*Oui.* I'm lak' yo de bes' mans I guide. But, firs' I got to let de 'oman know I'm ain' com' hom' so queek. She t'ink mebbe-so we git keel—we bus' to hell on de rapid—we go over de fall—we git teep ovaire on de lak an' git drowned, eh?"

Porter was still smiling. "Can you write a letter your wife can read?" he asked.

Pierre nodded emphatically: "*Oui,* sure—me, I'm educat. Not so mooch educat een de Eenglis'. De *français,* I'm write heem good—*bien!*"

"All right, then, Pierre." As he spoke, Porter reached into an inner pocket and drew forth a flat leather wallet. "The time has come when I'm going to show you how much I really think of you. Do you see these bills? Each one is worth one thousand dollars." Pausing, he passed one to the guide, who with wide staring eyes handled the scrap of paper reverently as with his finger he verified the number of cyphers following the figure 1.

"*Mon Dieu!*" breathed the awed guide, "Me I'm ain' know dere ees mor' as twenty dollaire een wan beel! Wan t'ousan' dollaire—wan leetle piece papaire!" Clutching it tightly, he passed it back. But Porter only laughed.

"Keep it, Pierre," he said. "It's yours. And here's four more just like it. I told you the time had come to show you how much I really think of you. Now, I guess you feel able to go on with me, don't you?"

Pierre Gatineau sat as one paralyzed, clutching the bills in his hand. Finally his lips moved: "Fi' t'ousan' dollaire! Fi' t'ousan' dollaire!" he murmured the words slowly, as though striving to comprehend the stupendous sum.

"Yes—five thousand dollars—and it's all yours. It's a present from me. Now, I'll tell you what I want you to do. You hit back to the post and tell McGregor to send that money down to your wife—see? Tell him to see that she gets it. Tell him it's a present from me. You can tell him we're figuring on going on indefinitely, but we can lay in supplies as we go—Owl River Post—DuBrochet, maybe—wherever we happen to hit. Then you write your wife a letter and tell her you are going on with me. Tell her we don't know where we're going—but we're going to stay a long time—don't forget that—a long time. Tell her she'd better put the money in a bank somewhere. You understand that, do you?"

"*Oui*," answered the stupefied Pierre, as he knotted the bills into a huge handkerchief which he crammed to the very bottom of his trousers pocket.

"You better hit out now—tonight," said Porter. "You can be back here by daylight, and we can shove on."

It was near midnight when Pierre Gatineau, fairly gibbering with excitement, roused the whole post to witness his good luck. McGregor, the factor, who had known him always, rejoiced with him, and promised to see that the money reached his wife in safety. Then after an hour of laborious work with a pencil and paper, Pierre concluded the letter to his wife, and departed. At the post they heard him singing wild voyageur chansons until his voice died away in the darkness.

At daylight, when Pierre stepped from the canoe and started for the little tent, a figure rose up stealthily from behind a spruce as he passed. An ax swung high and its blade crashed downward with a sickening scrunch that clove the skull of Pierre Gatineau to the chin. Then, very methodically John W. Porter proceeded with a knife he had brought for the purpose, to sever the damaged head from the body, and with studied skill, to detach the left arm at the elbow. "They'll believe he cut off the arm to prevent identification by that old buckle scar," he said. "And about the time I'm climbing the Chilkoot Pass, the police will be searching all Canada for Pierre Gatineau—murderer and robber of John W. Porter, the embezzler." He even smiled, grimly: "Most of 'em will say, 'served him right,' and there'll be no one to push the search very hard."

Stripping the body, Porter carried it to a swamp not too far distant, and threw it in the mud. Returning, he wrapped the arm and the head in Gatineau's clothing, wiring it stoutly to a large stone. This package he loaded into the canoe. Pulling off his own clothes, he burned them at a small fire, being careful to leave just trace enough of the scorched material to be identifiable as his own. His keys, also, he left in the pocket, so that they would be found when the police sifted the ashes. Then he rigged out in rough clothing, shaved his face smooth, for the first time in ten years, broke his pince-nez on the rocks as though it had been knocked off in a fight, and hastily striking his tent, loaded the outfit, and pushed out onto the river that flowed out of the lake of the post. Twenty miles away, he sank his gruesome package in the waters of a small, deep lake—and paddled on.

CHAPTER XIX

The Police Take the Trail

THREE men filed solemnly out of detachment headquarters of the North-West Mounted Police, and Inspector Costello stepped to the door and summoned Sergeant Burns and young Corporal Downey, who were pitching horseshoes in the rear of the building. As the two officers stood before his desk, the inspector leaned back in his chair and regarded them critically. When he spoke it was with a drawl that instantly commanded the attention of the two, for it was a common saying among the younger members of Costello's command that: "When the old man drags his words you can bet hell's broke loose somewhere."

"Thim three astute citizens that jist wint out the door, is the vice president, an' a couple av the directors av the Farmers' an' Drovers' Bank, at Cranch. Thirty-wan days ago today the presidint of the bank disappeared wid two hunder'd an' fifty thousan' dollars in cash, an' these gintlemin has begun to suspect that the bank's be'n robbed."

"A quarter of a million!" exclaimed Sergeant Burns.

"Thirty-one days!" gasped Downey. "An' they're just beginning to suspect him?"

"Aye," answered the inspector, dryly. "A quarter av a million—an' thirty-wan days. Ut looks like they was a little slow in the head, but 'tis not so bad as ut sounds. The presidint is off on his vacation, which he ain't due to show up fer a couple av weeks yet. 'Tis his custom to go fishin' fer six weeks every summer, an' on his way this time he was to stop off in Winnipeg an' arrange wid the Exchange Bank to ship the two huner'd an' fifty thousan' in cash to the Cranch bank in thirty days. The thirty days was up yiste'day, an' whin the shipmint didn't come, they wired the Exchange Bank an' the bank wired back that the presidint, Jawn W. Porter, his name is, had took the cash along wid him instead av arrangin' fer ut to be shipped."

"Thirty-one days' start with a quarter of a million dollars," repeated Corporal Downey with a sickly grin at Sergeant Burns. "Why—he could be half way around the world, by now."

"Aye—he could," assented Inspector Costello, "an' that's why I called in the two av yez instead av a couple of constables. But, av he's gone *all* the way around the world ye've got to git him. Ut's the biggest robbery iver pulled in this district, an' be the way he worked ut, ut looks like ye've got a mighty smart thief on yer hands. Go git um, now. Ye kin work together, or work alone, as ye like. Av ye work together an' find ye disagree, then ye kin each follow his own theory. Ye've a cold trail to follow—but, good luck to yez."

Inquiry in Cranch developed little beyond a photograph and description of the missing president and a statement of facts above noted. Porter's wife could tell nothing of her husband's whereabouts, stating that he never discussed his hunting and fishing trips with her. She professed to believe that in two weeks, when his vacation was at an end, he would return and be able to give a satisfactory account of his actions: which was also the belief of many of the townspeople.

From a sportsman friend of Porter's they learned that he frequently went into the wilds by way of Little Turtle Post.

At Winnipeg, they learned from the Exchange Bank that Porter had left the building carrying in a brown suitcase the cash for which he had duly receipted and deposited securities. The bank officials supposed he had gone direct to Cranch, and had no inkling of anything wrong until the Cranch bank had wired thirty days later. The transaction had roused no suspicion, as Porter had frequently carried large sums of cash between the two institutions.

Inquiry revealed the fact that a ticket to the end of steel at Little Turtle Lake had been sold on the day Porter had disappeared with the cash. An hour later the two officers were on the train, where the conductor told of having carried Mr. Porter, who frequently rode with him. Porter had gone into the wilds, but in so far as the conductor knew, he had not returned.

At the post, McGregor, the factor, told of the arrival, the outfitting, and the departure of Porter and Pierre Gatineau, and of Pierre's return at midnight with the five thousand dollars that Porter had given him. Whereupon the two officers took heart. The trail although still cold seemed much less dim.

Late the following afternoon the two found the campsite on the river. A half dozen crows rose from the edge of a nearby swamp and perched noisily upon adjacent trees. A few moments later the two officers were examining a badly decomposed body from which the head and the left arm had been removed.

"Guess it's him, all right," opined Sergeant Burns. "This man would have been about six foot one. But what in hell did Gatineau cut off his arm for?"

"Same reason he cut off his head, I suppose,"

suggested Downey. "I'm bettin' we'll find he had a scar or some mark on that arm. Let's prowl around a bit an' then bury him. I don't suppose there's a Chinaman's chance that the guide cached the stuff around here, but we might locate it."

"He's probably clean out of the country with it by this time. But we'll hunt around. Might find something," agreed Burns.

"Here's his glasses—what's left of 'em," called Downey, holding aloft a ribbon upon the end of which dangled a remnant of the banker's pince-nez.

"Yeah, and here's some pieces of his clothes that didn't get all burnt up," added Burns. "We'll pick out what can be identified, and then sift the ashes for the buttons."

Sifting the ashes netted not only the buttons, but also a bunch of fire-blackened keys. For several hours the officers searched for sign of a cache and finding none, applied themselves to the task of burying the body. This accomplished, they returned to Little Turtle with the story of their find.

"So now," concluded Sergeant Burns, as he finished to the last detail, "We've got the Frenchman to hunt instead of this Porter. And, believe me, I'm glad it broke that way. This guide will stick to the back country—to the only kind of a life he knows. He'll have to show up here an'

Sergeant Burns laughed: "There you are, McGregor—you're prejudiced. I don't blame you. I'd stick up for a man through hell and high water, who'd saved my life—you bet! But you can't get away from the facts. You'll know different when we bring him in with the cash."

"Aye," answered the Scot. "When ye bring him in wi' the cash, I'll know."

The sergeant turned to Corporal Downey who had been a silent, but interested listener, albeit his attention seemed to be focused upon the whittling of a chip. "Come on, Downey. We can't do any more good down here. Let's go."

"Go where?" asked the younger officer, his eyes on a shaving that curled from his knife blade.

"Well—first we'll go to Beaver Falls and put Gatineau's woman through her paces, and pick up that five thousand before she gets it spent, or put a stopper on it if she's stuck it in some bank. Then we'll report back to the inspector an' post descriptions of this Gatineau all over Canada. He'll show his face somewhere before long, and then we'll have a hot trail."

Corporal Downey was one of the youngest non-coms in a hard-boiled force of men who can hope to rise only through merit. He did not know then—nor did any man know, that the name of Corporal Downey was to become a byword in the service. There would never be a

Sergeant Downey, nor an Inspector Downey, nor a Superintendent Downey. For a reason known only to himself he was to steadfastly refuse promotion. But down through the years sergeants, and inspectors, and superintendents, and even commissioners were to seek his counsel, and to act on his suggestions. In the outlands among red men, and white, the name of Corporal Downey, or more affectionately, Old Man Downey, is a name to conjure with.

Another shaving curled from the keen edge of young Downey's knife. He did not look up. "You go ahead, Sarge," he said. "I guess I'll poke around a bit, up here."

Sergeant Burns sneered: "Going out for a record, eh? Well, good luck to you! Going to step right out on a canoe trail thirty-three days' old and *'get your m-a-a-n!'*"

"Yump," smiled the younger officer good-naturedly, ignoring the sneer. "Maybe I will. I've got a hunch, Sarge. Maybe if we kind of talked things over a bit, you'd stick along."

"Oh, I would, eh? Well, let me tell you, kid —when I need to talk over a case that I've worked up with any rookie that ain't dry behind the ears yet, I'll sure let you know. The Inspector may have known what he was up to when he told us we could separate if we wanted to—I don't. When *I* learnt policing, if a sergeant said 'come,' by God, a corporal came—and he didn't stand around and argue about it, either."

"That's where the trouble is, Sarge," said Downey, gravely. "I ain't learnt policin', yet—an' maybe I never will."

"It's a damned cinch you never will if you go kihootin' off on your own when you've got the chance to play along with someone who has," snorted Burns in disgust. "But go ahead. Damned if I'm going to waste my time. Inspector Costello will sure be tickled when he finds out he's got a man that can follow a month-old water trail. So long!"

CHAPTER XX

Corporal Downey Plays a Lone Hand

WHEN Sergeant Burns's canoe was but a speck on the lake, Corporal Downey tossed away his chip, pocketed his knife, and spat with accuracy upon the chip. "What size of a man was this Gatineau?" he asked.

"Weel, he was a big mon. I would say risin' o' six foot. But, lad, yon sergeant's right aboot the trail bein' too cold to follow. What wi' the country half water, an' Pierre knowin' it the way he does, an' a braw mon wi' the paddle, ye could na' hope to follow him. I do na' believe he kilt Porter nor robbed him—but, he's gone somewhere, an' that's a fact."

"Yump—that's what I figure. The money's gone, too. Now, about Gatineau—you said he broke his leg. Did it cripple him? Was he lame?"

"No. We'd a doctor from the railroad camp to set it. It was broke in three places—both bones just below the knee, an' the big bone just above the knee, an' agin aboot half way to his hip. But they never give no trouble after they healed. He kin travel all day wi' no more limp than ye've got."

"How long ago was it?"

"'Twas four year, come September."

"Which leg?"

"'Twas the right leg. He stud like this, an' helt back the logs ontil I got free."

"I don't suppose there's any picture of him?"

"Nae, prob'ly not. Pierre wad na' be the mon to be gittin' his picture took. Ye'd know him, though, by a scar on his right cheek where a stub raked him when the logs of the bear trap caught him. I'm tellin' ye all this, lad, because when ye find him, if ye ever do, ye'll find oot he's nae criminal. Spite o' the case yon sergeant has got worked up agin' him."

"Maybe you're right," admitted Downey. "I expect I'd better be goin'. I'll need a canoe, an' some grub."

It was a gruesome job the young officer had set for himself—the disinterring of the month-old body—a gruesome, and a most disagreeable job to laboriously scrape away the decomposed flesh from the bones of the corpse's right leg. When it was finally accomplished, he washed them in the river, and balancing them on a log beside his little fire to dry, he proceeded to cook his supper.

The meal over he lighted his pipe and regarded the three bones with satisfaction. Each showed unmistakable signs of having been broken at the exact point indicated by McGregor. Each had healed perfectly, showing only a slight thickening at the point of fracture. "It was McGregor's sayin' that the man had made too many fool plays for Pierre Gatineau that started me thinkin' that maybe the killin' had be'n the other way around. An' when he mentioned the busted leg, I knew I could prove it. Lookin' at all them plays from Porter's angle, they're pretty damn' smart. The question is where do I go from here? The Sarge an' McGregor are right—the water trail's too cold to follow."

For a long time Corporal Downey sat staring at the photograph of the missing banker which Sergeant Burns had discarded as soon as he believed the man to have been murdered. He studied the eyes, the nose, the ears, the hair, and even the poise of the head, and spent an hour trying to envision the face smooth shaven—without the pince-nez which he knew, now had been deliberately broken and left as evidence. Wrapping up the photograph carefully with the bones, he placed the packet in his duffel bag and crawled between his blankets.

A few days later the young officer showed up in Cranch, and went directly to the Porter home. The washed-out "widow" sat primly facing him in the parlor. News of the embezzlement and murder had reached her through police channels, and the shock of it was plainly visible in her manner—though Corporal Downey shrewdly divined that the carefully spaced sniffles, and the dabbing with the handkerchief at dry eyes, were more in the nature of a sop to convention than the expression of a soul-searing grief. Why, he wondered, should this woman be feigning a grief that should be terribly real? Even though her husband had been proven an embezzler, Downey reasoned that an average woman would hardly recover so quickly from news of his murder. She must have hated him, he reasoned. Why? Some other woman, possibly? The thought gave him his cue.

"I'm here to ask a few questions, ma'am," he began in a kindly tone. "I know it's hard on you, an' I won't bother you but a few minutes. Of course you know the money ain't be'n found, yet —an' you might be able to give some information that would help us to pick up the—the murderer, an' recover the money besides. Now, did your husband have a scar on his left forearm?"

"Yes. A very pronounced scar, reaching from near the elbow almost to the wrist on the—the front of the arm, I suppose you would call it—

the side corresponding to the palm of the hand."

"Thank you. That would account for the murderer cuttin' the arm off the body. Now, you see, we don't know whether Mr. Porter carried *all* the money he took out of the bank north with him. There's a suspicion that a certain woman might have a considerable part of it—or know where it is. I know it's a kind of an awkward question to ask you, ma'am. But—do you know if there was any woman he was—er—interested in?"

Downey noted a sudden hardening of the eyes, and a tightening of the muscles about the woman's mouth that could, by no stretch of the imagination be ascribed to the emotion of grief. Breathlessly he awaited her answer. His random shot had told.

Suddenly the woman rose from her chair: "Wait here," she said, and hurriedly left the room. In a few moments she was back, and pausing before the small center table, fairly slammed a photograph upon it. "Is that the woman?" she demanded, in a voice thick with venom.

Corporal Downey picked up the picture and studied it—a full-length portrait of a beautiful girl in some sort of fancy-dress costume. Across the face was written in a feminine hand the words, "Nadu, alias Kitty." At length Downey raised his eyes from the picture: "Yes," he said, gravely. "I'm pretty sure that's her. What's her last name? I might know then, for sure."

"Her last name!" cried the woman, hoarsely. "How do I know her last name? The hussy! I know nothing whatever about her! I found that *thing* in my husband's pocket on his return from Winnipeg a month or so before he disappeared."

Corporal Downey nodded: "Would you mind if I kept this picture?" he asked. "It might help in locatin' her."

"Certainly keep it! I hope you do locate her! Possession of stolen money is a crime, isn't it? I hope you put her in jail for life! Be sure and tell her her lover was murdered—and describe how his head and his arm were cut off. I think she'd like to hear all about it. I wish I could tell her."

"Yes-s'm," said Corporal Downey, rising and reaching for his hat. "Yes-s'm, I wish you could. Well, good-day, ma'am. I'm obliged."

"W-h-e-e-w," he breathed, as he walked rapidly toward the station. "I played with a hunch, all right—an' it sure was loaded."

In the office of the Chief of Police of the city of Winnipeg, Corporal Downey laid the photograph on the desk: "Know that woman?" he asked.

The chief nodded with a grin: "You're barking up the wrong tree, Corporal. I was wondering how long it would be before you Mounted Police would run across that trail. Of course, *we* ran it down the day we got word that Porter had lammed out with the dough."

The air of superiority conveyed by the patronizing tone was not lost on Corporal Downey who heaved a well-feigned sigh of relief: "Well, now that's fine, Chief. It'll save me quite a bit of proddin' around. I sure hate it when women gets mixed up with policin'."

The chief interrupted with a laugh: "You fellows don't know anything about real policing. Why, in a city the size of Winnipeg, we do more policing in a week than you fellows do in a year! When you come to run up against real policing, son, you'll learn that women are mixed up in about half of it. Fact is, when anything is pulled off, the first thing we do is hunt for the woman in the case. That's how we happened to check up on Nadu the Sublime. It's like this: When we get word to check up on Porter's movements in the city, he's been gone better than a month. But we find out he bought a ticket for Little Turtle within an hour of the time he left the bank. The Mounted found that out, too, and a couple of your men hit out after him, and a couple of days later they located his body.

"The day after he beat it, the newspapers printed Porter's picture, and the ink wasn't hardly dry till a couple of dames came busting into this office with the paper in their hand. They sure were gratuitous with their information. But, that's the way with women—let one of 'em get jealous of another and there's nothing she won't do to gum her game. These women were actors down to the Olympic—a little skinny one, and another that run mostly to bust and hips. They claimed they knew Porter under the name of Mr. Jones of Edmonton. It seems that he'd throwed parties for 'em down at the hotel, and he'd got caked in on this Nadu the Sublime, another Olympic star, that done fancy dancing.

"They said that the night before Porter disappeared he and this Nadu had gone to the hotel together after the show—and that's the last any of them had seen of her. She didn't show up for the performance the next night, and when the manager went to her boarding house he found out that she'd paid up and left without saying where she was going—just took what stuff she could stick in a suitcase and left all the rest of it. Of course, the manager didn't report it to the police—she had a right to go if she wanted to, and leave as much of her stuff in her room as she pleased—the Porter disappearance didn't break till thirty days later. When it did break, these high-minded females done their duty as citizens and tipped us off. But, as I said, there's nothing to it. We checked up on the story and found out that the girl boarded the train for Vancouver several hours before Porter drew the money out of the bank. Manifestly, she couldn't have had any of it with her. And you know Porter hit north from here. We figured they would get together—and maybe they did intend to—but when your men found Porter's body—that closed the case as far as we're concerned. It looks like it was up to you fellows to run down this guide that's got the dough. You're pretty good at that, I guess—chasing a man through the brush—but that ain't real policing, like the problems we're up against."

The telephone rang sharply and the chief picked up the receiver. When the voice ceased speaking, he scowled fiercely as he answered in short clipped sentences: "Book him! Book every one of 'em you pick up! I'm going to stop this sidewalk spitting if it takes every man I've got on the force!"

As the man slammed up the receiver Corporal Downey picked up his photograph and placed it in his pocket. "I'll be goin', Chief. Much obliged," he said with just the suggestion of a grin twitching the corners of his mouth. "I guess you're right—you city police is up against problems we don't know nothin' about. Suppose they was to pass a law out our way prohibitin' a man from spittin' on the prairie? Wouldn't we have a hell of a time enforcin' it? Take me, now—I'd rather be chasin' murderers through the brush. So long."

From the chief's office Corporal Downey made his way to the Olympic Theater and waited until the conclusion of the matinée. He accosted the ingénue whom he recognized from the chief's succinct description. "Did you know the woman known as Nadu the Sublime?" he asked.

"Sure, I knew her. She horned in on the show with a bum dance act, an' you'd 'a' thought she was the Virgin Mary's twin sister the way she wouldn't drink or smoke or swear. She thought she was better'n anyone else—an' if I couldn't dance on crutches better'n what she could, I'd go jump in the river. She come in off a road show that went bust—an' I don't wonder, if they was all like her. Nadu the Sublime—hell! Her name was Kitty Flannigan—an' she come from somewheres up in Alaska or somewheres—Forty Miles was the name of the burg—an' to hear her tell it, you'd think it was London or Paris or some place where there *was* somethin'. But with all she stuck up her nose at us, she wasn't no better'n what she ought to be—runnin' to the hotel nights with this guy Jones, he called himself, but he was this hick banker, Porter, that dug out with a barrel of dough an' a married man, at that! Me an' my friend spotted him the minute we seen his picher in the paper. She'd lammed out before he did—figured on meetin' up with him out on the coast somewheres, I guess. But some guy croaked him before he got there—an' I bet she's wishin' to hell she had her job back. But Mr. Palm wouldn't touch her with a ten-foot pole, the way she done him—an' if he did we'd all quit. We're decent girls tryin' to make an honest livin' an' we won't stand for associatin' with no grifter like her."

"Thank you," said Corporal Downey, as he withdrew a photograph from his pocket. "This is the woman, is it?"

The girl's lip curled nastily: "Yes—that's her. Stage picture—took a lot of touchin' up to make it look like that. Her hands looked like a couple of hams."

Downey produced another photograph. "Do you know this man?"

"Sure—that's him! Jones of Edmonton, he called himself. He was a good spender, all right—but anyone would have know'd he wasn't nothin' but a hick—fallin' for a bum like her. Say, gi'me that picher, will yeh? You don't need it, now he's dead."

Corporal Downey smiled: "Sorry," he said, pocketing the photograph, "but it belongs in the files. Good-day."

Four days later Corporal Downey was a passenger on an overcrowded boat steaming northward from Vancouver.

CHAPTER XXI

An Attempt at Claim Jumping

BACK on Bonanza the Yukon Kid doubled his force of workmen and bit deep into the gravel of the two claims—his own, and Kitty McGuigan's. Upon his return he had, in brief, terse sentences, told the sourdoughs of his trip to Seattle and his unsuccessful search for Kitty. The old Forty-Milers, the men who had known the girl since babyhood, listened in sympathetic silence. It was Old Bettles, dean of the sourdoughs, who voiced the sentiment of the camp.

"Don't you worry, Kid. She'll come back. She was borned an' raised on the Yukon. An' it don't stand to reason that anyone that's got any sense, an' know'd this country like she knows it, would stay in a place like the States, does it? Not by a damn' sight, it don't! You jest go ahead an' work them claims fer all they're worth, an' set tight. We all know how you feel about it—an' we feel sim'lar. It's too bad you don't drink, 'cause it's one of them times, amongst others, that calls fer a good drunk. She'll be showin' up one of these days, a-fetchin' my oranges—an' when she does, by God, we'll make them old Roman feasts you read about look like a soup line!"

So, grimly and efficiently, the Kid mined his gold. He bought claims on Hunker, on Eldorado, on Ophir, and on a dozen other creeks. With a light stampeding pack he explored the hills, and prospected dozens of tiny feeders and dry gulches.

"The Kid's changed," observed Moosehide Charlie one day, as a little group of sourdoughs stood at the bar of the Tivoli.

"His heart ain't in his work, no more," agreed Swiftwater Bill. "He ain't smiled since he come back."

"His heart ain't, but his brains is," said Old Bettles. "If one out of ten of the claims he's bought, an' recorded pans out, he'll be the richest man on the Yukon."

"Er the brokest," commented Camillo Bill. "He paid thirty thousan' in dust fer a claim on Sulfer, an' jerked his men out of the shaft in a week. A man can't stand that clip long."

"Yeah, but on Eldorado he bought a claim fer a thousan', an' two foot below the bottom of the shaft he run into a pay streak that run better'n forty dollars to the pan."

"He buys 'em, an' sells 'em, an' gives 'em away, an' abandons 'em till it would make yer head swim," said Moosehide.

"He calls claims, the chips in the game," grinned Old Bettles, "an' he shore strews 'em liberal. That's gamblin', all right—the biggest kind of gamblin'. I'll bet right now he's worth a million."

"An'," said Swiftwater Bill, "he's cut Kitty in on the half of all of it."

"I wonder where she is?" mused Camillo.

"Wherever she is, if she don't come back pretty quick, she'll find herself ownin' half the Yukon," said Bettles.

"The Kid give Father John twenty-five thousan' fer his mission, to start a little horspital where even a chechako could go if he got sick or hurt," said Camillo.

"Yeah," added Swiftwater, "an' he give them 'piscopals the same. I was talkin' to the archdeacon."

"More chips in the game," sneered a chechako, who had listened at the edge of the group. "He's gamblin' to keep out of Hell."

"Is that so!" bristled Old Bettles, belligerently, "well, let me tell you, young man, he don't have to keep out of Hell! When you git there the Kid'll be the first one you'll see! He'll be b'ilin' up chechakos fer dog feed!"

One day late in the fall, the Yukon Kid stood

talking to a little group of sourdoughs close beside his original claim on Bonanza, when a man stepped up and addressed him abruptly: "Wher's this here Kitty McGuigan, which she's filed on the claim next to you?"

"Who wants to know?"

"Me. Boggs is the name. Jake Boggs."

The Kid glanced sharply into the eyes that peered at him from above a blond beard liberally stained by tobacco juice. "Oh, so it's Boggs, is it? You didn't tell me the name the last time we met."

The man grinned truculently: "Still sore, be you, about that joke me an' my pardner tried to play on you up the river—the time we made out like we was goin' to rob you?"

"I told you then, that you paddled a hell of a ways to pull off a damn' poor joke."

"Yeah," admitted the man, "an' you was right, at that. You damn' near scair't us to death, thinkin' all night you was goin' to hang us—an' settin' us afloat the way you done in the canoe. But some chechakos found us floatin' downriver, an' they untied us, an' give us a paddle. It was a poor joke, all right—it was on us."

"You hadn't learnt, yet, that the Yukon Kid always pays. It was lucky for you that chechakos found you instead of sourdoughs. With that 'Thief' sign on you, they'd have passed you on clean to the ocean."

The man scowled. "You ain't told me, yet, wher's this Kitty McGuigan."

"That's right."

"You mean, you ain't a-goin' to tell me?"

"How'd you guess it?"

"Well, then, I'll tell you an earful. That there claim filed next to yourn, an' that you're workin' along with yourn, wasn't never filed by this here Kitty McGuigan, which she wasn't even in the country when it was staked. She'd gone outside, an' you filed the claim in her name."

"That might be news to you—but, it ain't to me."

"Well—mebbe this'll be news to you, then. That claim wasn't filed legal. She had to stake it herself to hold it—an' she was outside. I'm givin' you notice to git yer men off that claim right now. It wasn't filed legal."

"It's legal enough so all the boys respect her right to it," answered the Yukon Kid, evenly.

"You might fool a lot of damn' boobs into thinkin' it's legal," retorted the man, "but you can't fool me. It wasn't only yesterday that me an' my pardner heard a man tellin' another about how her old man jumped out of a canoe, er some damn' fool thing, to save yer life, an' how you filed her on this claim to kind of pay her back."

"The Yukon Kid always pays."

"Yeah—well, this time you paid with phoney

money. She ain't got no rights to that claim whatever—an' neither have you."

"But—surely you wouldn't jump a woman's claim—an orphan, at that?"

"The hell an' I wouldn't! Call it jumpin', or whatever you want. It's straight business with me. It ain't my fault she's a woman, nor an orphan, neither. I come into this damn' country to git what I could. I didn't come fer my health, by a damn' sight! Me an' my pardner's got a claim on Hunker, but it ain't no good. So when we heered that fella talk yisterday, we seen our chanct. Accordin' to him, this here Kitty McGuigan claim is one of the best ones on Bonanza."

"It's as good as any," answered the Kid, mildly. "But, no one that's half a man would jump her claim, after he knew the circumstances."

"To hell with the circumstances! That ain't nothin' to me! I come here fer gold—an' if I'm smart enough to git it by filin' a claim that ain't never be'n filed legal, I'm goin' to do it. If everyone else up here is damn' fool enough to pass it up, I ain't—an' you kin bet yer life on that. The law is the law—an' fer onct, I've got it on my side!"

"You mean, you're goin' down to Dawson an' file Kitty's claim?"

"Like hell he is!" cried Old Bettles, unable

any longer to restrain his wrath. "Git a-goin', Kid! Don't stand there augerin'. Git down to Dawson, an' file it yerself! We'll keep this son of a bitch so busy clawin' fists out of his eyes, he won't never see Dawson!"

"Is that so!" sneered the man. "You don't think I'm damn' fool enough to come up here an' tip off my play till it was cinched, do you? My pardner pulled out fer Dawson last evenin'. The claim's already filed in our name! Go git yer men off our claim! An' I ain't so sure we ain't entitled to all the dust you've took off that claim right from the start! I'll have the law looked up. We filed it legal—an' it looks like we'd ort to be entitled to all that's on it, er ever was on it. This here Kitty McGuigan never had no rights at all. It's every man fer hisself in this country, an' the devil take the hindmost!"

Moosehide Charlie scowled at a red-coated figure that strolled past on the other side of the creek. "If it was in the old days, before the law come in," he growled, "we'd call a miner's meetin' an' hang you fer the good of the country!"

"But, as it is," interrupted the Yukon Kid, deliberately removing his mackinaw, "I'm goin' to give you one of the thoroughest lickin's a man ever got. Peel down, damn you, an' take what you've got comin'! The Yukon Kid always pays—an' there won't be no phoney money in this payment!"

Instead of complying, the man glanced wildly toward the retreating back of the red-coated figure across the creek: "Police!" he yelled, at the top of his lungs. "Police!"

The red-coated one paused and glanced toward the little group of sourdoughs—a group that was being rapidly augmented by the men from nearby claims, many of whom had knocked off for their midday lunch.

On the edge of the crowd Old Bettles waved the officer on his way.

"That's Corporal Bush," he said with a grin. "He's a damn' good guy. Yell louder, chechako! There's times when he's a little deef."

And the chechako did yell louder. But officer Bush passed on.

The Yukon Kid stepped closer, and Boggs turned to run, only to find his way blocked by a circle of eagerly expectant miners who thrust him ungently back into the center.

His eyes narrowed to slits, the Kid advanced another step. "Peel down, you yellow cur, an' collect what's comin' to you. An' quit your squawkin'. It's goin' to take more gold than you'll ever take out of that claim to fill in your missin' teeth."

From the standpoint of a fistic encounter, the fight that ensued, if fight it could be called, presented but a sorry spectacle. The Kid drove his fists with a merciless force and precision that dyed the blond beard crimson in the first thirty seconds. Boggs lashed out wildly with his fists, and aimed vicious kicks at the Kid's middle, and then contented himself with covering his face with his arms, and charging blindly against the closely packed circle of spectators in vain attempts to find a weak spot. Everywhere he was met by heavy hands that shoved him back against the Kid's crashing blows, until a fist finally landed with a solid thud on the corner of the jaw just under his right ear, and he collapsed like an empty sack.

"It's too damn' bad about Kitty's claim," said Camillo Bill, as the crowd turned in disgust from the crumpled form on the ground. "Of course, we all know you've cut her in, full pardners, on all yer stuff. But, that was a damn' good claim, an' we're sorry to see her lose it."

A crooked grin twisted the Kid's swollen lips where one of the chechako's flailing blows had landed: "What do you mean—lose it?" he asked.

"Why—like he said—the law's on his side. The claim wasn't filed legal. We all know'd that—us sourdoughs. We didn't give a damn—an' we figgered the chechakos would never know. We shore hate to see a damn' skunk like him git away with it. But, at that—I wouldn't of took a lickin' like he done fer any claim."

"He took the lickin', all right," answered the Kid. "But, he didn't get away with nothin'. You boys don't suppose I'd let a damn' chechako play me for a fool, do you? Not by a jugful, I wouldn't! I know'd the filin' wasn't legal when I recorded it. But, it was a sourdough stampede, then. No chechakos was in on it. An' I know'd you boys know'd it wasn't legal—an' I know'd there wasn't one of you that would jump it if it was the only good claim on the crick. I know'd, too, that it wouldn't be long before the chechakos would come swarmin' in on us. So sixty days after I'd filed my own claim, I went back to the recorders an' filed hers in my own name. Yup— I jumped Kitty's claim myself!"

"But," exclaimed Old Bettles, "it's in her name, ain't it?"

"Sure, it is. After I refiled it, I transferred it over to her, for value received, in case somethin' might happen to me before she come back. The transfer's on record. This slimy bastard's pardner will find out when he tries to jump it, that Kitty holds the claim by purchase: an' not by filin'."

"Well—I'll be damned!" exclaimed Old Bettles, eyeing the younger man in undisguised admiration.

"Hooray fer the Yukon Kid!" cried Moosehide Charlie. "Bring on yer chechakos!"

The man on the ground had struggled to a sitting posture, and had listened to the Kid's explanation. "You've beat me agin'," he muttered thickly, as he rose to his feet. "But, I'll git you yet."

"What's all the rookus about?" asked Corporal Bush, strolling leisurely into the group.

"Arrest that man!" demanded Boggs, pointing to the Kid. "He damn' near killed me! It's assault—that's what it is. I know my rights!"

Old Bettles shook his head: "You wouldn't have no case, Corporal," he said. "On account there ain't no witnesses to no assault. What we figger is that this here party is prob'ly subject to the nose bleed. Loan me yer keys, an' I'll job one through the back of his neck. They claim that's good fer the nose bleed. An', while yer at it, jest run through yer book an' see if there ain't some further penalty fer attempted claim jumpin'. The nose bleed don't hardly seem adequate."

CHAPTER XXII

Two Hundred Thousand for a Claim!

With things running smoothly on Bonanza, the Yukon Kid redoubled his activities on other creeks. He bought claims lavishly—recklessly, men said—paid thousands for claims that never yielded a dollar in dust—and tens of thousands for claims of proven value. At no time could he even vaguely estimate what he was worth. Men said "more than a million." The Kid, himself knew that if luck broke his way, it was nearer six, or eight, or ten millions—and that if luck broke against him, he was worth a staggering figure less than nothing. He grubstaked worthy chechakos, and saw to it that no sourdough, down on his luck, wanted for anything in the way of outfit or supplies. He would disappear into the hills for weeks at a time, prospecting on his own account—to appear suddenly in Dawson and paint the town red with free whisky for all and sundry—albeit he, himself, never touched whisky.

Young in years, he was already one of the elder heroes of the great new land, and as such, was the subject of many a garbled feature story mailed back to the States, by the little army of newspaper correspondents that swarmed in on the big stampede.

"The Luck of the Yukon Kid" became a byword along the river, and whenever he filed a new claim on some far creek or river, a stampede was sure to follow in his footsteps.

But, as Swiftwater Bill had said, his heart was not in his work. With a hundred hirelings digging the dust from his claims, he would sit alone beside his little fire in some gulch among the high-flung hills, with his thoughts on Kitty McGuigan. There was no longer any thrill for him in the finding of gold, nor in the possession of gold. Stark worry gnawed at his vitals, and in his heart was an ever-growing fear that Kitty McGuigan had followed Big Tim into the Beyond.

Eagerly, in the seclusion of his shack, he would scan each new batch of reports from the detective agencies—and return them to their envelopes with a sigh of bitter disappointment, as he drew checks for amazing sums in the way of expenses, upon a fund he had deposited in a Seattle bank.

Just on the edge of winter he paid two hundred thousand dollars in dust for a claim on

Hunker. The deal was noised about as the biggest transaction ever negotiated in the Yukon. Chechakos gasped. Old-timers shook their heads, and voiced their misgivings.

"The Kid's gone plumb crazy," opined Moosehide Charlie.

"Not if he takes out more than his two hundred thousan', he ain't," defended Swiftwater Bill.

"Hunker's got some damn' good claims—but none of 'em that I'd lay out two hundred thousan' on—nor nothin' like it."

"Two hundred thousan' is a hell of a big chip to toss into any game," opined Old Bettles. "It looks like the Kid's runnin' hog-wild."

"I wish to hell Kitty would come back before he plumb loses his head," said Camillo Bill. "He sent nine sled-loads of grub to some starvin' Siwashes—an' flour fetchin' two dollars a pound!"

"Yeah, an' they say he's figgerin' on buildin' better'n a mile of flume along the side of a mountain, 'way off to hell an' gone in the hills, to run water into a dry gulch where he's staked three claims. Burr McShane says it'll cost him two, three hundred thousan', if it costs a dollar! Cripes, a man can't keep peelin' two, three hundred thousan' off his roll, no matter how big it is!"

"He kin if he wrops three, four hundred thousan' back onto it agin every time," insisted

Swiftwater Bill. "It's like bettin' yer hand in a poker game—sometimes it's good—an' sometimes it ain't."

"Yeah, but the ante's too damn' high," said Moosehide.

"If I had the Kid's luck," retorted Swiftwater, "the higher the ante was, the better I'd like it."

"Speakin' of antes," said Camillo Bill, with a grin, "he went down to Cuter Malone's the other night an' busted that damn' Sam Cronk in a poker game. Sam had beat pore old Jerry Tindall out of his claim on Hunker, an' the Kid heard about it. It seems that old Jerry had give the Kid a canoe, onct, back on Forty Mile. The Kid never fergits. So, when he heard about what Sam done, he sticks around till he ketches Sam in a game, an' he sets in, an' lays fer Sam an' busts him—skins him clean down to bed rock—won his two claims, an' his dust, an' even his dogs an' his outfit. Old Jerry's watchin' the game, an' when Sam gits up from the table, the Kid gits up, too: an' he tosses Jerry a sack of dust, an' walks over to the bar an' transfers Jerry's claim back to him—which Sam Cronk had jest transferred it to him. 'Here's fer that canoe—back on Forty Mile, that time,' he says. 'The Yukon Kid always pays.'"

"An' by God, he does, too!" exclaimed Old Bettles. "Both ways from the middle. I shore wouldn't want him layin' fer me. His luck's too damn' good!"

The creeks froze, and as winter clamped down on the northland, the men of the Yukon settled down to chopping cordwood and burning slowly into the ground, throwing the gravel onto dumps to be sluiced out in the spring.

The Yukon Kid set a crew to whipsawing lumber, and built a shack close beside the mouth of his two-hundred-thousand-dollar claim on Hunker. He moved over from Bonanza, and between lone prospecting trips into the hills, kept a keen eye on the gravel that his men heaped beside the mouth of the shaft. Melting ice, he made frequent test pannings of the dirt that grew richer as the shaft deepened.

Returning from one of his forays into the hills, he was greeted one day early in December by his foreman whose usually jovial countenance presented an air of doleful foreboding: "They struck bed rock two claims above us at forty foot—an' we're down thirty. What's more, they didn't find nothin' to brag about when they hit the rock. She run about like the last ten, fifteen foot of it had run."

"Well, we haven't hit bed rock, yet. She might shelf off like she did on Forty Mile above Goose Crick."

"Yeah. She might," admitted the foreman, lugubriously. "An', she might shelf up, too. I tell you, Kid, I've sweat every time I've drove in my pick, since they hit the rock, for fear I'll hear her ring."

"Save yer sweat fer summer, Joe," laughed the Kid. "Winter sweatin's bad. You might take cold."

"The chances is, she don't shelf one way er another, an' if that's the case, we only got ten foot more to go, an' we're through. An' that means that you won't take fifty thousan' out of this hull claim—an' you give two hundred thousan' fer it. You might see somethin' to laugh about—but, I don't."

"Listen," said the Kid. "This claim is just the same as all my other claims—just a chip in the game—that's all. It's a yellow chip—an' yellow chips come high. But, hell, a man can't expect to win every time he tosses in a yellow chip!"

The foreman, an old sourdough from Forty Mile who had unsuccessfully staked on Ophir, shook his head dolefully. "A hundred an' fifty thousan' is a hell of a loss fer any man to take. An', you've got to think of Kitty, Kid. The talk is that you've cut her in, full pardners on everything you've got. If that's so, half of these here chips yer tossin' into the big game is her chips. There ain't a one of us old-timers that wouldn't go to hell fer her—er you neither, as fer as that goes. An' we'd hate to see you lose."

"Look here, Joe," replied the Kid, regarding

the man seriously. "You knew Big Tim. An' you know how he passed out. Nobody could accuse him of not havin' guts, could they?"

"Hell—no! Big Tim——"

"All right, then. Kitty's a chip off the old block. She's got just as much guts as Old Tim had. If she was here she'd play the game just like I'm playin' it—the way Old Tim told me to play it the day we sat alone on Bonanza an' fingered them little sacks of coarse gold we'd dug out of the grass roots, the time you fellows down to Forty Mile wouldn't believe Carmack had made a strike. She's a big game, Joe—an' me an' Kitty's playin' it big. We'll make millions—or we'll go broke. An', whichever way it goes, we've had a run fer our money, an' when the chairs is shoved back from the table, an' the chips is all cashed in, by God, we'll laugh! Don't go playin' Kitty McGuigan fer no piker, or you'll lose."

A horny hand shot out and grasped the Kid's hand in a grip of iron: "Yer right, son! I hadn't looked at it jest that way. Here's hopin' that bed rock shelfs off a mile!"

Other shafts hit bed rock on Hunker. The claim next below the Kid's found it at fifty feet, and its owner started a new shaft. On the morning of the twenty-second of December Joe's pick rang on the rock, and he looked up to see the Kid peering into the shaft.

"I heard it. Clean her out, Joe, an' come on

up. We'll be hittin' fer Dawson fer Christmas. The boys are prob'ly whoopin' her up, already."

"What'll we do now?" asked Joe, an hour later as he and the Kid and the windlass man and the wood chopper, sat down to their midday meal.

The Kid grinned: "Well, you boys will prob'ly get drunk, an' I'll get some poker played durin' the next week er so. Wish licker didn't make me so damn' sick."

The windlass cranker eyed him with deep concern. "I b'lieve if you'd go at it right, you'd make a go of it," he opined. "Any man's stummick is liable to go back on him after a night's drunk. The trouble is, you prob'ly never kep' at it. The way to do is to go right after it agin in the mornin'. It'll damn' near kill you, an' sometimes a man's got to swaller eight, ten drinks 'fore he kin make one stick. But when one sticks the others will, an' then yer all set fer that day —yer hands quit shakin', an' yer head'll most likely quit achin', an' you kin have a hell of a good time till next mornin'—an' then you've got it all to do over agin'."

"I'm afraid I'll never make a good drunkard," laughed the Kid.

"Well—some don't," replied the man, seriously. "I wouldn't worry none about it, if I was you, Kid. I know'd another feller, onct, that didn't drink, none. He was in the machinery business back in Sauk Center, Minnesota, wher' I come from—an' he was well liked. Folks won't think none the less of you because you don't git drunk—if yer square in other ways."

"You aimin' to sink another shaft on this claim after Chris'mas?" asked Joe.

"Sure," answered the Kid. "I've still got faith in this claim. I've got a hunch she's goin' to pay out."

"I s'pose we might's well clean her up," replied Joe. "But, as fer her payin' out—er anythin' like payin' out, at two hundred thousan', I think yer playin' a bum hunch. With the three of us workin' here, we won't be takin' out much more'n wages the way the top gravel runs."

"All right," grinned the Kid. "Call it wages, then. Anyway, that's something. An', by the way, cover the mouth of the shaft so she won't fill up with snow before we get back. We'll be bringin' out a sled-load of giant, an' the shaft'll be a good place to store it."

"Giant! What the hell would we be wantin' with giant? Figgerin' on blastin' down through bed rock?"

"No," grinned the Kid, "but I ran onto a rock proposition back a-ways in the hills, an' I figure to give it a play. I don't know nothin' about quartz gold—but I want to shoot down the corner of a cliff, an' see what she looks like."

Word that the Hunker claims were petering

out reached Dawson ahead of the Kid. Hunker and Sulfer were deep gravel creeks, and men had been waiting expectantly to see what bed rock would show. The sourdoughs were discussing the outlook when the Kid arrived at the Tivoli.

"We're sorry about Hunker, Kid," said Moosehide Charlie. "We all kind of expected there'd be somethin' big at the bottom of that deep gravel."

"Yeah," answered the Kid. "So did I. But I ain't lost faith in Hunker yet."

"Ain't buyin' no more claims there, be you?" asked Camillo Bill.

"Well, I might. Just now, though, I'm interested in a rock proposition. I'm takin' some drills an' a quarter of a ton of giant back with me to shoot down a face on a cliff."

The sourdoughs, placer miners all, gazed inquiringly into each other's faces. Had anyone but the Yukon Kid made the statement, it would have been greeted with uproarious derision. But the Kid—they hadn't forgotten their premature scoffing at his scheme for winter mining—and now winter mining was the established order. The Kid was smart. And, yet—he had paid two hundred thousand for a claim that wasn't worth fifty thousand. Maybe the Kid was slipping. All remembered the few curious, half-cracked old characters who had drifted into the North, mumbling incoherently about "the mother lode," and spent their solitary lives chipping futilely at hard rock among the high hills. And now, the Yukon Kid, admittedly the shrewdest of them all, was fooling around with hard rock!

Old Bettles was the first to speak: "Was you, by chanct, expectin' to find the mother lode?" he asked.

"Well," answered the Kid, seriously, "it stands to reason there must be a mother lode. This placer gold that we've been getting out is all float. It's a cinch it had to start somewheres."

"It ain't where it started; it's where it's at now that I'm interested in," opined Swiftwater Bill.

"I found an outcroppin' that looks like quartz," said the Kid.

Old Bettles shook his head dolefully and demanded a round of drinks. Raising his glass, he eyed the younger man. "So long, Kid," he pronounced somberly. "We won't be seein' you no more. But, years an' years from now, long after we've skun all the dust out of these here cricks an' turned the country back to the Siwashes, they'll be runnin' acrost an old, old man with a three-foot beard an' no seat in his pants, back in the high hills, a-peckin' at the hard rock with a hammer. 'It's a *Tah*,' the young ones'll say. But the old ones'll shake their head. 'No,' they'll say. 'It's the Yukon Kid. He's still huntin' the mother lode.'"

The Kid joined in the laughter of the sourdoughs, and later, at the faro layout, he rubbed elbows with Boggs, the chechako. The man regarded him with a leering sneer: "I hear you've got a two-hundred-thousan'-dollar hole in the ground on Hunker. Buyin' any more claims over there? Me an' my pardner's got one we'd like to unload on some sucker. It's an inland claim—lays right up agin the rim. I hear how yer goin' in fer hard rock minin'. This claim ort to suit you fine—the rock wall comes up out of the ground right on the claim, an' sticks up in the air a hundred foot er more."

The Kid answered the sneer with a grin: "I'm still holdin' down the Kitty McGuigan claim on Bonanza," he reminded. "An' that's worth a damn' sight more'n any two hundred thousan'. I guess you can keep your claim on Hunker, Boggs, or Doggs, or whatever your name is. I've got a location out in the hills that'll make Bonanza look like a shoestring. When I get my discovery stakes set, I'm goin' to let some of my friends in on it. An', believe me—you won't be among 'em!"

CHAPTER XXIII

The Yukon Kid Stakes a Claim

WHEN the week's celebration was over, the Kid and his three men returned to Hunker and lowered the ten cases of giant into the shaft for storage. Work was begun on a new shaft at the lower edge of the claim, and many times during the day the Kid would grin to himself as he noted that the man, Boggs, was keeping close watch of his movements, from his claim which lay, as he had said, against the base of the valley wall, with four or five inland claims intervening. The Kid's boast of a rich proposition out in the hills had occurred to him on the spur of the moment in a spirit of pure deviltry as he talked to the man in the Tivoli. He knew that Boggs would be watching with a stampeding pack all ready to follow him into the hills, and he planned to lead the man on a wild-goose chase that would tax the endurance of any chechako.

The strong cold was on when, one morning

YUKON KID STAKES A CLAIM

just before daylight, the Kid harnessed his dogs, and headed into the hills. From the vantage point of a spur of rock that jutted from a high ridge, he chuckled to himself as he watched the two chechakos toiling up the long slope on his trail in the early gray of the morning. All that day the Kid threaded the hills, purposely choosing the roughest going that was possible even for his own superbly trained dogs. That night he camped in the shelter of the only clump of trees in a wide, wind-swept moose pasture, chuckling in unholy glee as he thought of the discomfort of the two followers who would be forced to make a fireless camp. Next morning, he crossed a sparsely timbered ridge, halted at noon in a narrow little valley, boiled a pot of tea, and devoured his lunch. When he was certain that time enough had elapsed for the others to be watching from tne rim, he got up, gazed carefully and suspiciously all about him, and proceeded with every evidence of haste and secrecy to stake out a discovery claim. When the stakes were in, he struck off down the valley, recrossed the ridge at a point several miles below, and headed for Hunker.

When the Yukon Kid disappeared down the valley, two parka-clad forms rose from behind an up-jutting rimrock.

The larger of the two bared a hand to the cold and pinched the icicles from his overhanging mustache. "Well—here we be," he said. "He's got his discovery stakes in on this crick that he told me, hisself, would make Bonanza look like a shoestring. 'I'm lettin' my friends in,' he says, 'an' you won't be amongst 'em.' Wonder what he'd say if he know'd we set here an' watched him plant them discovery stakes?"

The smaller man stamped about in the snow and beat his arms over his chest. "Le's git a-goin'. I'm damn' near froze. When his friends comes in they'll find me an' you filed on 'Number 1 Above, an' Below Discovery.'"

"Oh, no they won't," grinned the other. "They'll find you filed, either above er below, whichever looks best to you. An' they'll find me filed on 'Discovery.'"

"What! Good God, Boggs, you don't mean yer goin' to change his stakes!"

"Sure, I'll change 'em. Why not? Me an' you kin use that discovery claim can't we?"

"He'll kill you, sure as hell! An' if he don't, them other sourdoughs will!"

"He won't kill no one—an' neither will them others. The reason is that we'll knock him off before he gits to the recorder's——"

"Not by a damn' sight!" interrupted the other, a look of terror in his eyes. "He's too smart fer——"

"He ain't too smart fer nothin'!" Boggs cut in, angrily. "He jest thinks he's smart! If he'd of be'n so damn' smart he wouldn't of bragged to me about this here location till after he'd got his stakes in an' the claim recorded. He didn't think I was smart enough to keep cases on him till he come out here to stake. He got up an' pulled out in the dark of the mornin', an' then picked out the roughest trail he could find, figgerin' that no one could foller him. But I fooled him, damn him! He didn't pick out no trail I couldn't foller! An' then he camped last night so anyone that might be follerin' would have to camp cold. But we done it."

"Yeah, an' I'm damn' near froze yet. Seems like I never will git warm agin."

"Quit yer squawkin'! We got claims here that'll let us set back an' take it easy, like he does. You don't never see him shovellin' no gravel, do you? Not by a damn' sight! He hires it done, an' all he does is set around an' buy claims, an' go an' hunt new ones. But he's got to the end of his rope now! I told him I'd git him—an' I will!"

"Yeah—jest like you got him that time when he was packin' all that dust outside! An' jest like you got him back on Bonanza, when you made that play fer Kitty McGuigan's claim! Looks like you'd learnt sense enough by this time to lay off'n that hombre."

"Is that so? Well, listen to me, thickhead! He got the best of me them two times because he was lucky. 'The Luck of the Yukon Kid' is a kind of a sayin' in this country. But luck's got to change sometime. They all say that. They're sayin' his luck's changed already, on account of that two-hundred-thousan'-dollar claim that petered out on him—but they don't know the half of it! I be'n studyin' it out while we was mushin' up here. He's got to go back by the way of Hunker to git to the recorder's in Dawson. He won't be in no hell of a hurry to file, because he don't know anyone follered him out. He'll stay anyways one night in his shack on Hunker —an' that shack's right on the edge of that two-hundred-thousan'-dollar shaft! He might figger on hangin' around there a week er two before goin' to Dawson, seein' he jest come back from there. He'll figger on stoppin' at Bonanza an' lettin' his friends in on this here new strike, either comin' er goin'. But—he won't never git to Bonanza—nor neither to Dawson! He'll git to his shack sometime tomorrow, an' we'll git to ourn. Then, tomorrow night, me an' you slips over an' drops a go-devil down on top of that giant he's got cached in the bottom of that shaft. There's ten cases of it down there, an' when she lets go, she'll blow him an' his hull damn' claim plumb off the map. Then, me an' you slips down to Dawson an' files the two claims. An' bein' as we're chechakos, that filin' won't start no stampede, like if the Kid had filed—sixty days later, we'll file us a couple of more, an' agin', mebbe sixty days after that. I tell you we're rich! Richer'n that damn' Yukon Kid ever thought of bein'. He was a damn' fool to think he could buck me an' git away with it."

"But, cripes," exclaimed the other, "there's three other men bunkin' in that shack. We'd blow 'em all to hell."

"Well, it ain't our fault if they're bunkin' there! We didn't tell 'em to, did we? We ain't to blame if them three picked 'em out a dangerous place to bunk in, be we? If they git blow'd up along with the Kid, that's their hard luck."

"But—it's murder!"

"S'pose it is murder? It was murder fer the Kid to put us in that canoe that day with our hands tied, an' no paddles, an' a sign on us which said we was thieves. It was jest our good luck that some chechakos found us. If it had be'n sourdoughs we'd of be'n goin' yet—if we hadn't starved to death, er drowned. An' that lickin' the Kid give me over on Bonanza! That was so damn' clost to murder there wasn't no fun in it. He's got it comin'. An', them others has got to die sometime, ain't they?"

"Yeah," admitted the other. "So've I. But, I'd hate like hell to git hung."

"You stick with me, an' you'll git rich. But, don't try no monkey business, er hangin'll look good to you beside what I'll do. You know too damn' much about what I'm a-goin' to pull—see?"

"What if the giant don't go off?" demurred the man. "It's prob'ly froze."

"It's winter powder. It won't freeze."

"What if it don't kill the Kid? We'd be in a hell of a fix, then. What with them stakes changed."

"It'll kill him, all right," replied the other, confidently. "But, if it don't, we'll knock him off somewheres between Hunker an' Bonanza. An', if somethin' come up so that wouldn't work, we kin always slip back up that crick an' put his stakes back on that Discovery claim, an' I'll file another claim along side of him. Hell—that Discovery ain't the only good claim on that crick! Didn't he say it was goin' to make Bonanza look like a shoestring?"

Descending into the valley, Boggs proceeded to remove the Kid's stakes and substitute his own, while the other man staked Number 1 Below Discovery. Then after caching the Kid's stakes where they could be recovered in case their plans went awry, they struck out for Hunker, passing rapidly down the valley.

"What's a go-devil?" asked the smaller man, nervously, as the two crawled between their robes for the night. "You said you was goin' to shoot off that giant with a go-devil."

"It's a dingus they use in the oil fields fer

YUKON KID STAKES A CLAIM 221

shootin' a well. I worked in the fields, onct, an' I seen 'em do it lots of times. It's nitroglycereen they use down there, but, I'll use giant. I've got some, an' a cap, an' some fuse. I'll make up a good stiff shot, an' cut the fuse long enough so we kin git away from there. Then, we'll slip up to the shaft an' light it, an' drop it in. When she goes off, all the giant in that hole'll go off, too, an' there won't be enough left of the Yukon Kid to pick up the pieces."

CHAPTER XXIV

The Giant Lets Go

AFTER supper, on the day the Kid returned from the wild-goose chase he had led the two chechakos, he and Joe sat at the rude table, and checked off various claims on a roughly sketched plat of Bonanza.

"I'll be movin' back to Bonanza, I guess, after I shoot down that cliff face. I want to open up a couple more of these claims I bought over there before spring, so we can sluice out on the first water. You stay here an' keep nickin' away at this one."

Over at the stove, the windlass man and the wood chopper were washing up the dishes.

Joe filled and lighted his pipe. "A lot of 'em's losin' faith in Hunker," he said. "I don't believe we'll take much better'n wages out of this claim. You might better take us all over on Bonanza."

The Kid shook his head; "No. You boys stay here. I may be wrong, but somehow, I've still got faith in this claim. It's a hunch, I guess—an' a man's a fool that don't play his hunches."

The door flew suddenly open admitting the cold air in a swirl of fog. A fog-blurred face appeared in the doorway, and a voice shrill with excitement rang through the room.

"Come out—quick! It's sure death! It's murder!"

As the Kid rose from his chair the whole world seemed suddenly to collapse in a dull, heavy roar, pierced for an instant by loud cries, and by the sharp snapping and cracking of wood. He felt himself hurled, now this way, now that, as he ricocheted from a bunk stanchion to the wall, and from the wall to the wreck of the overturned table.

The next thing he knew a man was passing a rope about his middle, and he was being carefully extracted from a mass of débris that seemed to have lodged in the mouth of the shaft. The voice of Joe was in his ear:

"Stidy now, Kid! Jest let yerself go, an' we'll git you out."

Men crowded about the shaft mouth. Someone had kindled a fire, and the flames fed by the slivered lumber that had been the shack, leaped high, lighting the scene with a weird brilliance. Other men arrived, their shadows distorted by the leaping flames, throwing grotesquely moving shapes upon the snow.

Eager hands reached out and drew him from the mass of wreckage to the trampled snow.

"Are you hurt?"

In a daze, the Kid moved his arms, his legs. As someone untied the rope from about his waist, he got slowly to his feet and gazed about him. The still air was heavy with the pungent odor of burned powder.

"What—happened?" he asked, as his brain cleared.

"The giant in the shaft let go," explained someone, "an' caved in the lip of the shaft, an' the shack tumbled in. Most of it wedged in the mouth—but some went on down."

"Who's that?" inquired the Kid, and without waiting for an answer, stepped to a blanket-covered form that lay near the fire, and threw back a corner of the blanket. Instantly he recognized the face of the kindly chechako who had begged him not to hang Boggs and his partner that night on the river—the face of the man who had flung open the door of the shack and called his frantic warning just before the terrific crash that had turned the world into chaos.

"Bronson's his name," someone was saying. "Him an' his pardner's got that inland claim up agin the rocks next to Boggs's. We found him layin' there on the lip of the shaft with his head stove in. A foot more, an' he'd of went to the bottom."

THE GIANT LETS GO 225

"Wasn't he in the shack, Kid?" asked a man. "If he wasn't, how come he's here?"

Joe limped forward and was about to reply, when the Kid forestalled him. "Yes, he was in the shack—over by the door. He was prob'ly blow'd out, an' a timber hit him." Dropping to his knees, the Kid examined a long gash high on the man's forehead from which blood still welled slowly. "Someone get a bandage!" he called, sharply. "This man's alive! An' I've got five hundred dollars for the man that gets him alive to the hospital in Dawson! An' five thousan' for the doctor that saves him! There's a hole in his skull—but, men have lived to laugh at a busted skull!"

"I'm goin' after that five hundred!" cried a man. "Tie up his head, an' I'll be here with my dogs by the time you git done!"

As men scurried excitedly about, the Kid whispered in Joe's ear: "Don't say nothin'. Someone touched off that giant—an' he knows the answer." Aloud, he asked: "Are you hurt?"

"Not bad. Only my hip, an' it ain't broke."

"Where's the other two?"

For answer Joe pointed to the shaft. "They must of went on down. The hind end of the shack, nearest the shaft, got it the worst, an' they must of went to the bottom along with the stove. The front end, where we was, stuck in the shaft, an' I clim' out, an' seen you was wedged in beside the bunk, an' then the boys come, an' we got a rope on you so you couldn't slip on down, an' then we worked you loose. Ain't you hurt none?"

"Not a scratch, that I know of. But we've got to go down after those others."

Joe shook his head: "It ain't no use," he said. "If the fall didn't kill 'em, that powder gas would. We'll let a candle down. I'm bettin' she'll go out before she gits halfways to the bottom. It would be sure death fer a man to go down there."

"Hell!" cried the Kid, "that gas is liable to hang in there for a day or two! I ain't goin' to leave those boys in there without tryin' to get 'em. They might be alive! There might be an air pocket on the bottom, or somethin'."

"You won't git no one to go down," opined Joe.

"They're my men," snapped the Kid. "It's up to me to get 'em."

"You mean—yer goin' down yerself!"

"You're damn right, I'm goin' down!"

"But—the windlass is all jammed up——"

"To hell with the windlass! There's enough of you here to lower me an' yank me up by hand. I'll wrap a blanket around my head an' breathe as little as possible."

"How you goin' to see with a blanket around yer head?"

"Couldn't see anyhow, with all that smoke. I can feel."

"The stove was a-goin' when it went down, an' plenty of light wood went on down, too. It's liable to be all afire down there."

"Fire—hell! You jest told me a candle wouldn't get halfway down."

"But the stove'll be hot."

"I ain't after the stove, an' I ain't afraid of burnt fingers. Come on—get a rope!"

Overriding a storm of protest from the assembled miners, each and every one of whom predicted that he would never come up alive, the Kid made them wrap a blanket loosely about his head, imprisoning as much pure air as possible. They knotted a windlass rope firmly under his arms.

Seated on the lip of the shaft, he gave his final instructions as a hundred eager hands grasped the rope. "She's fifty feet deep, boys. Let out the first forty-five fast—then ease her up. When I give two jerks, haul like hell. An', remember, you'll be haulin' a double load."

"No double loads!" exclaimed a bearded miner, who pushed to the Kid's side, and thrust a coiled rope into his hands. "Take this extry rope an' tie it around one of 'em. Then give us the jerks, an' we haul you up fer air. You fetch the end of this rope with you, an' we haul him up. It's too resky—haulin' double, without no windlass. The lip of the shaft's rough—it might cut yer rope—an' then where in hell would you be?"

"All right!" called the Kid, "here goes!" He slipped over the edge, and the rope payed out rapidly as it slipped through mittened hands. It slowed, and the next instant, the Kid's feet struck solid bottom. But, it was not the flat, nearly horizontal bottom of the shaft as he had last seen it. His feet shifted in loose gravel that had fallen in from the caved lip, and he stumbled among loose rock fragments. A metallic sound told him he had kicked against the stove, and the next moment his foot touched a yielding object. Stooping swiftly, he passed his rope about the body of a man, and knotting it securely, laid the coil beside the body, and grasping the loose end, jerked twice on his rope. Instantly he was jerked clear of the bottom, and rose rapidly, bumping the frozen gravel of the wall. His head felt a trifle light, and his lungs struggled for air. The pungent fumes of the powder had penetrated his blanket, and with lips tight-pressed, he reduced his breathing to a minimum, despite the frantic pumping of his lungs. After what seemed a long, long time, hands grasped his arms. He was jerked from the hole, and the blanket unwound from his head. He lay there sucking in the cold pure air

THE GIANT LETS GO

in great deep-drawn breaths, as the men hauled away on the line they had taken from his hand.

"How about him?" he asked, as they removed the limp form of the woodchopper from the hole and laid it on the snow.

"Dead! All smashed to hell! He never know'd what hit him. There ain't no use goin' down after the other one, Kid. No man could be alive—down there."

"I'll know that when I see him layin' here beside the other," answered the Kid. "Let's get it over with. Come on—wrap this blanket."

The second descent was a repetition of the first, the Kid locating the other man without much trouble, jammed in between two slabs of broken rock. He, too, was dead—both, evidently killed instantly by the fall.

The two bodies were decently composed and placed on the roof of a nearby shack to fre_ until such time as a grave could be burned into the iron-hard ground.

Borrowing robes and blankets until they could salvage their own or procure new ones, the Kid and Joe took possession of a shack on an adjoining claim, whose owner had tired of winter mining and gone down to Dawson.

"Who the hell touched off that giant?" queried Joe, as the two sat alone in the bare little shack, with a fire roaring in the stove.

"You don't s'pose that there Bronson done it, an' then got cold feet, do you?"

"Not in a thousan' years," answered the Kid. "But, he knows who did it. He give us the warnin'—but, it was too late."

"By God!—I'll bet it was that damn' Boggs—fer you knockin' hell out of him over on Bonanza, that time. I'll git the boys, an' we'll go hang the son of a bitch!"

Joe was on his feet, reaching for cap and mittens, when the Kid laid a restraining hand on his arm. "Hold on, Joe," he said. "I believe you're right. But, we can't prove it—not unless Bronson gets well. You keep your suspicions under your hat. Boggs ain't liked since he made that play for Kitty's claim, an' the boys would hang him on damn' slim evidence—prob'ly on suspicion, once they got started. But we've got to remember that there's a chance that he didn't do it. We don't want no innocent man hung. Besides, since the police come into the country, hangin' by miner's meetin' ain't so good, except on far-away cricks like Halfaday. Jest set tight till we see how Bronson comes out. If he lives, we'll see Boggs hung by a regular trial, if he done it. If folks gets to askin' questions, tell 'em we don't know how it happened. A spark from the stove pipe might of touched her off—or a rock fallin' down from the lip."

"Huh," grunted Joe. "But s'pose Bronson

dies, which it's likely he's dead a-ready, a-bumpin' hell-bent down to Dawson on a dog-sled."

"Then, we'll try some other way to find out who done it," answered the Kid. "Tomorrow, we'll begin tearin' the wreckage of the shack out of the shaft, an' rig the windlass, an' clean out the bottom."

"What the hell's the use of cleanin' out that shaft? She's plumb down to bed rock. She ain't worth a damn, an' the stuff we crank up won't be, neither. The stove'll be smashed, an' everything else, barrin', mebbe, some blankets, an' tin dishes."

A slow grin twisted the Kid's lips. "I told you I was playin' a hunch on this claim. An', my hunch says, clean her out."

"Huh!" snorted the unimpressed Joe.

"Yup. Listen, Joe. What would happen if you was to touch off a hell of a big shot of giant right on top of bed rock?"

"Nuthin', except you'd prob'ly blow hell out of everything in the country that was loose."

"But—what would it do to the bed rock? Would it break it up in slabs an' chunks?"

"Hell—no! Bed rock goes on down from where you strike it clean to—to—well, to the middle of the earth, I s'pose. I ain't never heard no one say what laid in under bed rock. There don't no one know. How could they?"

"An' it wouldn't slab off?"

"Not without you drilled it, an' put in yer shots—like shootin' down a face of hard rock, it wouldn't."

"That's what I think, too," agreed the Kid. "An that's why I believe my hunch is workin'. Joe, the bottom of that shaft is full of rock slabs!"

"What!" The old miner's eyes were wide with incredulity.

"Yes sir—rock slabs! Of course, with my head all done up in that blanket, I couldn't see nothin'. But, I could feel. They seem to be about eighteen inches, or two-foot thick."

"Gawd A'mighty!" exclaimed Joe, after several moments of stunned silence. "Then, she wasn't bed rock—an' we're down into new gravel!"

"Old gravel, you mean," corrected the Kid. "Damned old."

"Shore! An' she might be plumb rotten with gold!" Once again, he reached for cap and mittens. "Come on, le's git to work on that shaft. We kin light us a fire to see by!"

"Wait till mornin', Joe," counseled the Kid. "We've got all winter to find out what's in the bottom of that hole. Let's roll in."

CHAPTER XXV

In the Bottom of the Shaft

It took several days to clear the mouth of the shaft and rig the windlass. In the meantime the dog-musher had returned from Dawson and reported that he had delivered Bronson alive at the hospital, and that the doctor had got right to work on him.

"An', it was Doc Kinsolving, too—not old Doc Pettus," added the musher. "You bet, he knows his onions! The way he had them two young doctors, an' them women nurses, steppin' around was a caution. Hell, they had his clothes off, an' his head all washed up an' shaved around where it was smashed, an' him on a bed with wheels, an' more kind of saws, an' hammers, an' pinchers, an' scissors, an' long shiny punches, an' things, strung out on platters than a man kin shake a stick at.

"I hung around till they fired me out of there, an' then I hung around outside the door. Every little while one of them women nurses would come out an' go back in there with somethin', an' I'd ask how they was comin', but they never said nuthin'. They're too stuck up fer their britches! Jest 'cause they kin wear them white dresses an' white hats, they think they don't have to talk to no one. Two, three hours later, they opened the door an' they all come out, an' a couple of 'em was wheelin' Bronson out on that there bed. They'd throw'd a white cloth over him, an' he looked dead as hell to me—never wiggled a toe. But Doc Kinsolving claimed he wasn't. He claimed he couldn't see no reason Bronson shouldn't git well, barrin' a silver plate he'd have to wear in his head. 'Course, I seen he was kiddin' me about the plate, so I come right back at him. 'That's a handy way fer a man to pack his plate,' I says. 'A fella kicked me off'n his land onct, an' I had the Doc gouge out a place fer a whole set of dishes where it hurt worst.'

"Doc looked like he was goin' to git mad, fer a minute, then he throw'd back his head, an' laughed. 'Yer all right,' he says. 'You done a good job, gettin' him clean down from Hunker.'

"'Yeah,' I says, 'but I wisht to hell I was a doctor, at that. I win five hundred fer eighteen hours of damn' hard mushin'—an' you git five thousan' fer two, three hours work in a warm room with four, five folks to help you.'

"The Doc laughs agin: 'But, out in the hills,' he says, 'you're liable to bust into a pay streak that'll win you five million—so I guess we're all about even.' He's a good guy, Doc is. I wouldn't wonder if Bronson got well."

For two months, the Yukon Kid and Joe worked the claim. They cleaned the débris from the bottom of the shaft, raised the rock fragments from the shaft at night, and buried them in the snow. From the moment they excavated the first shovelful of dirt from beneath the two-foot shell of rock crushed by the blast, they knew they were into gravel different from any that had showed on Hunker—different from any either had ever seen on any creek. It was much lighter-colored than other gravels—so light, in fact, that it later came to be known throughout the North as "the Hunker white pay streak." And, it was rich. After the first half-dozen test pans had been washed in the shack, old Joe raised his rheumy eyes sparkling with excitement from the little pile of yellow grains, to the face of the Kid.

"Gawd, Kid, yer hunch was right! Whoever it was touched off that giant, shore blow'd you into a million—you an' Kitty McGuigan!"

But there was no sparkle of excitement in the eyes of the Yukon Kid as he slowly nodded his head: "Yes—an' Kitty McGuigan ain't here," he answered in a dull, listless voice.

"But, she'll come, Kid! She'll come! Hell—we're her folks! She's got to come back to us!"

"She may be dead," said the Kid, his eyes on the yellow pile.

A frown of disapproval succeeded the sparkle of excitement in the rheumy old eyes: "Dead! What d'you mean—dead? She ain't no deader'n what you be! She's too young to be dead! Yer a damn' young fool, an' it's time someone told you to turn around an' take a good look at yerself! You ain't had a good laugh sence you come back from outside! You go mopin' around, an' can't think about nothin' but pilin' up the gold —an' all because you couldn't go back down there to Seattle an' find that gal right where you thought she'd be at! What did you think—that she'd broke her leg er somethin', that she couldn't move around a little? Didn't you never stop to think that whilst she was down there in the States she'd want to kind of take a look at different places? There's the Washin'ton Monymint, an' mebbe there's another World's Fair goin' on like the one they had in Chicago awhile back, er mebbe she slipped down to Cuby to see the fightin'. 'Cordin' to what the chechakos tells, the army is knockin' hell out of them Spanish, er niggers, er whatever they got down there, on account they blow'd up a boat, er somethin', an' Kitty might of took a run down there to see the fun. Hell!—you couldn't blame no one fer not

THE BOTTOM OF THE SHAFT

wantin' to hang around Seattle—what with the rain, an' all—an' that there aunt you said she knocked hell out of. Buck up, now! When she gits a eyeful of them States an' things, she'll come back. Anyone'd think you didn't have no guts!"

The Kid smiled. "You're all right, Joe. But if Kitty had be'n doin' any of those things I'd have known about it. I've got two big detective agencies hunting for her."

"Yeah, an' the hull kit an' caboodle of 'em ain't worth the powder to blow 'em to hell! All the detectives in the States was huntin' Jesse James fer years an' they couldn't find him—an' all he done was to change his shirt an' his name, an' set there right in under their noses, livin' in a big town with his wife, an' kids, an' he'd of be'n settin' there yet, between trains an' banks he robbed, if that damn' stinkin' little Bob Ford hadn't snuck up an' shot him from behind! Detectives—hell! All they're good fer is to shake down saloon keepers fer drinks! The only way they'll ever find her—if she goes up an' tells 'em who she is—an' then, they'll make her prove it!"

Day after day the two worked the new-found pay streak, running little exploratory tunnels close under the shell of rock. They removed little gravel to the surface, and that little they covered with snow.

Busy with their own claims, others paid them

small heed. To the few who made casual inquiry as to how they were coming, the two replied that they were tunneling a little along the surface of the rock to see what they could find—making no mention, of course, of the fact that it was the *under* surface of the rock.

And these tunnelings elicited a curious fact—that in two directions the white gravel petered out into a dark, sandy mixture that contained almost no gold whatever. In the other two directions, the white streak persisted.

For several days after making this discovery, Joe worked the shaft alone, while the Kid put in the daylight hours apparently roaming idly about the rims of the valley. On the fourth evening of this, he returned to the shack to find Joe cleaning up a test pan.

"Look," cried the old man, as he pointed to the pan whose bottom was butter-yellow with coarse gold. "She's as good as the best on Bonanza! My Gawd, Kid, Hunker's paved with gold!"

The Kid smiled and shook his head: "How about that black stuff our tunnels hit, to the north an' south?"

"Prob'ly jest dead pockets, here an' there."

"That ain't the answer. But I think I know what the answer is. We're into the gravel of an old, old crick—a crick so old that the shell rock covered it, an' the fifty or sixty foot of Hunker gravel covered the shell rock, since it quit runnin'. That black stuff we run onto was the banks of the old crick, an' the white stuff is its bed."

"You mean a crick that onct run crossways to Hunker?"

"Exactly. An', I believe it crossed the Hunker valley, not once—but twice. Like this." Taking a piece of paper, the Kid sketched a rude map in the shape of a horseshoe, the lines crossing and recrossing the Hunker valley. "I've been out on the rims for four days, an' I believe I've doped it out. There's two notches in the rimrocks acrost the crick—one almost opposite here, an' the other nearly half a mile below. The old crick flowed in at one of those places, made a big ox-bow, an' flowed out at the other. The ox-bow bend—the toe of this horseshoe, you might call it, is right up against that high face of old rock, on this side of the valley—right where Boggs an' his pardner, an' Bronson an' his pardner have got their inland claims. An' if that's true—those two claims are goin' to prove the richest claims of all, because right in that sharp bend, against that rock face, is where this old crick would have deposited most of its gold."

"What you goin' to do?" asked Joe, his eyes on the map.

"Do! I'm goin' to buy claims! I'm goin' to buy every claim I can clear acrost the valley in two lines runnin' from those notches to that rock face!"

"They'll think yer crazy—buyin' up inland claims," said Joe dubiously.

"Good! The crazier they think I am, the cheaper I'll get the claims! I'm goin' to start in tomorrow. There ain't very many of 'em—ought to buy 'em all in a couple of days. When they see I'm buyin' some, an' passin' up others, they'll be sure I'm crazy—but they won't tumble till it's too late, that I'm buyin' 'em in a regular pattern—like this map shows. It's a hunch, I tell you—the biggest hunch I ever had!"

"You better play it then!" grinned Joe. "My Gawd, if yer right they'll be talkin' about the luck of the Yukon Kid clean down to Afriky!"

And, the Kid did play his hunch. As Joe had predicted, men said he was crazy. He passed up creek claims, and bought inland claims. He would buy one claim—and pass up those adjoining. There was apparently no rhyme nor reason to his orgy of buying. Because he was the Yukon Kid, men for the first couple of days, signed over their claims on his promise to pay. He was known to be rich—and he was known to be square. But, when he kept on buying, there were those who asked to see the color of his dust. For answer, the Kid asked and received forty-eight-hour options, and leaving Joe on the claim, he harnessed his dogs, and headed for Dawson.

THE BOTTOM OF THE SHAFT 241

At the recorder's office, he recorded the transfers he already had, and filed the claim he had staked the day he led Boggs and his pardner on their grueling trip into the hills.

Hastening to the hospital, he found Bronson sufficiently recovered to be discharged.

"It was damn' white of you, Kid, an' I'm thankin' you," said the man. "They tell me you give Tom Britton five hundred in dust fer haulin' me down here—an' the doctor five thousan' fer fixin' me up. That's a hell of a lot of dust, Kid. I may never be able to pay it back."

"You try it, sometime, when you feel a hell of a lot stronger, an' see how you come out," grinned the Kid. "What I want to know is what you was goin' to tell us—that night you stuck yer head in the door?"

Bronson's eyes narrowed: "I was tryin' to warn you to git out of the shack. I was goin' to yer shack to see if, mebbe, you wouldn't buy out my claim. We ain't doin' no good there—hardly takin' out wages, an' I thought if you'd give me enough to git back to the States, I'd quit. My pardner he feels the same way. When I got almost to the shack, I seen two men slippin' along the bank an' then they stopped right at your shaft. It wasn't so very dark, an' I hung back in the scrub an' watched, an' d'rectly, a match flared up, an' I seen the splutter of a fuse, an' then the burnin' fuse disappeared down the shaft, an' the men run like hell. I happened to think of all that giant you had stored down there, so I run as fast as I could leg it to warn you. But, I didn't git there in time. An' the next thing I know'd, I woke up here in the hospital with my head all wound up in forty rod of band-ages."

"Who were the men? Did you get a good look at 'em?"

"Yes," answered Bronson, "I did. I expect I'd ort to of let you hang 'em that night on the river when they tried to rob you. It was Boggs an' his pardner. I s'pose he was tryin' to pay you back fer that lickin' you give him back there on Bonanza when he tried to jump the girl's claim."

"Yes," answered the Kid. "That—an' other reasons."

"They tell me that two of yer men was killed when that giant let go. They're goin' to let me out of here today, an' I was goin' down an' tell the police about what I seen that night. I already told the doctor, an' he said I better wait till I was stronger before tellin' the police. They'd prob'ly ask a lot of questions, an' mebbe, want me to go back to Hunker with 'em. An' there wasn't no hurry, as long as Boggs an' his pardner wasn't tryin' to pull out. I s'pose they figger they got away with it."

"Yes," replied the Kid. "That's just what they

figure. Are you fit to go back, now—tomorrow?"

"Yes, the doctor says I'll be all right back on the claim, if I kind of take it easy till spring. I couldn't go outside till then, anyhow, with the strong cold on. Might it be, Kid, that you'd buy me out, along toward spring? You wouldn't take no hell of a lot out of the claim—but you'd easy git back more'n I'd ask."

"Yes," smiled the Kid. "If you want to sell out when spring comes, I'll take the claim off yer hands. But, come on, let's go talk to Corporal Bush. I expect he'll want to go back up to Hunker with you. I'm in a hell of a hurry. I'm buyin' up a few more claims along the crick, an' I've got to take up a load of dust—an' some more giant."

"Giant!" grinned Bronson. "Gosh sakes, it looks to me like you'd had about enough of giant! That other sure didn't do you no good!"

"I want to shoot up some rock," smiled the Kid. "Maybe I can do us both some good with the next shot."

CHAPTER XXVI

The Yukon Kid Always Pays

EARLY next morning, with two hundred pounds of giant, and many thousands of dollars' worth of dust on his sled, the Kid pulled out for Hunker, pausing before his departure to revisit the recorder's, and to grin at the two entries that followed his own. Boggs and his partner had followed him down, as he figured they would, and had filed above and below his Discovery.

On Hunker, he paid off his obligations, and readily bought the remaining claims that he wanted at practically his own figures. Not sensing any plan to his buying, the sellers were glad to unload at his first offers, as they saw that he was turning down far more claims than he bought.

"He's crazy as hell," growled a man whose claim he had turned down. "It's like playin' roulette with a system—some numbers he plays —an' most of 'em he won't look at! What in hell will he do with all them inland claims? They ain't a damn' one he's bought, that's payin' better'n wages."

"He claims he's playin' a hunch," supplied another. "He's hell to play his hunches, the Kid is. An', he's got rich at it, too."

"Yeah—but, he ain't got so damn' rich on Hunker! Look at that two-hundred-thousan'-dollar hole where the giant went off! A few more hunches like that, an' the Yukon Kid will be moochin' drinks down to Dawson. Then what'll them noospaper guys say, that's touted him up fer the big noise along the Yukon?"

Two days after the Kid's return, Bronson showed up in company with Corporal Bush. The Kid met them at his shack, and the three strolled toward Bronson's claim.

As they passed his adjoining claim, Boggs called out a greeting; "Hello, neighbor! Glad to see you back! Damn' clost call you had that night." He turned to the Kid with a fatuous grin: "The Kid, here, he ort to warn folks when he's goin' to shoot off his giant. Guess he's more intrusted, now, though, in buyin' up claims, than shootin' down hard rock, ain't you, Kid? I hear yer playin' another hunch. Buyin' some—an' leavin' others. What'll you give me fer mine, here?"

"What'll you take?" asked the Kid, indifferently. "I ain't buyin' any claims, only here an' there—an' the price has got to be right."

"Oh—I'll make the price right," grinned Boggs. "Facts is, me an' my pardner's got a sweet little proposition back in the hills. Yeah—one that'll make Bonanza look like a shoestring, accordin' to yer own tell. You thought you was damn' smart that day you hit out before daylight, an' took a hell of a rough trail so no one couldn't foller you. But we was onto you, all right—an' we follered you—an' we sunk our stakes right in side of yourn. That time you told me you was goin' to stake a proposition that would make Bonanza look like a shoestring, an' let yer friends in, an' I wouldn't be in on it—from that time on, we never lost sight of you fer a minute. An', when you staked, we staked. An' we follered you to Dawson—an' when you recorded, we recorded. So, it looks like we was goin' to be neighbors—don't it, Kid?"

"Maybe," scowled the Kid. "So, you got in on that, did you?"

"We sure did!"

The Kid sneered: "You're jest the damn' fools I thought you were. Those claims'll never show a color. There's nothin' but muck in that valley—not a color in a ton of it. What'll you take for those two claims. I'll give you your entry money back."

"Haw, haw, haw! That's a good one! Don't

play us fer that much of a damn fool! If that crick's good enough fer you to file on, it's good enough fer us."

"I'll give you fifty thousan' apiece for 'em."

"Like hell!"

"A hundred thousan', then."

"No. If they're worth that to you, they're worth it to us."

"Two hundred thousan' apiece. An' that's my limit."

"Not enough," sneered the other. "I wouldn't sell fer a million. Tell you what I'll do. I'll sell you this here claim—if yer so hell bent on buyin' inland claims—an' it won't cost you nothin' but jest enough to winter us through. Give us a thousan' in dust, an' she's yourn. You'll take out a lot more'n that—but, we won't have no time to bother with it. We want to start in on the new claims."

"Write out the transfer, then," said the Kid. "Here's yer thousan'." The man disappeared into the shack, called his partner, and returned a few minutes later with the paper which he turned over in return for the dust.

"Want it weighed?" asked the Kid.

"No, it hefts about right. What's a few dollars, one way er the other amongst friends?"

"Would you give us a thousand dollars apiece for our adjoinin' claim?" asked Bronson. "It's twict as much as you give him—but, we need it all, an' you'll take out more'n that."

The Kid shook his head: "No," he said, shortly. "I'm just pickin' these claims up, here an' there. Seein' I've got Boggs's, I won't be buyin' yours."

Bronson flushed. "But—you told me back in Dawson that you'd buy it!"

The Kid smiled. "I told you I'd buy it if you wanted to sell it in the spring—an' I will. But you won't want to sell, Bronson—not for a million! The Yukon Kid always pays."

"What do you mean?"

"Wait an' see. Joe an' a couple of boys'll be up here with the giant in a few minutes. I jest give 'em the signal. I'm goin' to fire a hundred-pound shot in the bottom of my new shaft that I jest bought off'n Boggs, here. If my hunch is right, that shot'll put me into the richest gravel that's ever be'n uncovered. Your claim is right over it, too. An' that other hundred pounds of giant I brought up is for you."

Boggs grinned: "Shoot all you want to, Kid. The bottom of that shaft's right down on bed rock. Mebbe you figger on shootin' on down through it."

"Yeah," answered the Kid, "that's exactly what I do figure. You see, when that giant let go in my shaft, it smashed down through what all of us on Hunker thought was bed rock. But it ain't. It's jest a shell a couple of foot thick. It let me down into the bed of an old stream that looped back an' forth under Hunker in a big horseshoe bend. These claims I've be'n buyin' are the ones that I figure lie on top of the bed of that crick. An' these two ought to be the richest of 'em all. They're right at the toe of the horseshoe. Most of the gold would be deposited where the crick hit this rock wall an' doubled back. See those two notches on the opposite rim? That's where the old crick come in an' went out. You'll notice that all the claims I've bought line up between here an' those notches."

Boggs uttered a sneering laugh: "An' that claim you staked up that other valley—I s'pose there's one of these here old cricks runs in under that, too!"

"No. There's nothing under that, so far as I know, but jest plain muck."

"I take notice you was willin' to pay damn' high fer muck," retorted Boggs. "If we'd of took you up, what would you of done with four hundred thousan' dollars' worth of muck?"

"I didn't buy any muck," reminded the Kid. "I knew you'd turn the offer down when I made it. I just quoted those big figures to take yer mind off of this claim, Boggs. I didn't buy any muck—but, I've just bought a hell of a lot of coarse gold—tons of it, maybe—for a thousan' dollars in dust. Even back as far as my claim is from this bend, Joe an' I have be'n takin' out from twenty to sixty dollars to the pan—an' it's in the top gravel of the old crick, at that. I've trimmed you to a turn, Boggs. The Yukon Kid always pays. This was to pay you back for tryin' to jump Kitty McGuigan's claim. Here comes Joe with the powder."

The sneer died from Boggs's face. Somehow, the Yukon Kid's words sounded convincing. His face went white with rage.

"Don't you put that powder in that hole!" he cried. "I repudiate that sale! Here's yer dust back! It's guilty knowledge, er *caveat emptor,* er latent defects, er duress, er somethin'! I know my rights! I'll have the law on you!"

"Yer damn' right!" echoed his partner, "we don't stand by that sale!"

The Kid smiled grimly. "Yer a great hand, ain't you, Boggs, to holler fer the law? You claimed the law was on your side when you jumped Kitty McGuigan's claim—an' now you're proclaimin' the same thing again. Maybe yer right about the law bein' on your side. Yer damn' soon goin' to know." He turned and nodded at Corporal Bush: "Arrest 'em both, officer, fer murder."

"Murder!" cried Boggs. "What d'you mean —murder?"

"Fer the murder of those two men—my woodchopper, an' my windlass man—in my shaft that night you touched that giant off."

"It's a lie! We don't know nothin' about that night!"

"Oh, yes you do," said Bronson. "If you'd have got me along with those two others you might have got away with it. But I lived, Boggs. An', when the time comes, I'll tell the judge an' the jury how I stood within fifty feet of you an' yer pardner, here, that night, an' seen you light that fuse an' toss the shot into the shaft that touched the giant off. I run to the shack to give 'em warnin'—but, I wasn't quick enough. The Kid, here, told me that night back on the big river, that you'd murder someone if you was let stay in the country. I see, now, he was right. But you won't murder no one else, Boggs—not after I've told my story."

As Constable Bush slipped the manacles onto the wrists of Boggs's partner, the man burst forth into a perfect frenzy of rage and terror. "I told you!" he cried, striking at Boggs with his manacled hands, "I told you it was murder if anyone got killed! I told you not to touch off that giant! An', now, damn you—we'll both git hung!"

CHAPTER XXVII

Homeward Bound

SICK at heart and with eyes brimming with tears, Kitty McGuigan turned from the crowd that milled and churned about the Vancouver pier alongside which lay a steamer booked to sail for the North that very day.

She had stepped from the Winnipeg train the day before, and had immediately purchased an outfit, differing in no essential from the one that had scandalized the Widow O'Brien when she had arrived from the Yukon more than two years before. And it was with eager anticipation of once again seeing her beloved Yukon that she hastened to the steamboat office and demanded a ticket to Skagway for tomorrow's boat. The man shook his head. Every available inch on that boat was sold out. He couldn't promise a ticket even for the next boat. He couldn't even say when the next boat would sail. She might be able to sail in a week—two weeks

—a month—there was nothing certain. The unprecedented rush to the goldfields had disrupted schedules, and thrown all northbound shipping into a hopeless confusion.

In vain the girl pleaded, cajoled—stormed. The man was sorry. He thought it possible—just barely possible—that she might be able to buy the booking of some prospective passenger—but she'd have to go pretty high. Men were offering double, and even triple, money for passage, but they rarely found a seller.

At the pierhead she found herself in the midst of a confusion of duffel and men gone mad. Her head in a whirl, she plunged into the shoving, cursing maelstrom, vainly trying to make herself heard. Those who listened to her offer to buy passage either laughed or profanely declined to sell, but for the most part they pushed her aside without notice. It was quite some time before she realized that half the men in the crowd were trying to buy passage.

Weary and discouraged, she turned away and, her eyes blinded with tears of disappointment, all but ran into a man who stood directly before her, blocking the way. Startled, she glanced up, and for the space of seconds stood staring wide-eyed into the bearded face of a big man who stood smiling down at her.

"Camillo Bill!" The name rang in her own ears thin and hysterical.

"Yep—it's me, all right. You ain't fergot yer old friends, have you, Kitty? But—it 'pears to me yer headed the wrong way!"

Despite her effort to control them, Kitty felt hot tears trickle down her cheeks. "Forgot you!" she faltered. "Why, Camillo, I just *love* everyone on the Yukon!"

Camillo Bill's laughter boomed loud: "Well, that's quite a contract, Kitty. Damned if *I* do. The old river ain't what she used to be—all gummed up with chechakos. Look at 'em!" With a gesture of contempt, he indicated the milling horde. "They won't pan out three men to the boatload! But—where you headin', Kitty? Ain't you goin' in?"

"Oh, I can't go! They won't take me! They say the boat's full, and there's no room. I've been trying to buy a passage here, but no one will sell."

"Ain't no room, eh? Well, well! Where's yer pack?"

"I left it across there in that store."

"Come on, then. Let's go. My stuff's be'n on board since mornin'."

Crossing to the store, Camillo Bill swung the girl's pack to his shoulders and led the way back to the pier, Kitty following close at his heels. At the gate in the iron fence that had been thrown across the pierhead, Camillo shoved half a dozen men aside. The gate swung open and as

Kitty, her heart thumping like a trip hammer, followed Camillo, the gate snapped shut behind her, and a detaining hand was laid on her arm. Her heart seemed to stand still as a voice sounded in her ear:

"You got a ticket, lady?"

Camillo Bill whirled at the words. "Ticket—hell!" he roared. "Who wants to know? Course she's got a ticket! She's got mine!"

"But——"

"Butt yer damn' head off!" bellowed Camillo Bill, glaring at the uniformed gateman. "Go roll yer hoop, son. An' whenever you feel like throwin' me off yer damn' scow I won't be hard to find—I'll be up in Cap' Mason's room."

As she hurried down the pier beside the big man Kitty glanced up into his face: "I won't take your ticket, Camillo. I'll stay behind before I will."

"You got to," grinned Camillo Bill. "Bunk an' all. Cap' Mason don't know it yet—but he's goin' to bunk double this trip—an' I sure aim to git my share of the bed."

Camillo Bill had been among those lucky enough to secure a cabin. Unlocking the door, he swung Kitty's pack to the bunk, picked up his own, and paused to face the girl in the narrow little alley: "There you be, Kitty—snug as a bug. Jest make yerself to home. See you later. Got to go find Jack Mason an' break the news to him that his bunk's got to carry double this trip."

"But—your ticket——"

"Hell's bells, girl! This here ain't our boat! Let someone else worry about the tickets!"

When Camillo Bill disappeared down the passage, the girl stepped into the little cabin, threw herself onto the bunk, and burying her face on the pillow gave way to a flood of tears. Only a short half hour before, buffeted and ignored by the milling chechakos, baffled by insurmountable difficulties, she had turned heartsick from the pier—then, the face of Camillo Bill indistinct through the mist of tears, and the big voice of Camillo Bill in her ears—and the insurmountable difficulties had vanished like mist before a summer sun. A sweep of the mighty arm, and the chechakos went spinning from their path, a bellow of the mighty voice and petty officialdom busied itself elsewhere. And here she was—bound for home at last!

"Home!" She breathed the word, and her tears flowed afresh as she wondered what home would be like—home without Big Tim—without Tommy Haldane! But, no—she hated Tommy Haldane! Tommy, who had refused to say the word that would have allowed her to remain in the North. Tommy, who had made a miserable failure where the other sourdoughs who had been in on the first rush had made good!

With a shock like a dash of cold water, a face appeared before her mind's eye—a neatly trimmed imperial, and a black ribbon dangling from a pince-nez. A suave voice sounded in her ears, and a soft hand seemed to caress hers. Home—with Mr. Jones of Edmonton—who would rob a bank for revenge!

Vaguely she realized that the boat had got under way. The bunk vibrated to the throbbing of the engines, and somewhere men were shouting. She was dry-eyed, now—dry-eyed, and staring up at the low ceiling. It seemed hours that she lay there—the future a chaos her brain groped dully to fathom. No Forty Mile. No Circle. No Big Tim McGuigan. No Tommy Haldane. A big strange camp—thousands of sweating chechakos, pitting the creeks and the valleys, shearing the hills of their timber—and Mr. Jones of Edmonton!

A knock roused her, and the voice of Camillo Bill sounded from beyond the door. "Grub-time, Kitty. An' Cap' Mason wants he should meet you. When I told him you was Big Tim's girl, he says you got to set up next to him at the table, an' I agrees, providin' I kin set on t'other side of you, an' share his bunk fer the trip, an' git my passage throw'd in to boot—so we calls it a bargain."

Kitty found herself smiling. Dear old Camillo Bill — homefolks — the sourdoughs never change. "Just a minute," she answered, and as she dabbed at her face with a damp washcloth, she realized that her fists had been clenched until the nails left little red moons in her palms.

"Mighty proud to meet you, Miss McGuigan," the voice of Captain Mason was as hard and as hearty as the grip of the powerful fingers that closed about her own. Kitty was conscious of a sudden spasm of terror. $1,000 REWARD! The headline seemed to blaze before her eyes. She had been Kitty Flannigan so long. She was conscious that her eyes had shot a furtive glance about her, but if anyone within hearing had recognized the name they gave no sign of it. The voice was booming on: "Yes'm— mighty proud to know Big Tim McGuigan's girl. It takes a *man* to do what he done, Miss. The sourdoughs ain't never forgot—an' the chechakos will know about it, too. They say the Yukon Kid has ordered a monument to set up opposite where he went down that'll cost him twenty-five thousan' dollars time it's in place." The girl's eyes blurred with sudden tears. It was Tommy Haldane's life Big Tim had saved at the expense of his own. But, it was this Yukon Kid she had read so much about—this chechako

—who was spending his money to commemorate the deed!

As the long twilight lingered, Kitty stood beside Camillo Bill at the rail, and drew the good salt air deep into her lungs.

"Tell me about it, Camillo," she said, "—about my father."

When he had finished the simple narrative the girl stood silent, looking out over the dark waters. She found herself speaking, and her own words surprised her: "Oh, Camillo," she said, "I loved Tommy Haldane! I could love him now—if—if he hadn't proved a failure!" She noted the peculiar glance with which the man's eyes sought her face, and hastened to explain. "It isn't that I care for the gold! I could have starved in a tent with Tommy. I loved him. But he had his chance—the same chance you all had—you who were there at the first. And you all made good—all but Tommy. If he only had *done things*—have found gold, and lost it. Even if he had scattered it to the winds like Swiftwater Bill, and McMahon, and Jimmy the Rough did, I could love him for it—but to fail—that I can't forgive!"

"H-u-m-m," said Camillo Bill. "What do you mean—fail?"

"Why—fail! Fail to make good. Fail to be anybody! Fail to get gold where everyone else is getting gold! Fail to be mentioned in a land where everyone else is written up in the newspapers! Oh, I've kept track of you—all of you! I know what you've been doing. The Sunday papers have long stories about Moosehide Charlie, and you, and Old Bettles, and Swiftwater Bill, and Jimmy the Rough, and McMahon—and this Yukon Kid, too—but never a word about Tommy Haldane! I must meet the Yukon Kid, sometime. I want to thank him for —for the monument to my father."

"You'll prob'ly meet him," said Camillo Bill, a smile widening the lips behind the blond beard.

"Tell me about him," urged the girl. "You see, he's come into the country since I went outside. How could any chechako go in and do the things he's done? The papers say he's the richest man in the North. And they say he's got hundreds of men working for him, and that he gives away more gold in a year than most men ever see. And that he can travel through a country that would starve a wolf. Maybe a good deal of it's lies, but——"

"No—there ain't no lies in what you've jest mentioned. The Kid, he's smart. It was him that first doped out winter minin'! He located a couple of the best claims on the crick—an' bought a lot more—an' he's kep' about four jumps ahead of the rest of us ever sence."

"Do you like him, Camillo? Is he skookum tilacum?"

"Yes, Kitty, he's skookum tilacum, all right. I'd call him the best man in the North."

"Now, tell me about Tommy Haldane," she said. "What's become of him? Where is he?"

"Well—seems like he don't stay in no one place long. Come to think of it, I ain't even heard his name spoke in more'n a year."

There was more than a touch of bitterness in the girl's voice: "Probably working for the Yukon Kid," she said.

Camillo Bill nodded gravely: "Now you mentioned it, seems like he was workin' fer the Yukon Kid, last I heard."

A flush mounted to Kitty's cheeks, as she thought she detected a smile behind the beard. "You wouldn't laugh, Camillo, if you thought of Tommy Haldane as I—as I once did," she said. "And, there's something I must tell you, Camillo. I'm not Kitty McGuigan, now—I'm Kitty Flannigan——"

"Hell's fire! You ain't gone an' got married!" The thunderous disapproval of the big man's voice startled, even more than it surprised Kitty.

"Why, no—I—that is—no, I'm not married —yet." Confused by the searching gaze of the pale blue eyes, she hastened to explain. "You see, Camillo, Flannigan was my mother's name. Back in Seattle the spring after I went outside, a man from Circle told me in a gun store that—that my father was dead—only he didn't know Big Tim was my father. And my money was almost gone, and my aunt had been nagging me because I owed her for a couple of weeks' board, and when I told her my father was dead she said it was a good thing. And then, something seemed to snap inside my head and I sailed in, and before I realized what I was doing she was lying unconscious on the floor, and the housemaid was screeching in the hall, and I was afraid the police would come so I ran away. I went to Tacoma and was working as cashier in the grillroom of an hotel. I told them my name was Kitty Flannigan, and one day the newspapers came out with notice of a thousand dollars' reward for Kitty McGuigan, offered by the Chief of Police of Seattle. I was afraid someone would recognize me, so I went to San Francisco, and after a while the reward notices stopped. But I've been afraid to use my own name ever since. I was scared most to death when you introduced me to Captain Mason—it was the first time I'd heard my own name mentioned in two years. Oh, Camillo, I'm afraid my aunt died and they want to catch me and—and hang me!"

Camillo Bill knew about the reward posted by Tommy Haldane. He knew, also, that operatives of several detective agencies, in the pay of the Yukon Kid had been, for more than a year, searching for trace of the missing Kitty McGuigan. Camillo Bill loved the dramatic—and here was a chance to stage a scene the like of which the Yukon never saw. He knew that the Yukon Kid was off on a trip with Al Mayo, and that it would be a month or two before he would show up in Dawson. Tommy Haldane was the Yukon Kid, and Kitty didn't even suspect it! Kitty Flannigan was Kitty McGuigan, and he must see to it that her identity was kept secret so that no inkling of the girl's return would reach the Yukon Kid's ears until——

"Gawd!" he breathed to himself. "The Kid would give a million to be standin' where I am right now. What a hell of a night Dawson's goin' to see—when them two meet!" He'd slip around and wise up the sourdoughs. The chechakos didn't matter. Kitty McGuigan meant nothing to them.

But, in the meantime, he must say something. He cleared his throat, and the pale blue eyes looked grave: "H-u-m-m, well—they'll have a hell of a time hangin' you, onct you git back on the river. You see—knowin' you like the boys do—an' after what Big Tim done, an' all—I sure wouldn't want to be the party that tried it. I figure he'd be lucky if he lived long enough to git hung, hisself. 'Course if you bungled the job, an' yer aunt got well—that would be too bad, too—sayin' what she done about Big Tim. But I figure it might be jest as well to kind of lay low ontil we sort of find out how the land lays. Guess you jest better keep on bein' Kitty Flannigan fer a while. I'll speak to Cap' Mason, an' when we git inside I'll kind of slip around an' wise up the rest of the boys—an' somehow, amongst us, we'll figure out a way to square it. Remember, yer back amongst yer own folks, now. They can't no one bother you an' maintain no manner of good health whatever. You said you was cashier of a restaurant, or somethin'— well, Bob Henderson runs the swellest restaurant in Dawson, an' he'll be tickled to death to git someone fer cashier that he don't have to turn 'em upside down an' shake the dust out of their pants every time they go off shift. That'll give you somethin' to do till we git a chanct to sort of look around." Then the unwonted gravity dropped like a mask from the face of Camillo Bill. The blue eyes twinkled, and the bearded lips smiled: "By the way, Kitty—Old Bettles has skipped two birthdays waitin' fer you to fetch in them oranges."

The black waters blurred and merged with distant wooded heights, and the girl's voice was not quite steady as she answered: "I've got them with me, Camillo—and Swiftwater Bill's red necktie—and Moosehide Charlie's yellow shoes, size nine! I didn't forget, Camillo. There wasn't a chance in the world that I'd ever forget!"

In her bunk that night, as she lay wide awake listening to the steady throb of the engines, the words of Camillo Bill kept repeating themselves over and over in her brain: ". . . yer back amongst yer own folks, now." Her own folks. The littered beach at Forty Mile. . . . "Good-bye, Kitty." . . . "Good-bye." . . .

She was safe, now. Her heart seemed bursting with love for these rough men—with love, and with a mighty pride, as she remembered the words that had fallen from bearded lips as they spoke of her father—the man from Circle—Captain Mason—Camillo Bill. If only Big Tim could have lived to know the regard in which these men held him! Perhaps—some place—he does know. Then, her heart chilled, and the blood seemed to run cold in her veins as a face obtruded her consciousness—the face of Mr. Jones of Edmonton. The crook—the bank robber—the suave seducer of women. Thank God she had held him in his place! But—marry him! A shudder traveled to her very toes. Big Tim McGuigan's daughter married to a common crook! What would these men—her men—think of her then? Camillo Bill, Mooseheide Charlie, Old Bettles, and all the rest? Outwardly they might appear the same—for old time's sake. But how long would the thin veneer of suave respectability serve to cloak the soul of Mr. Jones of Edmonton, under the cold-eyed scrutiny of such men as these? They would not hate her for what she had done. They would pity her. In her heart Kitty knew that she could endure the hatred of these men—but never their pity. "Two hundred and fifty thousand dollars—a quarter of a million," she repeated dully—and the next moment she was sitting bolt upright, her bare feet on the cold floor, and her two hands gripping the edge of her bunk. "No, no, no!" she cried aloud. "Not for ten millions! *I'd die first.*"

A long time later, the face that passed with her consciousness into the oblivion of sleep was the face of Tommy Haldane.

CHAPTER XXVIII

Dawson

OF THE old Forty-Milers, only Moosehide Charlie and Bob Henderson were in Dawson when Camillo Bill and Kitty McGuigan stepped ashore from the steamboat.

With these two, Camillo Bill held conference at the end of the bar in the New Antlers saloon. "Gawd," said Bob Henderson. "She's in full pardners, on everything the Kid's got! An' she don't know a damn' thing about it! I wonder how it'll feel to have the richest woman in the world workin' fer me?"

"It'll feel pretty good to know that about half the dust you take in ain't stickin' to yer cashier anyhow," opined Moosehide. "I was figurin' on a trip up the McQuesten, but I guess I'll stick around. The Kid an' Al Mayo ought to be back in a month or two. Gosh! Think of Kitty McGuigan bein' right here in Dawson—an' the Kid's got half the detectives in the States huntin' her night an' day!"

"Won't there be a hell of a time when he hits camp!" exclaimed Henderson. "Fetch Kitty over to the restaurant, Camillo. I'm goin' on over an' fire the cashier."

"Remember, now," cautioned Camillo Bill. "Her name's Kitty Flannigan—not McGuigan. An' fer God's sake don't let her find out that the Yukon Kid is Tommy Haldane! What we want is fer him to walk right in on her—not neither one of 'em knowin' nothin' about the other."

" 'Tain't likely she'll find out," said Moosehide. "We'll put the boys wise if any of 'em drifts in—and the damn chechakos don't know the Kid's real name nohow."

So it was that Kitty McGuigan took up her duties as cashier of Bob Henderson's Eureka Restaurant. "It's like this, Kitty," explained Bob, as he inducted her into the little grilled cage. "Here's the scales, an' here's the dust box, bolted down so no one could grab it off on you. There ain't be'n no robbery in camp yet, but I ain't takin' no chances. Mostly the boys is orderly enough, but sometimes a bunch'll come in that's kind of feelin' their oats a little. The chances is you won't have no trouble handlin' 'em. But you can't never tell about chechakos. If they go to gittin' fresh with you, jest step on this here buzzer an' Joe'll come. You'll like Joe. He hangs out in the kitchen. He ain't so long on brains, mebbe. But he's willin'. He's a kind of a dishwasher, an' a handy man, an' bouncer. He loves a fight, Joe does—an' he's thorough. 'Course if any real trouble should break, sudden, here's a 'forty-five' where you can reach it, an' she's always loaded—an', if you step on this here dingus, it locks the doors."

With the passing of the days Kitty grew more and more nervous. She found herself scrutinizing each new face that entered the door. Some day, Mr. Jones of Edmonton would stand before her cage. Vainly she tried to visualize that meeting. Would she recognize him, shorn of the imperial and the black-ribboned pince-nez? What would he say? What would *she* say? One thing was certain—she would never marry him! She no longer viewed life through the jaundiced eyes of Nadu, the trouper. The very air of the big clean land had cleared her brain of the moral obfuscation that had allowed her to condone a robbery as a means to an end. When Mr. Jones appeared, she would return his expense money and send him about his business. But would it be as easy as all that? Suppose he should create a scene? Well—there was the buzzer—and Joe. She shuddered slightly—no, she would not call Joe. Once, only a few days before, she had stepped on the buzzer because a big drunken chechako was loudly demanding a kiss before he would pay his check. When Joe, the thorough, had performed his duty as he saw it, there were several chairs, and a table, and numerous dishes to be replaced with new ones, and the chechako had been carried out the door feet first. She did not want Mr. Jones injured—perhaps he did love her—in a way.

Other worries assailed her. Suppose some sourdough should come in and call her by name, and someone should overhear and would remember the thousand dollar reward? Then if the Seattle police should come—and the sourdoughs should rally to her defense—she closed her eyes, with a shudder.

Then—what of Tommy Haldane? In vain she had questioned Bob Henderson, and Moosehide Charlie, and Camillo Bill. She got only rambling, evasive answers that allowed her imagination full sway. Despite the fact that she kept repeating to herself that she hated Tommy Haldane, she knew deep down in her heart that she loved him—and that never in the world could she love any other man. It was obvious that he had dropped out of the picture. But why? Point-blank she asked Bob Henderson if Tommy had gone the whisky route—no, he didn't hardly ever drink no licker. Had he committed any crime? No, he was square as hell. Had he turned squaw man? No, he didn't 'pear to have nothin' to do with no women—white or red. Where is he? Well—he's somewheres out in the hills, I guess.

Doesn't he ever come into Dawson? Yes, he's in an' out—now an' agin'—like all the boys. He always eats here when he's in town—you'll meet up with him—sometime. Vague, unsatisfactory answers these—from lips unskilled in dissimulation. Kitty realized this, and behind the brave mask of a calm exterior she wondered—and worried.

Corporal Downey, N.W.M.P., in the garb of a prospector, stepped off the steamboat at Dawson and stared about him in amazement at the change that had taken place in the big camp since his transfer from the Yukon only one short year before. Tents and hastily constructed shacks had given way in a great measure to substantial buildings. Rafts of logs lay alongshore. And the whine of saws was in the air.

A man walked toward him, and he grinned as he recognized a sourdough he had known during his eight months of service on the river. As he was about to pass, Downey thrust out his hand: "Hello, Camillo!" he greeted. The man stared for a moment, and seized the hand in a mighty grip.

"Well, damned if it ain't Constable Downey! Didn't know you without yer uniform. Quit policin'?"

"No. An' it's Corporal Downey, now—not

Constable Downey. Only, keep your mouth shut about it—an' if there's any of the other boys around that know me, pass 'em the word. I'm up here to grab off a bad actor—bank looter an' murderer—an' it'll be better if folks don't know I'm a policeman. I'm not even goin' to report at detachment."

"Throw yer pack in my cabin till Bettles comes back. He's off in the hills, somewheres."

"Thanks, I may not be around here only a day or so. May drop on down to Forty Mile."

"Forty Mile! Hell's bells, there ain't no more Forty Mile—nothin' you might say, but a name. If yer man's headed this way, it's ten to one he don't git by Dawson."

"Maybe you're right," admitted Downey. "How's everyone—Swiftwater Bill, an' Bettles, an' Moosehide Charlie, an' the Yukon Kid?"

"Oh, they're all fine. Me an' Bettles is pardners on a couple of good propositions, an' Moosehide, he's settin' pretty with a good claim on Ophir. An' the Yukon Kid, figgers his dust by the ton—he's off in the hills right now with Al Mayo—but they'll be blowin' in pretty quick. Jimmy the Rough, he hit town last winter an' throw'd his dust to the rate of a hundred thousan' a month, an' then along in March he fell down in the snow an' froze to death. You remember Big Tim McGuigan——"

"No. I heard all about him, though. He died

just a little while before I came into the country. Jumped out of a canoe to save his pardner, didn't he?"

"He sure did. By God, there was a man! But—come on over to the shack an' toss yer pack in Old Bettles' bunk."

"Let's see, seems to me he had a daughter, or a son, or somethin', didn't he?" asked Downey, when the two had got their pipes going in the little cabin.

"Yeah," answered Camillo Bill. "Kitty, her name is." He smoked for a moment in silence, then grinned broadly: "Hell, we might's well let you in on it—it's a damn' good story—an' when the Yukon Kid hits town the blow-off will be tremenjous. They won't be no one sober fer a week, except the Kid, hisself. He don't drink no licker. It's like this——" For an hour Camillo talked, chronicling Kitty's departure from the Yukon, the death of Big Tim, Tommy Haldane's search for her and the posting of the reward, his own meeting with the girl on the Vancouver docks, her fear of the Seattle police that had induced her to take her mother's name, her return to the Yukon, and her belief that Tommy Haldane had proved a failure, and the uncomfortable wriggling and twisting of the sourdoughs under her questioning to keep from revealing the identity of Tommy Haldane.

At the conclusion, Downey grinned: "I sure

want to be there at the blow-off," he said. "I guess, after all, I won't go down to Forty Mile. I hope he blows in before my murderer shows up."

"He's due pretty quick. He figured on bein' back here by the first—an' it's around the twentieth, now. I look fer him in a week or ten days. Let's go an' eat. Bob Henderson's is the best dump in town—that's where Kitty's cashier. When I introduce her as Flannigan, don't let on you know different."

"I won't," said Downey. "An' don't ferget I'm just plain Downey—jest a prospector—not a constable nor a corporal, nor no other kind of a policeman."

She's the girl of the photograph, all right, thought Downey, as he and Camillo Bill dined at a little side table. An' she ain't told Camillo nothin' about Winnipeg, an' the Nadu the Sublime play-actin' stuff. The question is: is Porter here already, or is she jest waitin' for him to show up? It would be a damn' shame for a daughter of Big Tim McGuigan to go wrong.

CHAPTER XXIX

Corporal Downey Gives Advice

OLD Bettles sent word to Camillo Bill that he was needed out at the claims, and for a week Corporal Downey remained alone in the cabin and ate his meals at Bob Henderson's restaurant. He learned that Kitty roomed alone over the restaurant, and that she never entertained visitors. He deliberately cultivated her acquaintance, always pausing for a chat when he found her on duty. "He ain't got here yet, but she's expectin' him," he muttered to himself one day as he watched her swift scrutiny of each patron's face.

It was Kitty's habit to dine after the noon rush left the place comparatively empty. She had just seated herself one day when Downey strolled in. He paused beside her table and smiled into the upturned eyes of Irish blue. "Jest eatin' dinner? I'm late myself today. Mind if I set here, or would you rather eat alone?"

Her lips answered his smile. "No, indeed, I wouldn't rather eat alone. Bring a chair over and we can talk." She liked this young man who, although a newcomer in Dawson, was palpably no chechako. Furthermore, the sourdoughs all knew him, and liked him—and that was recommendation enough for Kitty. "Prospecting?" she asked, when he had seated himself opposite her at the table.

"Well, lookin' around a little. I ain't located exactly what I want, yet."

"But—everything's taken up that's any good, isn't it?"

"Yes—about everything that's any good."

"You've been on the river quite a while, haven't you? I notice you seem to know all the boys that are worth knowing."

"I put in eight months around here, but I be'n outside about a year. Jest come back about a week ago. Things sure has changed."

Kitty smiled: "I've only been back about a month. I was outside more than two years. When I went out there wasn't any Dawson. I used to live at Forty Mile."

"Forty Mile, eh? Why, that's where Big Tim McGuigan used to live! There was a man! I didn't know him myself. He'd—passed on before I come in. But shucks—I'd rather have the sourdoughs talk about me like they talk about him than to have all the gold in the hills. I suppose you knew him—Big Tim?"

Tears were very near to the surface in the eyes that met the steel-gray eyes across the white cloth. There was something clean and wholesome in those steady gray eyes—instinctively the girl knew that the mind that looked out through them was a clean mind. They were not like the eyes of the hangers-on about the stage doors of the theaters. Not like the eyes of—Mr. Jones of Edmonton.

"Yes," she answered, in a tone very low, and not quite steady. "I knew him—well." Suddenly an irresistible desire came over her to talk—to tell this man with the clean, understanding eyes —everything. He was no chechako. He was accepted by the sourdoughs as an equal. He was home folks. Never in her life had there been any woman confidante to whom Kitty could go with her joys and her sorrows and her worries. Nervousness—worry was pyramiding upon her as the days passed and she tried to keep her mind on her work, and her eyes on the faces that entered the door. Where was Mr. Jones of Edmonton? What would happen when she told him she could have nothing to do with him? What of Tommy Haldane? The sourdoughs were concealing something about Tommy—and, she couldn't even tell them about Mr. Jones of Edmonton. If she had told Camillo Bill right at first on the boat, when she had told him of her fear of the Seattle police, he would have understood. But—at that time she had not yet found herself—her perspective had not yet shown Mr. Jones of Edmonton in his true malignancy. Into her jaded and jaundiced life, surrounded by jealous and hateful associates, encompassed within the four walls of a theater, and the four walls of a miserable room, he had come as a fairy prince—as a savior who would snatch her forever from her intolerable surroundings, and set her down in her own big clean North. But the keen salt air in her lungs and the sight of the towering wooded heights of the Inside Passage had cleared her brain—had transformed her, even before she had set foot on the northern soil, from Nadu, the Sublime, to Kitty McGuigan, of Forty Mile. And, in the cosmos of Kitty McGuigan, of Forty Mile, Mr. Jones of Edmonton had no part. But, he existed, and he was a menace—a very real menace to her pursuit of peace and whatever of happiness the future held for her. She could not tell Camillo Bill, now— nor any of the others. They were square-shooters —all. They played her for a square-shooter. They would wonder why she had held out on them—there would be so much to explain.

But, this Downey—instinctively she felt that he would understand.

"I knew Big Tim McGuigan—and I know

his daughter. She is a—a friend of mine. And, she's here on the river, now. She's in trouble, and she needs—advice."

Across the table, the man nodded, slowly—and spoke no word. Almost unconsciously she began to talk. Food was set before them and remained for the most part untasted. On and on she talked, omitting nothing from the time of Kitty McGuigan's departure from Forty Mile. She spoke in the third person—made no apology for this course, or for that—stated facts—spared neither her subject nor others, albeit she mentioned no names. The man listened, interrupting with an observation here, a leading question there, and at times with a nod of understanding, or of approval. And, as she talked, with the steel-gray eyes always upon her face, her tense nerves laxed, she felt as though a vast smothering weight were being lifted from her heart.

When at last she had finished, the man opposite her sat for what seemed a long, long time, balancing a fork on his finger-tip. A slow smile curved his clean-cut lips.

"This friend of yours, now," he said, speaking slowly and distinctly. "She's had a mighty interestin' life. It's done her a world of good—hard knocks always does—when they don't kill. The only ones that survives is them that's fit to survive. An' she's proved that she is fit. It's like you said—back here in the Big Country with the air, an' the river, an' the hills—she's different than she was back there. All them cynical an' hopeless an' twisted thoughts is swept out of her brain like the dust an' the cobwebs they was. But when you come to think of it—it had to be that way. No daughter of Big Tim McGuigan's could have done no different. You see, most of what you've told me I know'd already. Some of it I had guessed. An' some I didn't know." The girl was staring aghast into the steel-gray eyes. "Yes," he continued, "I followed you here from Winnipeg. I'm Corporal Downey of the North-West Mounted Police. I'm up here after John W. Porter—the man you know as Jones of Edmonton. But he wasn't from Edmonton, he was from Cranch, an' the story he told you about his father's bein' robbed was a barefaced lie that he figured would work up your sympathy. He robbed the bank, all right, but he didn't rob it for revenge—he robbed it because he's a thief. An' not only a thief, but a murderer—as cold-blooded an' as mean a murderer as ever walked on two legs. What's more, he's got one wife already, so he couldn't have married you, if he'd wanted to. But you don't need to worry, Kitty— you won't mind if I call you Kitty, will you? The other boys do. You don't need to worry none about Jones of Edmonton, because I'm right here to take him off your hands."

"And you knew all the time that I was telling you about myself!" faltered the girl.

"Sure, I knew. An' I knew it was doin' you a lot of good to get it off your chest. There ain't nothin' you've told that'll ever git past me—you know that. An' I'm glad you told it, 'cause it was mighty hard for me to dope it out how any girl with eyes like yours could throw in with a crook like this John W. Porter."

"But—what will we do when he comes?"

"I'm watchin' all the boats, an' I'll drop in here three or four times a day—same as I've be'n doin'. I never seen this man, an' the picture I've got shows him with a beard, an' eyeglasses strung on a ribbon. He might git by me—but he's sure to hunt you up. It'll be up to you to stall him along till I show up, an' then tip me off. You don't need to have no compunctions about it, neither, after the way he lied to you, an' after killin' a poor guide to save his own hide, an' leavin' the man's wife an' kids to git on as best they can—an' leavin' his own wife, too. Hangin's too good for a skunk like him."

Kitty shuddered and covered her eyes with her two hands. "Oh, and only to think that I—that I——"

"Don't go blamin' yourself, Kitty. You didn't know what he was. An' feelin' like you did—low, an' downhearted, it's no wonder you grabbed at the first chance that showed up to get you out of it all. Most girls would have gone under. You done a damn' good job. Big Tim McGuigan would be proud of you."

"But—the Seattle police!" said the girl. "Suppose they should follow me up here as you followed me?"

Corporal Downey smiled: "I wouldn't worry about that, if I was you. It's a long way to Seattle from here. I don't believe your aunt died—folks don't, havin' their face punched. But if she did die, the police wouldn't have offered no reward in the papers. Don't you see it would have be'n the worst thing they could have done? It would have put you on your guard, an' you'd skipped out—jest like you did do."

"But—why should they offer a reward, then?"

"I don't know much about city police," grinned Downey. "You didn't spit on no sidewalk, did you?"

The girl looked puzzled: "What?"

"Just a way of speakin'. They prob'ly wanted to git track of you—one reason or another. That would be hard to say, offhand. Maybe folks noticed you'd disappeared, an' they wanted to know what become of you—anyway, it's a safe bet it wasn't nothin' serious."

There were tears in the girl's eyes as she raised them to meet the gray eyes across the table: "Do you know, Corporal Downey, do you know that

—somehow—you have made me feel—feel happier, than I've felt in many a long day. If—if only I knew about—about Tommy Haldane—— But the boys won't tell me! They're keeping something back. I feel it—and it—oh, it must be something terrible!"

"Well, now—suppose you jest kind of set tight. An' I'll kind of nose around. 'Course it might take a little time 'fore I git holt of anything definite. I've got to stick pretty close around here. But don't worry too much. Mostly, things turns out to be not so terrible as they might be. So long, Kitty. I got to be goin'. There's a steamboat due today, an' I want to be down there when she docks."

Kitty sat for a few minutes dabbing at her eyes with her handkerchief, while through a round hole cut in the green door that led to the kitchen, Joe, the big-framed dishwasher and bouncer, glared at Downey's retreating back until it disappeared through the door. "Huh—make her cry, would you? Goddam you! Make her cry! I'll learn you! Make her cry!" And, mumbling and muttering, he slammed the thick dishes about during half the afternoon.

CHAPTER XXX

The Sourdoughs' Banquet

HARDLY had the steamboat docked when down the plank came Camillo Bill, closely followed by Old Bettles, and Al Mayo, and an upstanding younger man whom Downey instantly recognized as the famous Yukon Kid.

Camillo Bill hailed the young officer loudly: "Hey, Downey! You remember the Kid! Sure you do—you was askin' about him the other day."

"Sure I do. Hello, Kid! How's everything?"

"Fine as frog hair, Downey. Back in the Big Country again, eh? They can't stay away, can they, Bettles?"

Corporal Downey noted that while the lips smiled, the deep-set eyes held a somber, almost a tragic expression, that somehow gave the impression of age to the otherwise youthful face. There was nothing about the Yukon Kid, with his checked shirt, and his worn and clay-spattered trousers to proclaim him the richest man in the North. To the casual observer he might have passed for any one of his hundred or more workmen. Only the curiously direct gaze of the haunting eyes, and the decisive, short-clipped sentences proclaimed him a leader of men. He turned to speak to Al Mayo, and Camillo Bill tugged furiously at Downey's sleeve.

"We ain't got much time—an' you got to listen to me. Me an' Bettles doped it out when we run onto the Kid on the boat. We let Al in on it, too. Here's the play. You got to stick around with the Kid, while me an' Al an' Bettles slips around an' wises up the old-timers. We told the Kid there was goin' to be a sourdoughs' banquet down to Bob Henderson's restaurant at seven o'clock. That ain't no stall—but we got to hurry like hell to git it goin'. I'll see Bob an' git a big table fixed up kind of far back from the door, so we kin see the fun when he steps in an' him an' Kitty sees one another. Gawd A'mighty—the Kid'll go through that wire cage like a rock through a winder! Remember, your job's to stick to him like a louse to a Siwash till quarter to seven, then herd him down to Bob's place, an' we'll be there with all the champagne there is in Dawson stacked alongside us. He'll head fer the barber's first to git a shave an' a haircut—an' you git one, too, an' that'll kill a lot of time. Talk minin' to him—talk anything—but don't let him go into Bob's till quarter to seven—an' it's half-past five, now. I got to go."

Camillo Bill, and Al Mayo, and Old Bettles filtered away into the crowd, and Corporal Downey turned to the Yukon Kid. "I suppose we better take in the sourdoughs' banquet, tonight," he said.

"Sure, the boys'll have a good time. An' we might as well eat there as anywhere."

"I expect we'll *all* have a good time tonight, Kid. Gosh, it feels good to get back on the river."

"Yes, it's always good to get back. You still in the police?"

"Yes—ain't advertisin' it, though, this trip. I'm tryin' to locate a murderer."

Abruptly, the Yukon Kid asked: "What chance has a person got of disappearin' absolutely without leavin' a trace?"

"Not much. Why, you figurin' on disappearin'?"

"Do you remember Big Tim McGuigan?"

"No—he died jest before I come in."

"He died to save my life."

"Yes—I know."

"He had a daughter. Sent her outside to an aunt's, just a few weeks before he died. I love her. Besides that, I promised Big Tim to look after her. She disappeared the next spring—in Seattle. I advertised in the papers for a while, an' offered a reward. It did no good. I'm hirin' a couple of big detective agencies in the States to locate her. They're no good, either. What'll I do?" The two were walking up the street. Not far ahead was the sign proclaiming Bob Henderson's Eureka Restaurant. Kitty's cage was visible from the window.

In front of the barbershop Downey halted abruptly. "Git a shave," he said. "An' a hair-cut. I need one, too. I'll be thinkin' it over."

"Is there a chance you can help me?"

"Yump. I find folks. That's why they sent me here. If you ain't found your girl by the time I pick up my man here, I'll find her for you."

"You'll what?" A hand gripped Downey's arm till it seemed the bone would crush.

"Sure—I'll find her." The tone was matter-of-fact—casual. It was as though he had stated he would find a lost ball in a weed patch.

"Good God, Downey! You're not kiddin' me?" The tragic eyes were fairly glaring into his own as Downey answered.

"Not a chance. There's only so many people in the world. Women's easier to locate than men in the western parts—there ain't so many of 'em. Other way around in the East. But—east or west, if you ain't found her before I go back, I'll find her."

"But—how long will it take you?"

"Oh—couple weeks, maybe."

"By God, Downey, you find that girl, an' you'll never have to do another lick of policin' as long as *you* live! I'll give you a half million in gold!"

"I like policin', Kid. An' we ain't supposed to take tips."

The barbering took the better part of an hour, during which time Downey felt that the eyes of the Yukon Kid were always upon him.

From the barbershop the officer led the way into the New Antlers saloon where he drank sparingly, and the Yukon Kid not at all. When, from his position of vantage that commanded Bob Henderson's door, he noticed that no more sourdoughs were drifting into the place, he looked at his watch. "Well—quarter to seven," he announced. "Suppose we loaf over to the Eureka?"

As Downey swung open the door and allowed the Yukon Kid to precede him, he was conscious that his heart was beating a bit faster than was its wont. He liked the Yukon Kid, and he liked Kitty McGuigan, and never would he forget the tragedy in the eyes of each as they had spoken to him of the other. He felt a sudden compunction at thus being a party to this public meeting. Somehow it seemed more fitting that they should have met in private. But, no! They belonged to the Yukon—both. There were no chechakos here —the men who had foregathered to witness the

THE SOURDOUGHS' BANQUET

reunion were the men who loved them—their own folks. Only he, himself, was a comparative stranger, and he felt that he was here as of right.

Directly before him, his frame blocking the doorway, the Yukon Kid stood as though frozen in his tracks. From the interior Downey heard a sound of swift movement, then a voice sounding as though torn from a woman's very soul:

"Tommy! Tommy Haldane!"

And then, the Yukon Kid **was** no longer blocking the doorway, and Downey could see the form of Kitty McGuigan crushed in a mighty embrace. For long moments they stood so—while the sourdoughs cheered and cheered.

Suddenly aware of the pandemonium that had broken out about them, they turned to face the table of cheering men with eyes blurred by the tears that trickled unashamed down their cheeks.

Moosehide Charlie was on his feet, bellowing to make himself heard: "Kitty McGuigan," he said. "Meet the Yukon Kid!"

His long finger was pointing at the man whose arm was about her waist, and Kitty drew away and shot a startled glance into the eyes that now held no hint of tragedy.

"The—Yukon Kid!" she faltered, as though trying to grasp the import of the words.

"Yes, Kitty," grinned Tommy Haldane. "That's what they call me, now. How **you** going to like being Mrs. Yukon Kid?"

"I'll love it! But—Tommy——" The sentence was drowned by the voice of Old Bettles who, drunk already, stood bawling his song with glass and bottle weaving uncertainly.

> *"In the days of old,*
> *In the days of gold,*
> *In the days of 'forty-nine . . ."*

Camillo Bill interrupted. "I claim the thousan'-dollar reward, Kid! It was me that fetched her in! An' believe me, it'll cost you a damn' sight more'n a thousan' to pay fer this fuzzy water!"

"They'll run wide open in Dawson this night!" laughed the Kid, "an' the more, the merrier!"

"Did you have a hard time keepin' him corraled, Downey?" called Al Mayo.

"Hell," grinned Corporal Downey. "You couldn't of pried him loose from me with a crowbar!"

Whereat the Yukon Kid favored him with a happy grin: "You're a cocky young policeman —you are! At that, you had me guessin'. Somehow—I almost believed you when you told me you'd find her for sure."

"And he told me he'd find you, too," announced Kitty, happily.

"I guess he found us," laughed the Yukon

Kid. "He's one policeman that sure can deliver the goods!"

Stooping, he kissed the girl squarely upon the lips—when suddenly a voice rang sharp from behind Downey who stood just inside the doorway. "What's this?"

Kitty turned at the sound of the voice, and Corporal Downey saw her face go dead-white as she stared with horror-widening eyes at the smooth-shaven man who stood just inside the doorway. Instantly Downey whirled, and quick as a flash his left hand shot out and closed about the left hand of the man in the doorway. With all his force he jerked him forward, at the same time ripping the sleeve from his shirt and disclosing a forearm upon which showed a long livid scar. The bit of byplay had apparently passed unnoticed by the sourdoughs across the room, who, all talking at once, were busy with bottles and glasses.

"The jig's up, Porter," growled Downey, as he dodged a terrific blow from the man's right. At mention of the name a spasm of rage distorted the banker's features, and the next instant he had whipped a gun from his pocket.

With a scream Kitty leaped to her cage, at the same instant that the Yukon Kid lunged at the man who all but had the gun on Downey. There was a sharp report, and the Yukon Kid staggered backward and toppled to the floor.

Across the room the sourdoughs were staring spellbound as Downey fought with everything that was in him for the possession of the gun. Again Kitty screamed as her foot found the buzzer, and the next instant Joe charged through the green door like a bull, and with the bellow of a bull he snatched up a chair, swung it high and brought it crashing down on the head of— Corporal Downey: "Make her cry, will you? Goddam you! Make her cry! Le'me go! Gimme another crack at him!"

Corporal Downey had almost succeeded in getting hold of the gun when there was a blinding flash of light, and the world seemed to go black, and to whirl dizzily. He staggered backward, his muscles laxed. And Porter, realizing that his one hope of safety lay in killing this man who had solved his identity, raised the pistol until its muzzle was almost against the breast of the officer who had brought up against the wall.

Downey's head was clearing. He stared into the muzzle of the gun, but his muscles refused to act. Instinctively he braced to withstand the shock of the bullet.

There was a deafening report. The gun muzzle lowered, and John W. Porter straightened suddenly, spun half around, stared in horror-stricken bewilderment for a moment, and pitched forward upon his face.

Downey gazed about him. A thinning fog of blue smoke eddied in an air current above the wire cage where Kitty, a big black "forty-five" in her hand, was staring in frozen horror from the inert form of the banker to the blood-stained one of the Yukon Kid. As Joe once again swung his chair above his head, Downey raised a feeble arm to ward off the blow just as the man with his uplifted chair crashed to the floor with three sourdoughs on top of him.

A six-gun dropped to the desk, overturning the gold scales.

The girl in the cage had fainted.

"What's it all about?" asked the Yukon Kid half an hour later as Kitty put the finishing touches on the bandage that circled his forehead where the bullet from Porter's gun had glanced from his frontal bone.

"Nothing to worry about, Tommy," smiled the girl, with a glance into the steel-gray eyes of the young officer. "Corporal Downey's man showed up—that's all."

"An' Kitty got him," grinned Downey, ruefully. "But I jest run through the pack he'd set there in the doorway, an' this here package I've got in under my arm is about a quarter of a million dollars in bills. I've had policin' enough fer one day—come on—let's eat!"

"Got to have a toas' firs'," proclaimed Old Bettles, as with drunken gravity he managed to step from a chair to a table-top with a bottle and a glass in his hands. Weaving uncertainly, he slopped a drink into the glass: "Here's to the Yukon Kids—bosh of 'em!" He waved the glass, distributing its contents impartially upon the crowding sourdoughs, tossed the empty glass to the floor where it shivered into a thousand pieces, and tilting the bottle, drained it. "Now I'm goin' shing y' li'l shong:

*"In the days of old,
In the days of gold,
In the days of 'forty-nine . . ."*

THE END

Robert Duffek
354 East 81 St.
New York — New York.